Victor Suthren is Deputy Curator of the Canadian War Museum and has written extensively on eighteenth- and nineteenth-century history. He has a great deal of sailing experience which includes crewing on schooners and going on adventurous voyages in small boats to retrace the sailing routes of the eighteenth-century wars. He lives with his wife and three children in Ottawa.

By the same author

The Black Cockade
A King's Ransom
In Perilous Seas

VICTOR SUTHREN

Royal Yankee

GRAFTON BOOKS

A Division of the Collins Publishing Group

LONDON GLASGOW
TORONTO SYDNEY AUCKLAND

Grafton Books
A Division of the Collins Publishing Group
8 Grafton Street, London W1X 3LA

Published by Grafton Books 1989

First published in Great Britain by
Hodder & Stoughton Ltd 1987

ISBN 0-586-20429-6

Printed and bound in Great Britain by
Collins, Glasgow

Set in Ehrhardt

1

The dawn of 10 November, 1739, was breaking in amber, cloud-hung glory over the face of the Caribbean Sea. As the blood-red disc lifted behind the rain curtain of a distant squall line, it turned the hissing flanks of the long grey swells first golden, then indigo, flecking with white as they swept westward under the steady Trade Winds. The neat, cotton-ball rows of cloud that marched slowly westward also glowed a brilliant peach until they brightened as the sun continued its climb. Two grey gulls which had ridden out the night on the sea surface spread their wings and thrashed aloft, circling in the growing light for their first meal. To them, and to the broad panorama about them, the sun brought in a few swift minutes' first light and then the promise of heat. And these in turn fell over the form of the lean, graceful ship which was tracking south-westward across the long lines of swells, heeled well over from the press of its straining canvas.

The ship was a topsail schooner, with the trim line and rig of a Bermudaman: sleek and comely, seventy tons of Bermuda cedar driven by the Western Atlantic schooner rig that gave her a turn of speed far beyond what most wallowing hulls of her age could hope to achieve. The tan-coloured body of the ship was not as bluff and fat as most vessels, and the lovely line of its sheer was picked out in the painted black of the waterline wales and the trim of its upperworks. As the hull rolled, the white underbody gleamed in the sun, still almost clean and unfouled by the growth of weed and barnacle that bred on the hulls of ships in the warm Tropic seas. Beneath the sturdy bowsprit and the slim, reaching spar

5

of the jib-boom an exquisite figurehead rode, in the form of a young girl: Grecian in delicacy, with beautifully carved drapery slipping from one white shoulder to reveal a small, high breast, a hand touching the throat, the other shading the painted brown eyes that stared out towards the pitching horizon below a goddess's hairstyle of loosely gathered curls.

Two-masted, the ship carried three broad triangular head-sails: foretopmast staysail, jib, and jib topsail. On both the raked foremast and the taller mainmast, a gaffed foresail and mainsail were drawing, their canvas arches set well out to starboard as the schooner boiled along on a broad larboard reach. Above the gaff foresail, a broad square topsail bellied out from its yard, and set between the masts, a rectangular staysail added to the power that drove the ship on its swift way off to the south-west, leaving a foaming wake beneath the simple, unadorned stern, with its row of stern lights – the windows of the after cabin – and the carved, yellow-painted lettering that gave a name to the schooner and the exquisitely womanly form of her figurehead: *Athena*.

'She's French, sir. Look at the steeve of her jib-boom.' The midshipman standing on the canting quarterdeck of the schooner handed a long brass telescope to the tall figure that stood at his side.

'Is she, by God?' Lieutenant Edward Alan Mainwaring, Royal Navy, captain of His Britannic Majesty's Schooner *Athena*, six guns, peered through the smoky lens. He was tall, closer to six feet in an age when most men were closer to five. His hair was dark, a sort of sun-dusted brown, and unruly; it was gathered back at the nape of his neck and tied simply with black ribbon. His face was clear featured and strong, with intelligent blue eyes under straight nearly black brows and an aquiline nose almost aristocratic in its shape, were it not for the prizefighter's break in its arch. His long, straight jaw framed a mouth now pursed in study, but which

6

was full and expressive. His frame was broad shouldered, narrow at the hips, and with a lean grace that had more the air of a buckskin hunter's muscular athleticism than a stumped and hernia-crippled seaman used to hunching under the low deckheads of warships. He wore a plain black tricorne jammed down over his eyes against the glare of sun and sea, and his clothing was loose and practical: canvas trousers falling wide to old hose and salt-rimed buckle shoes; a buckskin waistcoat over a checked shirt; a black silk scarf knotted casually at the throat; and a threadbare brown coat with docked skirts and plain brass buttons, now all green from salt. In age, he was in his twenties, but to his easy carriage there was added an air of steely resolve, and in his eyes there was a wary perceptiveness that spoke of a hard life and early responsibility.

Edward Mainwaring was an American; a Massachusetts man native to Old Town, a seamen's village on the island of Martha's Vineyard. To his speech, his manner and his ways, any Englishman would have attached the adjective 'Provincial', which was interchangeable with American; but in Mainwaring's presence it would have been difficult to use that adjective with the condescension it usually implied. There was too much warning in those clear blue eyes. To Mainwaring himself it mattered little whether it was fashionable to be a Jonathan – as the English called the American colonials – or not; his New World origins and ways had not yet proven themselves to be an obstacle in his planned career in the Navy of His Britannic Majesty George II.

Athena lifted and pitched down with muffled thunder over a swell, and Mainwaring lowered the glass to give the midshipman a slight nod of approval. 'You've a keen eye, Mr Pellowe,' he said. 'Worth a guinea more of the prize money if we take her, I warrant.'

7

The midshipman, a blond youth barely into his teens, grinned and swallowed. 'Th – thank you, sir. But – ?'

Mainwaring's eyebrow rose. 'Yes?'

'If that's a Frog, what's she doing here, sir? I thought these were Spanish waters, tight as a nut.'

Mainwaring raised the glass again, studying the distant shape, which was fine now on the starboard bow. 'Steering due west,' he murmured. Then he lowered the glass. 'Could be any number of things. Outbound from Cayenne. Trading into Cartagena or Porto Bello. Even a rogue slaver.'

'But, sir, don't the Spanish *guardacostas* – ?'

'Interdict the French?' Mainwaring squinted up at *Athena*'s scarlet masthead pennant. 'They're meant to, lad. The Dons are bloody protective of their monopolies. But then they might've let this plump little bird through to be useful.'

Mainwaring snapped shut the long glass. 'Pass the word for Mr Hooke and the master-at-arms. And tell them we'll go to Quarters if she holds that course.'

'Quarters? Aye, aye, sir!' There was a gleam in the lad's eye as he hurried off down the ladder to *Athena*'s waist.

Ship-rigged, thought Mainwaring, his eyes on the small shape ahead. *Sprits'l, tops'ls and t'gallants. Jib and mizzen brailed in, main course ducked up. All in all, a tidy package easing down the Trades, and ripe for taking. Yet . . .*

'Zur?'

Mainwaring turned to find the burly figure of Isaiah Hooke, *Athena*'s sailing master, at his elbow.

'That ship, Mr Hooke. What d'ye make of her?'

Hooke shaded his eyes with one shovel hand. 'B'loike o' wot, zur?'

'Her rig. Set of her canvas. Look naval to you?'

'Dunno, zur.' He shifted an enormous plug of tobacco to the other cheek. 'Them topm'sts is French naval fashion, right enough. Or mayhap Spanish,' he said, after a moment.

'Same size. An' no loose sheets, or buntlines needin' over-haulin' loike as some traders yew'd see.'

Mainwaring pursed his lips. He opened the long glass again and handed it to Hooke. 'Try this.'

Hooke hefted up the glass and squinted. After a moment he lowered it and spat thoughtfully to leeward.

'You'll have to be more specific, Mr Hooke,' said Mainwaring, with the lift of a corner of his mouth.

'Well now, zur, she c'd be only armed t' the weatherdeck, on account o' damage or cargo below. Or out in ballast, an' wiv her ports caulked.' Another brown jet arced over the leeward rail, and he wiped his mouth with the back of a hand. 'Ain't sayin' she's naval, zur. Can't say she ain't neither.'

'That hull, for instance,' said Mainwaring, accepting back the glass. 'About the size of a sloop of war, or a corvette. Twenty guns or so, wouldn't you say?'

Hooke nodded. 'Aye, zur. If she *is* a warship. More'n twice our weight o' broadside. An' handy in a seaway, too, bein' a Froggy hull.' He squinted at Mainwaring. 'Give us a fair fight, zur.'

'Or a fair packet of prize money.'

Hooke's oaken face split in a rare grin. 'Aye, zur,' he said, with a slow nod. 'Aye, it would!' The plug shifted again.

'Deck, there!' The foretop lookout's voice rang out over the sea noise.

'Keep her sou' west for the present, Mr Hooke,' said Mainwaring. He cupped his hands. 'Deck, aye?'

'Tops'ls an' t'gallants, sir! Three, four – no, *five* sail at least! Christ, more'n that!'

Mainwaring felt a shiver go up his spine. 'Where away?'

'Abeam, t'larboard, sir! Steerin' due east, by the look of 'em!'

Mainwaring swore and squinted against the sea glare off to

9

the south-east. Even at quarterdeck level he could see the faint pinpricks of mastheads along the wave-stippled horizon.

'Ten sail, now, sir! At least!'

Pellowe, the master-at-arms, had come lathering back up on to the quarterdeck. Like Hooke, he was without shoes, and the hard soles of his feet slapped on the ladder as he came up. In a moment he was at the rail beside Mainwaring.

'Think *they're* French, too, sir?' he blurted out. Then he flushed, aware of his impertinence. He writhed under what seemed to be an icy stare from Mainwaring until he saw the almost imperceptible smile on the Vineyarder's mouth.

'No, Mr Pellowe,' said Mainwaring. 'Any convoy at sea here – or any squadron – would almost certainly have to be the Dons. And it'll be damned bothersome if they are.' He poked a thumb skyward. 'In the next minute that lad in the foretop, or his mate in the main, is going to tell me that they're flying Spanish colours. And I'll be just a tad annoyed.'

Pellowe coughed. 'I – don't mean to sound stupid, sir, but what – ?'

'Vernon and the Fleet, Mr Pellowe. If the admiral managed to get the damned transports to do what he told 'em, they could be no more than fifteen or twenty leagues astern of us.'

'Oh,' said Pellowe. Then his face fell. 'Oh.'

'Precisely. The admiral needs surprise for the strike he plans at Porto Bello, eh? But if the Dons know we're coming – '

'Spanish colours, sir!' rang a shriek from aloft.

Mainwaring nodded. 'Aye, aye!' he barked in reply, and then looked back at the youth. 'If the Dons are aware of us, they'll have time to do any number of things to strengthen the place; booms, fireships, women with rocks in their bloody aprons, the lot.' He nodded at the Spanish vessel. 'That's why at the very least we have to take *that*. If we put about, then we give ourselves away for certain as a picket ship for the bigger fleet. Instead, we have to look like a grab-and-run privateer to 'em.'

Pellowe looked pale. 'Who are those others, sir?'

'Unless I miss my guess, that's a *flota* of Spanish men o' war, and no damned Plate Fleet. And likely to be old Admiral Pizarro himself.'

Pellowe's eyes narrowed. 'Christ, sir,' he said softly. 'On this track he'll – '

'Intercept Vernon in a day. Maybe two. And so much for surprise, or putting even one lobsterback or keen young bucko like you ashore at Porto Bello.'

Pellowe nodded, and the worried look increased. But Mainwaring was unconscious of it, for his mind was already racing ahead to a number of possibilities, even as he absently found himself studying the eager, ruddy features of the youth, who looked so damnably vulnerable that Mainwaring wondered how the boy's mother had been induced to let him be torn from her bosom and thrust into the harsh world of men at sea. Mainwaring felt a peculiarly cold logic rise out of nowhere and take over his mind, crowding out all sense of panicky stress. He let its calm flow over him, feeling a tinge of shame that Pellowe was now eyeing him in evident uncertainty and even fear, and that he was delighting in his own *sangfroid*. He pushed the feeling of sympathy from his mind and spat vigorously into the sea over the lee rail.

'We'll hold this course, Mr Pellowe,' he said briskly after a moment. 'I'll oblige you to make no more sail, and to fly no colours. Alter course only to keep our bearing on that Spaniard constant, as the wind allows. I'll return on deck in ten minutes, no more, and at that time I'll trouble you to call the ship to Quarters. But you are to call me the instant anything new takes place. Is that clear?'

Pellowe nodded vigorously, his eyes wide. 'Aye, sir!'

'Very good.' Mainwaring moved to the ladder, feeling an

11

odd tingle in the back of his neck as he glanced at the distant Spanish vessel.

He paused only long enough to fix a look on Isaiah Hooke. 'Mr Hooke! Give me five minutes alone and then join me in my cabin, if you please . . .'

The great cabin, like that of all schooners, was inaccurately named, for it was barely a cabin and in no stretch of the imagination great in size. A leather-covered settee traversed the stern under the slanting glass of the 'lights', or windows. Other than the narrow box bunk which swung slowly on its hooks to one side, the settee was the only place where a man could sit, with his back to the boiling line of the wake and a small table lashed down to ringbolts before him. Other than a battered sea chest to one side of the cabin door and a rack holding a cutlass and two long flintlock muskets on the other, there were no furnishings. Most of the cabin's space was taken up by the black and ochre bulk of two long three-pounder guns, which were snugged up by their breeching lines and tackles for heavy weather sailing. Lashed above them, in black iron racks bolted to the deckhead, were the gun tools: rammers, sponges, worms and handspikes.

Mainwaring tossed his hat on the settee and slumped down beside it. The dawn sun flooded in through the glass to warm his back and sent shifting squares of orange light swinging back and forth over the canvas-covered deck. It lit the dark corners of the cabin which, before dawn, had been lit only by the cloudy-glassed brass lantern which swung on a hook a few feet above the table. Below its feeble light Mainwaring had been studying a sheaf of papers and charts which were now spread out in a welter on the table, held down by the businesslike weight of a long flintlock pistol. Now his long brown fingers picked up once again a document that bore the heavy wax seal of the Admiralty Court of Massachusetts.

My disguise. And a licence to raise hell, he thought, as he hefted the letter-of-marque. *And all supposedly over that silly bastard's ear . . .*

The new war with the Spanish was all too plainly an effort by England to break the monopoly of merchant shipping into the sprawling Spanish Empire in the Americas, which the Spanish jealously guarded for themselves. For the benefit of British merchants and ship-owners, war had been declared on the basis of a ludicrous incident which had actually taken place some years earlier. A British-Jamaican vessel bound for England under the command of a certain Captain Jenkins had been taken by a Spanish privateer; Jenkins' ship had been looted, and his ear hacked off by a Spanish cutlass in a spasm of Latin enthusiasm.

Some Members of Parliament with heavy investments in the City had hauled Jenkins into the House, where he had made – or been coached to make – an impassioned little speech in which he avowed that while the Dons were making off with the cargo – the ear apparently being left behind – he had decided he would commend his soul to God, but his cause to his country. His country, insofar as it was represented by the comfortable gentlemen of the House, sprang indeed to his cause.

Pressure, Mainwaring reflected, had been building for some time in support of an attack on the Spanish over everything from the African slave trade to the Spanish interdiction of the English smugglers that swarmed to the coasts of Spanish America in search of cargoes. Jenkins' speech had given Parliament the pretext to loose the dogs of war, and even though few except those in the profession of the sea knew it, 'Jenkins' Ear' was already being made the name of the widespread sea war that was unfolding. Not that the lawless high seas were a peaceful world to begin with.

Mainwaring pursed his lips, watching the pattern of the sunlight's movements. 'At war over a damned thin argument.

More like a jest,' he muttered quietly. 'The Dons've done far worse than lop off ears. Still, in war there's promotion. And with one good prize we'd . . .'

'Cap'n?' A gruff voice sounded at the cabin door.

Mainwaring looked up. Isaiah Hooke stepped over the sill. He was shorter than Mainwaring, but deep chested and powerfully built. His stocky frame was clad in a tar-smeared pair of duck breeches opened at the knee to make pantaloons, a grimy checked shirt, and an old waistcoat of striped kersey. He had a scarlet bandana loosely knotted round his neck, and into the broad leather belt he wore round his waist was thrust a long seaman's knife on its lanyard. His thick, blond hair was 'hauled aft' into a tarry pigtail that reached to the small of his back, and in one ear, above the bulge of a tobacco-stuffed cheek, a golden earring gleamed. He was barefoot and hatless, with the coarse shovel hands of a veteran seaman, and his round, tanned face was a study in simplicity and directness.

'Though' yew'd loike t' know. Timothy, thar, up in th' maintop, says he caught a flash o' canvas on the nor'ard horizon jus' now. Mr Pellowe's lookin' at it in th' glass.' He wiped the back of one hand across his mouth. 'Could be the buggerin' admiral hisself an' his squadr'n. Leastwise, one o' his frigates.'

Mainwaring frowned. 'Damn. I don't like to think Vernon caught up with us that soon. If that Spaniard sees him – '

Hooke padded in, ducking under the beams to sit heavily on the barrel of one of the guns, his thick fingers splaying over his knees.

'We'd be whoreson unlucky. But it could be 'im, zur, ay? Christ, if it's a bloody *guardacostas* . . .'

Mainwaring shook his head. Standing to get a better look at the stained and water-marked chart, he pushed the royal

14

warrant and letter-of-marque to one side, and pointed a finger at the point below the great island of Hispaniola.

'I don't think so, Isaiah. Not this far at sea. Look here,' he said. 'Lead, latitude and lookout don't add up to precise pilotage. But unless I'm a fool or can't do an octant sight worth a damn we're right about – here.'

Hooke moved closer, scratching a flea bite under his shirt as he peered down at the chart. 'A hunnert leagues sou' west o' Cabo Beata. An' damned near due south o' th' Morants, ay?'

'That's if I'm right,' said Mainwaring. 'Tracking right across the course Vernon'd have to steer out of Port Royal.' His eyes met Hooke's. 'Make things a damned sight easier if that ship's a merchantman. And alone.'

Hooke scratched his thatch-like hair. 'That ain't the half uv it. Christ knows who we c'd beat off with *these* 'ere toys!' he said, jerking a thumb at one of the three-pounders. 'The *guardacostas* come armed t' th' bloody teeth. An' with enough garlic-chewin' Dons t' board us three or four times over!'

Mainwaring nodded. Hooke was referring to the swift, well-armed, small ships that the Spanish maintained in an endless war against the efforts of the English – and others – to infiltrate their trade and shipping Empire. They were heavily gunned, usually overmanned, and could either be a savage foe or a laughable enemy, depending on the mercurial Latin temperament of their crews at any given moment.

For a fully armed British or French warship, even a sloop, dealing with a *guardacostas* would have been a simple matter; for *Athena*, so similar in size and armament to the dozens of small, underarmed and undermanned New England merchant craft putting out under real letters-of-marque in the hopes of turning a quicker profit than the harsh sea usually allowed, it would be a fight to the death. Small ships like *Athena* relied on their speed and handiness to escape from

15

superior opponents; but such was Spanish shipbuilding skill that the *guardacostas* were, if anything, likely to be faster than the heavy northern hulls of their enemies. That a canny Yankee merchant, using the small reserve of profit which he had built up in his chandlery business in Old Town on the Vineyard, had been able to buy the Bermuda-built *Athena* as she lay seized for debts and sell her into a ship-poor Royal Navy, meant that Mainwaring was master of one of the few ships that might make a match in swiftness with the Spanish ships. But in arms and men – even the mixture of sturdy British tars and sinewy, hard Vineyarders that made up the *Athena* – Mainwaring and Hooke both knew the odds would be with the Spanish.

Hooke's eye gleamed at Mainwaring. 'What if he *be* a Don?'

'We'll have to fight him, Isaiah. And if necessary throw ourselves in the path of whosoever those topsails to the south'ard belong.'

The master's eyes narrowed. 'Christ, Cap'n. That'd be loike slittin' yer own throat.'

Mainwaring's smile was thin. 'Our orders are clear enough. Steer ahead of Vernon. Divert Spanish attention from his track to Porto Bello by doing what we can as a Yankee "privateer" along the Main. And if we see or intercept any ship – or ships – that may detect Vernon and warn the Spanish, we are to help keep that element of surprise in place.'

'By gettin' blowed out o' th' water?'

'If necessary. Vernon will turn away from any ship action his lookouts spot.'

Hooke shook his head. 'Damned hard articles, I say. Why, I . . .'

A young seaman in a red stocking cap thrust his head through the cabin door.

'Yer pard'n, Cap'n. Mr Pellowe says there ain't no vessel to nor'ard. Least not that he can see right now. But we're comin' down fast on the Spaniard, an' he says t' say that the fleet, or whatever, t' southward, seems to be alterin' course away from us.'

Mainwaring looked at Hooke. 'I think it's time we were on deck again, Isaiah.'

Ducking under the beams and out of the narrow door, the men swung up the companionway just outside and emerged into the open, their eyes slitted against the fierce glare of the sun off the scrubbed white deck.

Athena was punching swiftly along before the quartering wind, and as Mainwaring moved aft up the sloping deck to the tiny area which served as the quarterdeck – and therefore his private domain, even in a schooner – he threw a quick look aloft at the set of the schooner's canvas. Behind him, the main sheet tackle, shackled to the black iron bar of its 'horse' groaned and popped with the building force of the wind and its pressure on the great curving wing of the mainsail. Under *Athena*'s counter the sea was roaring and gurgling with a sound of speed that never failed to delight Mainwaring's ear.

'She flies on this point, Cap'n' said Hooke, at Mainwaring's shoulder. 'Christ, she's sweet!'

'Aye. And damned lucky we are for it,' said Mainwaring. 'I have a feeling we'll need every knot she can make before we tally up this cruise.' He looked aloft at the angle of the pennant which streamed from the mainmast truck, and spat over the lee rail. 'Larboard tack, now. I'll tell you when.'

'Aye, Cap'n.' Hooke moved to stand near the helm. He jerked a thumb off towards the south. 'Yew've a mind t' run up astern of him?'

Mainwaring shook his head slightly. 'Just giving us options, Mr Hooke. Just giving us options.' He loped off down the

17

deck and then clambered out over the rail to the foot of the windward main shrouds.

'Mr Pellowe!' he barked.

The midshipman had been peering into the binnacle box and started visibly at Mainwaring's voice. 'S – sir?'

'Call the ship to Quarters, if you please! And I'll ask you to hoist Spanish colours. Your may recall Mr Hooke relieved them from that unfortunate grenadier in Port Royal!'

Hooke looked at Pellowe for an instant, shifted his plug to the other cheek, then squinted up at Mainwaring, who was already ten feet off the deck and monkeying higher.

'Cap'n? No disrespect, but why'n hell *Spanish* colours?'

Mainwaring hooked one leg round the trembling ratlines. 'If he's not a Don or a Frenchman, we can hoist our own soon enough. If he *is*, it gives us a chance to close with him, eh? Hoist 'em!'

Hooke scratched his thatch. 'Hell,' he muttered. 'Just as soon hoist up th' old Red Duster, an' t' blazes with false colours. Still, orders be orders . . .' He turned and poked a finger at two hands coiling lines at the mainmast fife rail. 'Dirk? Yew'n Isaac get that damned greaser rag out o' my cabin an' run it up. Roundly, now!'

Beside him, Pellow cupped his hands and sought out the sturdy figure of Aiken, *Athena*'s boatswain, who was working with several hands to clear a fouled headsail downhaul.

'Mr Aiken! Pipe the hands to Quarter, if you please!'

Within a few moments the high, twittering call of Aiken's piping was echoing through the ship, but it produced no line of marine drummers resolutely thumping out the rhythm of 'Heart Of Oak' while hundreds of men thundered up companionways to their gun batteries. *Athena* was a small ship, and readying her for battle was a far less complicated process, though just as purposeful. Gundeck equipment in large warships was secured on racks overhead; but in *Athena*, it was only the guns in Mainwaring's cabin that were below decks. The ship's principal weaponry was mounted on the upper deck, and it was there that the organized tumult of casting guns free to operate, of setting out match and weapons tubs, of doubling up on key lines, lifts and halliards took place. For *Athena*, it was little more than the readying process a merchant vessel might have undertaken to beat off pirates; but the quick efficiency with which it was carried out was far from the manner of a merchantman's crew. *Athena* was, without doubt, a ship of war.

Meanwhile, Mainwaring had climbed briskly upwards, pausing in his progress aloft only when *Athena* heeled too far to make releasing a handhold safe. Soon the tarred shrouds narrowed until he could barely wedge his toes into them, and then he was hanging backward for a frightening moment as he wrestled himself out around the futtock shrouds before gaining the precarious perch of the main crosstrees. His heart was pounding almost painfully hard – more than the climb usually produced – and it annoyed Mainwaring that as calm as he might think he felt, his body was choosing to react otherwise.

The maintop lookout was a pimply Nantucket youth named Sawyer, with watery eyes and lank, blond hair that was whipped round his pinched face by the wind. 'She's right off the bows, Cap'n,' he said. This was accompanied by the levelling of a long, bony finger towards the horizon.

There was a bellow from ahead, in the foremast, and the bandana-swathed face of the lookout there peered round the foremast cap at them. 'Yew c'n see her floppy tops'l bunts, Cap'n! A trader, or I'm damned!'

Mainwaring shielded his eyes from the sea glare with one hand, the other wrapped in an iron grip round a topmast shroud as *Athena* heeled sickeningly beneath them. Then he reached behind to where he had thrust the big telescope into the back of his waistband and hauled it out to full extension, bracing his feet and trying to free his upper body and arms from *Athena*'s motion. By dint of effort he managed to centre the distant ship in the flat image of the glass and draw it slowly into focus.

'Ah.'

'Pardon, zur?' said Sawyer.

'That's a merchantman, by God. And Spanish, not French, by the look of her.'

Sawyer bared yellowed gap teeth. 'A prize, right 'nough, Cap'n!'

Mainwaring slammed the glass shut and thrust it back into his waistband. He swung dizzyingly out over the edge of the crosstrees and scrabbled for a grip on the futtock shrouds.

'That's as may be, Sawyer,' he said. 'Depends on things. Like your keeping a hawk-eyed watch on that vessel ahead instead of me, eh?'

The youth flushed, then grinned again.

'Then just mind you watch her!'

With quick agility Mainwaring went off down the ratlines, springing the last six feet to *Athena*'s deck with a thump that turned Hooke on his heel, stumping up and down beside Pellowe in front of the binnacle box.

Pellowe fingered his neckcloth as Mainwaring arrived at the rail. 'What is she, sir?'

'Queer ship,' said Mainwaring, his eyes narrowed in thought. 'No visible gunports. And her canvas is damned near all three sheets to the wind.'

Hooke had rolled closer. 'Then it ain't the greaser Navy, Cap'n?'

Mainwaring eyed him and shook his head, still thoughtful. 'Don't think so. The Dons may be hard to predict in a sea fight, but they build good ships. And the Navy ones I've seen are sailed well.'

'Well, then, hell's bells, zur, what're we a-waitin' on – ?'

Mainwaring scratched his chin. 'Just a feeling, Isaiah. I've had it before.'

Hooke and Pellowe glanced at each other and then looked back at Mainwaring in puzzlement.

He spat into the sea. 'Hunting, once, as a lad. With my father on the mainland, up the Connecticut way. My father'd stalked a four-point buck into a clearing. Took him all day to do it, and we were wet and hungry. He was all set to put a ball into him. But I had an odd feeling then; wouldn't let him draw back from half to full cock. You know the good click it makes?'

The men noded.

Mainwaring squinted out at the distant ship. 'The deer sprang away in the next instant, and we hadn't got up from our crouch when a French war party came right through the clearing, not ten yards away. Ottawas mostly, and a handful of Algonquins. Two French officers leading them. We would've died, without a doubt. And knowing the Ottawas, not easily.'

Pellowe followed his gaze towards the far ship. 'And you've got that feeling now, sir? About her?'

Mainwaring nodded, his mouth a tight line. 'Just a tad.' His eyes swung forward. 'You've piped Quarters. What about Abner and his guns?'

Hooke parted with a stream of brown juice over the side. 'He worked 'em last night agin, zur. Figgers he c'n give yew three guns workin' on one side. That's if ye'll not expect more'n two rounds a minute.'

Mainwaring winced. '*Two*? And just three guns?'

Another jet of juice. 'Hell, Cap'n, they mostly ain't Royal Navy gunners. Jes' Vineyarders. Need time t' work 'em up.'

'Time,' said Mainwaring. 'May not be enough, Isaiah.' He

took a deep breath. 'Very well, then, Mr Pellowe, you'll tell Abner I'll only want the bowchaser.'

Pellowe stared. 'The little three-pounder, sir? Naught else?'

'You heard me. Tell him. And for God's sake tell him to spike it over to the *windward* side of the fo'c'sle. The silly bugger almost blew the tack of the foretopm'st staysail last time!'

'Sir,' Pellowe grinned. 'He won't like that.'

Mainwaring's eye gleamed. 'Abner's a better shot when he's heated up. And we'll need a good eye today.'

Hooke was scratching thoughtfully at his stubble. 'What d'ye have in mind, zur?

Mainwaring smiled faintly. 'Something fairly simple, Mr Hooke. Let's run her down first, eh?'

Athena roared steadily on, as the sea around her gleamed a deeper blue with white flecks under the climbing sun. On the southern horizon the Spanish vessel was a miniature shape of white canvas above a red hull, the Bourbon ensign a flicker of white at her stern. Her lookouts would have been watching *Athena* now for a while. And that meant it was time, thought Mainwaring, to get the Spanish flag hoisted. Where in blazes was – ?

'Greaser flag goin' aloft, sir!' sang out Aiken's mate, a rat-like man named Slade, from the leeward taffrail. Mainwaring squinted aloft to see a tattered white ensign rising to *Athena*'s gaff. Unlike virtually any other rig, it was easier with a schooner to hoist the colours to a block at the mainsail peak than set this on a tall ensign staff at the stern; the mainboom, a murderous, mighty spar that overhung *Athena*'s transom, would have snapped off an ensign staff each time the schooner tacked.

'Keep a loose hitch on that flag halliard, Slade,' called

Mainwaring over the sea noise. 'We'll hoist our own colours again soon enough.'

Slade bared sharp teeth at him as he shambled loosely forward, tar-spotted canvas trousers flapping in the wind. 'Cleat'd with a slip knot, Cap'n. Yew jes' give the word, and, why, down she'll come like Poll's drawers!'

Mainwaring could not hold back a smile as he heard the cackle of laughter from the men near the helm. He squinted off to the south, seeing out of the corner of his eye Abner and his clutch of willing, if somewhat inept, gunners man-handling the slim little bowchaser over to the windward side of the foredeck. The Spanish ship was perhaps three leagues off now, the garish red and gilt of the hull visible to the naked eye.

It was time to make the first move.

'Sheets and braces, there!' Mainwaring barked through cupped hands. 'We'll harden up to a reach, Mr Hooke! Mr Pellowe! Your course will be due south, sir!'

'Aye, aye, sir!' chorused both men. Hooke growled at the helmsman, then bellowed down the deck. In moments the turns were taken off, and the last man was in place, eyes looking aft for the signal.

Pellowe and Hooke exchanged glances, and Pellowe nodded.

'Helm down, Harry!' said Hooke to the helmsman. 'Course due south. Heave in on those sheets there! Damnation, Jonah, you're like an old woman with that foresheet! Git the damned thing in!'

Athena heeled dramatically as the thick, capable hands of Burke, the helmsman, spun the broad oaken wheel. The schooner swung on to a course dead across the wind and the ranks of swells; the long finger of the bowsprit and jib-boom pointed now at the distant but growing shape of the Spaniard. Aloft, the foretopsail brace blocks squealed as the sail was hauled round to match as far as possible the drawing power of *Athena*'s fore-and-aft sails. It was this point of sailing that was the schooner's fastest, and it was now that the skill and good sense of her island builders became most evident; as she swung to her new course and her canvas was sheeted home, *Athena* lay over slowly on her leeward side and began to roar along with breathtaking speed. Awe for the power of their ship moved, unspoken, through all of *Athena*'s crew, as it will to men at sea; and like most men at sea, they let that spark of wonder lie unseen, deep in the sea chests of their souls. They swaggeringly spat over the rail or made rough humour with a messmate, sharing together the deceit that they were not moved, and touched, by the beauty of the creation their hands and strength brought to life.

Athena thundered on. The Spanish ship was now no more than a league, or three miles, away, and as Mainwaring braced himself against the weather rail abaft the helm, to watch how the ship was being steered, the Spaniard could be seen to be crowding on more sail. She was staying dead before the wind, on a westerly course, while the schooner raced southward across the wind to the interception. Seeing the flash of white, Mainwaring pulled the long telescope from its sheath by the wheel, where he had replaced it minutes before. It opened in one long pull, the brass tubes squealing within one another.

'He's hanging out more washing, sir,' said Pellowe.

'Yes.'

Mainwaring brought the image into focus. The Spanish captain had his men aloft on the t'gallant yards; he could see the small human figures laying out and struggling. Then, as he watched, the fore t'gallants'l dropped open from its yard, billowing out loosely and unevenly as it was sheeted home clumsily. It was odd how the ship looked in the flat image of the glass: a homely, squat duck, ruffling its feathers in a high gale, with all the grace of a flat-footed barnyard creature. The contrast with the smooth power of *Athena* could not be greater.

'Slow and sloppy. Didn't overhaul the buntlines. That's no *guardacostas*, that ship,' said Mainwaring.

Hooke stumped up to the rail beside him, cheek abulge with a fresh plug. 'She be showin' any guns now, Cap'n?' he asked.

The glass went up again. 'No. Wait. Yes. Two guns on the upper deck. Still no gunports visible. Could mean four, maybe six guns all told.' Mainwaring felt *Athena* lurch and yaw beneath him, and threw a glance at the binnacle box.

'Mind your helmsman's course, Mr Pellowe! Due south is where I want the ship's head!'

'Sir!' said Pellowe. 'Due south, Burke. For God's sake keep your mind on your task.'

'Aye, aye, sir,' muttered a contrite Burke.

'Six guns,' repeated Hooke. 'That lays fer trouble.'

Athena bent before a booming gust that sent the seas roaring along her rail, and Mainwaring clutched for a hand-hold to keep from slithering down the wet, slick planking.

'That's if they serve 'em properly, Isaiah,' he said, over the sea. 'And if they have a willing target.'

Hooke stared. 'What d'ye mean, Cap'n?'

Mainwaring handed him the long telescope. 'Here. Look at her stern gallery. What d'ye see?'

Hooke managed to centre the image of the Spaniard's sternworks in the glass: a mass of gleaming gilt and red paint. 'Stern lights, 'cross the transom. A gallery, like as to a man o' war. One o' them buggering' big stern lanterns wiv a statue on top. An' the stern staff. Naught else. What – ?'

'No stern chase ports?'

Hooke looked again. ''Course. They ain't no guns what'll bear aft!'

Mainwaring nodded. 'And that suggests we do what?'

'Simple. We just range up astern of 'em, nice as yew please. Keep out o' th' way o' them broadside guns an' let Abner bang away at 'em till they strike.'

'Right. And just what a privateer would usually do if he was worried about facing guns.'

'Aye. Hell, Cap'n, I'd wager a shillin' ye had that in mind t' begin wiv.'

Mainwaring nodded. 'I was hoping for no stern chase ports. Only option they'd have would be to smash out some of those stern lights and put a gun in the great cabin. Not a thing a Don officer would agree to readily.'

Hooke rubbed his hands, like a cook over a pot. 'What now, then, Cap'n?'

Mainwaring's tone was brisk. 'Mr Pellowe! Join us here, please!' The American waited for a moment until Pellowe had stepped quickly over. 'Stephen, I'll trouble you to get for'rard and see that Abner has that chaser well lashed down, with only a touch of slack on the breeching line.' He groped in a waistcoat pocket and handed a brass key to Pellowe. 'Here's a spare magazine key in case Abner's goes adrift. The lads will have to monkey their shot buckets up through the for'rard companion. And I'll want another cutlass tub aft, right here. Clear?'

'Sir,' Pellowe hustled off.

'And I'll trouble *you*, Isaiah, to make sure that you're well for'rard enough so that fore and main respond to some damned rapid sailhandling orders!'

'Aye, Cap'n!' And in the next instant, Hooke was padding off forward, the first orders lashing out from his lips at the knot of men gathered in *Athena*'s waist.

Mainwaring fixed a hard look at Burke on the wheel and then winked at him. 'Burke, you'll stay on the helm. But steer us foul and you'll live in the cable tier for a week. And for Christ's sake don't assume I've given you permission to die!'

Burke grinned wordlessly, pleased, and took a steely grip on the wheel.

Athena knifed over the back of a huge swell and heeled, the sea thundering under her bows and counter. The wind was building, and as Mainwaring wiped the spray from his eyes to peer ahead, he could see that the schooner was rapidly overhauling the wallowing, ship-rigged Spanish barge, so rapidly that the latter was only a sea mile away, if that.

Mainwaring glanced at the binnacle box and its swaying compass card. To keep on the track he wanted, he would have to bear away again, and curve in towards the Spaniard's stern. Steering for a point ahead of her would close the distance faster, but that odd feeling in Mainwaring's neck was so damned insistent: *Athena*, it said, *must not pass down that Spaniard's flank.*

He cupped his hands. 'For'rard, there, Mr Hooke! I'll trouble you to stand by to ease the sheets!' He waited until a knot of men, driven by Hooke's tongue, had scrambled past him and cleared away the mainsheet, matched by others who worked at the foresail and headsail sheets, and the tops'l braces.

'Ease the sheets, there!' he called. 'Up helm, Burke. Easy. A spoke at a time.' He watched the compass card as *Athena* swung under him, and the great booms winged out over the lee rail, the sheets squealing through their blocks. 'Now. Steady your ship's head on that, Burke! Steer west sou' west!'

'West sou' west. Aye, Cap'n!' Burke was putting all his considerable strength and skill into the steering now, his eyes flicking from the compass card to the foresail leech, to the streaming masthead pennant and back again.

Mainwaring peered ahead as *Athena* began a slow, pitching roll under the swells that lifted her under her counter. The

Spaniard was turned three-quarters away, still holding his westerly course, and with no visible reaction yet to the schooner's approach. Perhaps, thought Mainwaring, the false colours were doing the trick. Or were they merely pretending not to notice . . .

Aiken was at his shoulder, knuckling his brow. 'Lads are at Quarters, sir. Not as swift as most in King Ge-arge's Navy, bless 'im, but keen enough.'

Mainwaring nodded, still watching the Spaniard. 'Good. And the gunner?'

'Mr Pellowe says t' tell ye that Abner's loaded an' primed the chaser. The lads have monkeyed up ten rounds. And there's the extra cutlass barrel.'

As Aiken made this last statement, two bare-chested seamen staggered up the midships companionway with a barrel into which close to a dozen ancient cutlasses, hangers and knives of various patterns were jammed. They wrestled it to the mainmast foot, set it down with a thump, cursed it, and made off forward.

Hooke had come aft and was looking at the barrel. ''Tain't hardly the arms o' th' terror o' th' seas, is it?' he muttered, shaking his head.

Mainwaring had once more unlimbered the great telescope and trained it on the Spaniard. 'Eh? No. But we appear to be having some kind of effect, Isaiah. There's a lot of worried-looking gentlemen peering over the transom rail at us.'

'Think they've cottoned t' us, Cap'n?'

'I think not. Still . . .' He glanced up at the rippling ensign. 'We've perhaps five minutes until Abner gets off his first round.'

Hooke arced a jet of tobacco juice over the lee rail, and wiped his mouth on his sleeve. 'Aye. So?'

'Let's see if we can draw him out. Hoist our own colours!'

Hooke's tobacco-brown teeth bared in a sudden broad

grin. 'Aye, sir! Slade! Get aft, y' rot-gutted rat! Get th' greaser colours down! An' hoist our own!'

In the next minute the Spanish ensign was crumpled around Slade's feet, and with quick, steady hauls he was sending the bundled packet of *Athena*'s own colours up to the mainsail gaff peak.

'Lord!' said Hooke, at Mainwaring's elbow. 'Wouldn't I like t' see the faces over yonder when that breaks t' the wind!'

Mainwaring handed him the telescope. 'Then do so,' he said, and nodded at Slade.

Slade tugged on one fall of the halliard, and up at the peak, winging out over the water, the tightly packed roll burst open, and the blood-red British ensign streamed out, a breathtaking splash of colour against the deep blue of the sky and the white of *Athena*'s canvas.

Unable to contain themselves, the watching schoonermen scattered about the ship gave an involuntary cheer.

'Christ save me. Now *that's* true colours!' Hooke growled.

Mainwaring pointed with his chin, like a Pequod warrior, at the Spaniard. 'And what's that true colour doing to our Spanish friends?'

'Eh? Oh.' Hooke hefted up the glass. 'Well, they ain't – Sweet Jesus!'

'What is it?'

Hooke handed him the glass. ''T ain't good, zur. Look.'

The image of the slowly pitching Spanish ship filled the field of the lens. As Mainwaring's eyes adjusted, he saw that one of the heavily gilt windows of the stern lights across the ship's transom was vanishing as musket butts and axes smashed out glass and mouldings. In the gloom within, Mainwaring could make out a clutch of feverishly working figures wrestling with something heavy and bulky. He felt a cold knot grab at his stomach.

'Well, I'm damned,' he whispered, lowering the glass.

'Looks like we didn't fool him from the start, Cap'n,' said Hooke, sucking a tooth.

Mainwaring peered through the glass again. The red-painted muzzle of a ship's gun, it's bore gaping like an obscene mouth, was snouting out through the smashed stern light. 'Bloody hell. He's putting out a sternchaser.'

'How big, Cap'n?'

'Twelve-pounder, at least. Mayhap a sixteen. How in hell did they get *that* in there?' Mainwaring bit his lip in thought, lowering the glass.

'*Twelve*? That'll outrange Abner, fer sure!' Hooke swore luridly.

Mainwaring snapped the glass shut and thrust it back into its sheath. 'If we give the bastard a chance to use it!' he said, through tight lips. 'Get for'rard, Isaiah. Tend those sheets and tops'l braces smartly. I want every knot we can squeeze out of her!'

Hooke wiped his mouth. 'Aye, aye.' Then he paused in mid-step. 'What are ye goin' t' do, zur?'

'Rush in, Isaiah. Before he takes a swing at us with that big iron fist.'

'What, *board* him?' Hooke stared at him.

Mainwaring's tone was like a knife. 'We've got a choice, Isaiah: sit off and be pounded to gull meat, or go in and grapple with the bastard. Now which do you prefer?'

Hooke gave him a grin. And in the next minute he was loping forward, voice raised in a penetrating bellow. 'Sheets an' braces, lads! Let's make her fly!'

Mainwaring peered ahead. The Spanish ship was alarmingly close now, dead ahead over the bows. *Athena* was overhauling the other vessel at a frightening rate. It was still too great an angle for the gun in the Spaniard's stern, as *Athena* rushed in on the former's quarter. As long as the Spaniard held her course, and the gunners were not able to handspike the twelve-pounder round far enough, *Athena* might be able to come in alongside with only small arms fire to worry about. Except for that damned smooth side, where gunports *should* be –

'Cap'n! It's a whoreson of a long shot, but I c'd hit her now!' Abner's shriek echoed back from the foredeck, where he crouched with his little gun's crew round the bowchaser. 'Can I fire a Yankee ball into her arse?'

There was a burst of coarse laughter around the ship, and Mainwaring shook his head in mock disgust. 'Sweet Christ, Abner, you're a foul-mouthed bastard,' he roared through cupped hands. 'And no respecter of women. Aye! *Fire!*'

Abner's portfire arced down, and the little gun fired with a thump, the pink lancet of the 'huff' leaping head-high from the vent. The bursting cloud of acrid smoke from the muzzle was whipped away in a split second into tendrils twisting into nothingness around the bowsprit.

Athena sped on, foam wild around her bows as a broad swell overtook her. But Mainwaring was oblivious to the schooner's motion as he scanned anxiously, looking for the fall of the shot. It seemed an impossibly long time . . .

Then, in the next split second, he saw the ball slap into the back of a rolling, white-capped swell, a few yards astern of the Spaniard. The geyser rose in a glittering lance of spray as high as the ship's mizzentop before collapsing back into a drifting mist across her afterdeck.

Abner's piercing voice was ringing out again as his crew worked in frantic efforts to reload the gun. Pellowe, Mainwaring saw, had pitched in and was muscling a shot bucket forward from the companionway.

'Damned near, Cap'n!' called Abner. 'Had 'er quoin'd right down. Hell, next one'll strike home, sartin!'

Mainwaring cupped his hands. 'One more round, Mr Pellowe! Then have Abner and his lads get a blade in their hands! We're going to board!' And as he saw Pellowe's eyes widen in astonishment, he was already looking for Hooke's sturdy form at the foremast pinrail, where he was swigging off slackness in a halliard, the clump of men working with him all speed and energy.

'Mr Hooke!' Mainwaring called, gripping *Athena*'s rail as she heaved up her counter before another onrushing swell. 'Pick two hands each from fo'c'sle and afterguard and get 'em on the larboard rail with those grapnels we set aside last watch!' He took a deeper breath to bellow the full length of the schooner, 'Set a man each on every sheet to let fly when we strike her! The rest of you, get a weapon in your hands and form on the larboard side! We're goin' to run alongside the bastard and board him!' Mainwaring spat, trying to clear the sudden dryness in his throat. *If something hidden in that smooth hull doesn't do for us . . .* said a small voice in his head.

'Abner!' he went on, clearing the voice from his head with a shake. 'You and your gunners and the foremast and fo'c'sle hands cross with Mr Pellowe! Mainmast and afterguard, with Mr Hooke and myself!'

There was a general dive for the cutlass tubs. One seaman, brandishing a huge blade with an ancient basket hilt and guard, stared back at Mainwaring in momentary bafflement as he hefted it. 'What'll we *do* when we board 'er, Cap'n?' he cried.

'*Do*? Christ, Jonas, we *take* her!'

A burst of laughter swirled round the man, and his face split abruptly in a wild grin. 'Aye, sir!' he bayed, and made for the rail.

Mainwaring sprang to the binnacle beside the sweating, tight-lipped Burke. 'Steady as you go now, Burke,' said Mainwaring. 'No sudden changes of helm. Ignore it if they shoot. Just get us sweet and straight alongside of her.'

Burke nodded vigorously, afraid to talk.

Mainwaring squinted ahead. *Athena* was boiling in on the Spaniard so swiftly that the latter's shape was looming now over the pitching bows, a mass of red and gilt and luffing, flaxen-white canvas, a more frightening shape than it had seemed in the glass. Mainwaring felt a chill of doubt as he saw the dozen or so figures with slung muskets who were monkeying frantically up the ratlines towards the tops.

Damn me, am I a fool to attempt this? he thought. *This will not be easy . . .*

'Down a spoke, Burke! There! No nearer! Steer so that damned sternchaser can't bear on us!'

Burke nodded, eyes aflame, and found his voice. 'Aye Cap'n! Christ, she's close!'

Mainwaring cupped his hands. 'For'rard, there! Stay low till we strike her! Mr Hooke! The grapnels?'

From where he crouched, Hooke pointed at four men who hefted up grapnels and lines for Mainwaring to see.

'Good! Try and hook on at the shrouds! And tie 'em off quickly, or we'll lose her!'

The men nodded, eyes white with excitement. Mainwaring looked at their strained faces, feeling again the doubt. Perhaps he should have simply put *Athena* about when he saw the Spaniard, and let the two rival fleets sail on, now seemingly unaware of one another. The Spanish, if that was their identity, appeared to have turned away; and Vernon's ships, somewhere up there just over that northern horizon, were still safe and unseen. Why had he not –

'*Fire!*' Abner's cry rang out. The bowchaser's report was a sharp thump, jolting Mainwaring back into focus. The smoke swirled perversely up round the headsails, boiling round *Athena*'s bows and obscuring all sight forward. The Spanish ship disappeared from view, and Mainwaring had an image instead of *Athena*'s deck superimposed against a swirling white screen: there were about a dozen men a few feet

33

forward of where he stood, crouched with Hooke behind the larboard bulwark at the foot of the mainmast shrouds. Another ten or so were hunkered down in a knot at the foot of the fore, and Abner and his crew still crouched round their gun, with Pellowe a few feet aft of them.

'God damn that smoke!' Mainwaring raved, slapping the rail in frustration. 'Burke, you've got to get us in hard alongside her. Graze her, and we'll slide free! You've got to hit – !'

Burke was staring ahead, his eyes suddenly wide with shock. 'Jesus, Cap'n! *Look!*'

Mainwaring spun, and felt a cold fist hit his stomach. The smoke of Abner's last round had been ripped to shreds by the wind. But instead of revealing the Spaniard still bearing away downwind, it showed a frightening, much closer image: the Spaniard had hardened up swiftly to a reach across the wind, to starboard, and the gleaming red and gilt hull was an eye-filling shape steering dead across *Athena*'s bows, all towering, taut-bellied canvas and heeling, spray-rinsed hull lifting and plunging along.

And along her side, six carefully concealed gunports, so beautifully faired into the line of the hull planking and wales that they had been virtually invisible, were being hauled open. As Mainwaring looked on, the red muzzles of truck guns were snouting out, the cries and chants of their hauling gun crews and the squeal of their trucks carrying against the wind to Mainwaring's ear.

Above the guns, the Spaniard's canvas was being sheeted home with brisk efficiency now, and the sun glistened on the pike heads and musket barrels of the swarms of men who were suddenly appearing up hatchways to the waist and foredeck of the red ship. The Spaniard forged ahead with visible acceleration, and a large, spotless ensign rose snapping to the maintruck.

A trap! cried Mainwaring to himself. *God damn my stupidity. We are the prey*!

Ahead, Pellowe had sprung to his feet, pointing frantically with his cutlass, calling out. 'Captain! Look! She's – !'

In two swift paces Mainwaring was at the helm.

'Quickly, Burke! Down helm!'

'Wh – what, Cap'n? Did – ?'

'*Do it*!' Mainwaring was cupping his hands, bellowing at the top of his lungs over the wind and sea roar. 'Sheets and braces, Mr Hooke! Mr Pellowe! Drop those weapons and stand to the lines! We'll harden up to a reach! *Move*, if you want to live!'

Mainwaring's savage tone drove home the order. The cutlasses and weapons clattered to the deck and the men dived for the pinrails, scrabbling frantically at the coils. But *Athena* was already heeling with a thunderous roar under her lee bow, swinging in a great lunge off to larboard, the bowsprit dipping away from the red shape until the view forward was clear. A half-dozen men scrambled aft past Mainwaring and Burke to seize the great mainsheet, and in the next instant *Athena*'s blocks were squealing in high-pitched cacophony as the schoonermen hauled with furious strength to trim the ship's canvas. The spars creaked overhead, and the spray-rinsed, slick deck canted to an almost untenable angle, the abandoned weapons rattling down into the scuppers.

And then, in the next instant, the killing broadside Mainwaring had sensed a warning for was there.

As the Spanish ship heeled dramatically under the press of its tight, motionless canvas, a line of brilliant pink flashes rippled along its side, flashes that spat ahead of them billowing gouts of smoke that swirled and towered up through the Spaniard's masts like an enormous funeral pyre. A broken thunderclap of sound punched at Mainwaring and the straining *Athena*, and they stared as, in the swirl of the foaming wake where Mainwaring had turned the schooner away a moment before, six close-spaced shot splashes leaped up, glittering towers of spray that collapsed back into a drifting curtain of rainbowed mist.

Athena swung on, the sea hissing and leaping along her flank as she turned into the wind. Mainwaring's hand slapped down like a pistol shot on the hard wood of the rail.

'Damn me, are ye all struck dumb? Stand to your work!' As the schoonermen ceased gaping at the place where the shot had fallen and shook themselves into action, Mainwaring sprang back beside the wheel. 'Due south, Burke!' Mainwaring filled his lungs. 'Mr Hooke! Let her pay off to a reach, larboard tack! Quickly, now! The tops'l's luffing!'

He looked forward, where Aiken was struggling with several men to haul in the slack of the shaking foresail's sheet. The canvas was rippling with great, ear-jarring booms. 'Down slack on that, Aiken! Mr Hooke! Get that tops'l braced and sheeted round! She'll go aback in an instant!'

Mainwaring spun. The Spanish ship had come into the wind itself, its great foretopsail going aback with a clearly audible thump, the headsails rippling with dark, wave-like shadows crossing their faces.

He's turning. Pursuing us, the bastard, thought Mainwaring.

'Winton! Sawyer!' he barked. 'Down slack on that main sheet, there! Roundly, lads, with a will!'

The knot of men sweating over the mainsheet behind the wheel grunted with effort. The sheet squealed in its great blocks, and as the purchase did its work the great boom was hauled closer inboard, the sheet coiling like a vast snake round the legs of the men muscling it in. Beneath his feet Mainwaring felt *Athena* heel over and begin to plunge ahead.

From forward, Hooke was bellowing, 'That'll duck us away, Cap'n! Hell, he'll never catch – !'

'*Broadside, Cap'n!*' shrieked one of the mainsheet men in Mainwaring's ear.

'M'sieur? Capitán Rodriguez sends his compliments, and says that *Aguerra* is engaging the Englishman.'

Rigaud de la Roche-Bourbon, Chevalier d'Anjou and *capitaine de vaisseau* in the Navy of His Most Christian Majesty Louis XV of France, swung his white-hosed legs over the edge of the box bunk in the spacious and elegant great cabin of the Spanish sixty-gun ship *San Josefe*, and nodded to the swarthy seaman at the door.

'Is he?' he sniffed. 'Very well. My compliments to Señor Rodriguez, and I will be on deck directly.'

'*Si*,' breathed the man, and scuttled off.

It took Roche-Bourbon several minutes to wrestle into the blue and scarlet glory of his full uniform, unaided by the well-meaning attentions of Rodriguez' hunchbacked servant, who scraped and bowed, tugging ineffectually at a cuff here, a coat-tail there, jabbering in a breathy Spanish dialect Roche-Bourbon could not understand.

Roche-Bourbon sighed. *Our Spanish cousins and their damnable penchant for the niceties of regalia*, he thought. Were he back aboard his own stout sixty-four, the *Diamant*, he would be in the simple practicality of an unlaced frock coat and duck breeches, and be damned to silk and brocade.

Encumbered with cane, dress hanger and scented handkerchief, he emerged on deck, squinting at the glare, and climbed the gilt-banistered companion ladder to the quarterdeck, where Rodriguez and a good half-dozen necessary – or unnecessary – officers stood to windward of the helm, a clutch of figures ablaze in scarlet, gilt lace and wind-ruffled egret feathers. Rodriguez was a short, oily-skinned man with lank black hair and an enormous, wart-tipped nose. He was hopping from one foot to the other in excitement, wringing his hands like a fishwife over a tub of gutted cod. All about the weatherdeck of *San Josefe* a jabber of voices was flowing and eddying; it kept Roche-Bourbon from hearing Rodriguez' greetings and preposterous compliments, issued out from behind a wide smile that revealed in unpleasant detail the state of decay in the captain's yellowing teeth.

'You are too kind, my dear Capitán,' said Roche-Bourbon in flawless Catalan. What Rodriguez had said was easily guessed at. What was far more important was what he was now about to say. 'I understand the keen eyes of your fine lookouts have spotted something of interest?'

Rodriguez jigged to the other foot, beaming. '*Si*! The *inglés* has fallen into the trap of our *Aguerra*!'

Roche-Bourbon turned and peered forward. 'Where?'

'Fine on the starboard bow. They are still hull-down, and we are well hidden, as I planned. The lookout atop the main royal yard is watching!'

As I instructed, you oily little worm, thought Roche-Bourbon. 'Of course. So the Englishman will not have seen us.'

'Certainly not. So if by chance he slips through *Aguerra*'s grasp –'

All too likely, thought the Frenchman.

'He will think she was a vessel operating alone, instead of the vanguard of an invincible *armada* of His Most Catholic Majesty!' And here Rodriguez made a dramatic sweep of his arm towards the stern.

Roche-Bourbon squinted aft. The 'invincible *armada*' was impressive enough. Pitching along in red and gilt splendour astern of the *San Josefe* were eleven Spanish line-of-battle ships, hulking masses over sixty guns, all of them, in two ragged columns with luffing, sloppily trimmed canvas that Roche-Bourbon would not have tolerated for an instant in his own *Diamant*.

'Yes. Well, I hope you are right, Capitán. It is imperative, for all our sakes, that no English vessel sight and report us.'

Rodriguez snorted, pulling an enormous handkerchief from one sleeve and mopping his face. 'Pah! Admiral Pizarro would lead us to victory over the Englishman, Vernon, whether that dog knew we were coming or not! *Madona*, with a *flota* like this – !'

'Señor,' interjected Roche-Bourbon in an icy tone, 'I am acquainted with our illustrious admiral's enviable accomplishments as a lion of the sea. But may I remind you that Admiral Vernon's ships are at liberty in these seas, making for an unknown target we are meant to protect, and that he is at sea, not with a clutch of sloops and frigates, but with a very formidable force indeed – '

'*Si*, señor, but – '

'Which includes,' and here Roche-Bourbon flicked though the ordered jottings of his memory, 'the *Hampton Court*, seventy guns; the *Worcester*, sixty; the *Norwich*, fifty; the *Burford*, seventy; and the *Strafford* and *Princess Louisa*, which if I recall are both sixty-gun vessels. And they are commanded and manned by the usual sort of men the English send to sea!'

Rodriguez wilted, visibly shaken. The fighting merits of the seamen of Perfidious Albion were all too often the content of his nightmares.

Roche-Bourbon willed back his sneer of contempt and turned to seek out the vast hulk of Pizarro's flagship, the *Trinidad*, looming along in the rear of the formation. 'If, my dear Rodriguez, your – our – admiral is to have an opportunity to smash Vernon and save whichever hapless community the damned English intend to destroy – for that is evidently what they intend to do – we must *find* them, do you not agree?'

'*Si*,' nodded Rodriguez, still pale.

'And would it not be wisest if we had the advantage of surprise?'

'*Si*. Of course you are right.'

Roche-Bourbon sighed. 'I am going below again, with your permission. The flux still leaves me weak. If *Aguerra* takes the Englishman, which I sincerely hope, I trust you will bring any documents, or prisoners suitable for interrogation, to me at once. Is that clear? We *must* know Vernon's destination!'

Rodriguez nodded, twisting his handkerchief in his hands. 'And – and if *Aguerra* loses, señor?'

Roche-Bourbon paused at the top of the quarterdeck ladder. 'For your sake, my dear Rodriguez, I should pray she does not. For that schooner, if your first report of her rig was accurate, will outsail anything we have, and Vernon will have his warning,' he said smoothly. 'And we know what *that* would portend.'

Rodriguez nodded again, miserably. '*Si*.'

Roche-Bourbon descended the ladder out of sight, and Rodriguez spun round, squinting up at the distant lookout.

'Mother of God, *estúpido*, do you see nothing?' he shrieked up.

'They are so – so close, Capitán! I cannot tell if they yet fight with guns, or are boarding!'

'Aagh!' Rodriguez stumped to the rail, bowling aside one of his attendant officers, who caught his lacquered red heel on a ringbolt and fell with a squeal and a crash of cutlery to the deck.

'Blood of the Saints!' muttered the Spaniard as he stared westward to the tiny shapes on the horizon that marked all he could see of the distant fight. 'It is always *my* neck that comes in question. Always *my* responsibility. Why, in the name of the blessed Virgin Mother herself, did that wretched *inglés* get in the way?' And he pounded the rail with one chubby fist in frustration.

2

His Britannic Majesty's Ship *Burford*, seventy guns, rode majestically at anchor in the broad basin before the peninsula town of Port Royal, Jamaica. There was a deepening gloom, and dark rain clouds shut out the sun which a moment before had burned down on the crowded, roisterous town, the glassy face of the bay, and the dark green shoulders of the island rising in lush splendour to the north. *Burford* was not alone in the harbour; aside from the clutch of lighters and tenders, and the rough-hewn, slack-canvased island sloops that were everywhere, a half-dozen other line-of-battle ships of the Royal Navy rode in impassive grandeur in the bay's shelter. As the great ensigns of the Blue Squadron curled at their staffs, the crews of the ships looked at the onrushing dark arches of cloud and checked their cables or the gaskets on their furled canvases.

There was a similarly anxious look on the face of Isaiah Hooke as he steered *Athena*'s small longboat towards the looming oaken walls of *Burford*; at the boat's oars, Aiken and Slade and four other men looked glumly at the clouds and muttered until Hooke's growl silenced them. Beside Hooke, Edward Mainwaring shifted his small dress hanger round to a more comfortable position and glanced up at the threatening grey mass. 'Get me alongside her quickly, Isaiah. Then you and the lads pull for *Athena* for all you're worth.'

Hooke managed a quick smile as the first cat's-paw of the squall's wind ruffled the harbour face. 'Aye, zur. Quick as lightnin' we'll be.'

Abruptly, *Burford*'s mustard and black mass was towering

41

over them, faces peering down, and Hooke was barking quick orders for the oars to be brought in, and for Winton, in the bows, to stand by with his boathook.

'Boat ahoy!' rang down a tardy call from *Burford*'s rail.

''Bout bloody time,' muttered Hooke. '*Athena*!' Deftly he put the helm over at precisely the correct moment. He saw with some satisfaction Mainwaring's nod of approval as, under the watching eyes above, Winton had only to hook on gently, and Mainwaring but to step from the longboat's sternsheets on to the first of the splintery battens that led up *Burford*'s tumble home to the entry port far above.

'Nicely done, Isaiah,' under his breath. 'Now for God's sake get clear before that hits!'

'Aye, zur. Good luck, zur.'

Mainwaring nodded at him, clamped his hat firmly on his head, and with a prayer that he would not slip, began the climb like a bat on a cave wall. Below him the longboat pulled away smartly, Hooke's jocular mix of oaths and encouragement sending it surging through the water. Just as Mainwaring reached the entry port, the light went out as if a candle had been snuffed, and then with a rush a tremendous and instantaneous downpour fell on the scene.

Immediately drenched, Mainwaring heaved himself on to the vast expanse of *Burford*'s deck to see men and boys scattering in all directions, with the exception of an unhappy pair of boatswain's mates who were attempting to pipe him in a very liquid sort of way, and the slim form of a well-dressed gentleman who stood hopping from one foot to the other, gesturing for him to hurry up.

'Mainwaring?' he cried, through the hiss of the rain.

'Yes.'

'God damn and blast this rain. Name's Wetherall, inappropriately enough. Follow me!'

His hat cocks running like drain pipes, Wetherall, squelched off across the deck and led Mainwaring in under the half-deck. He opened a small doorway and bolted into the gloom within. In the next moment Mainwaring found himself standing with Wetherall, both men steaming like dogs come in out of rain, before a cabin door guarded by a lank-haired sentry in what appeared to be a colonial infantry uniform. Mainwaring had time only to blow a drop of water from his nose and ponder that the facings of the sentry were likely those of the Jamaica Garrison regiment when, in response to Wetherall's knock, a voice boomed from within.

Wetherall doffed his sodden hat, cursed the rain once more, and opened the door. '*Athena*'s captain, Lieutenant Mainwaring, to see you, sir.'

'And looking like a drowned rat as much as you do, no doubt,' said a not unpleasant voice from the interior. 'Be so good as to show him in before you go off to wring out.'

'Sir.' Wetherall stepped back, winked at Mainwaring, and shut the cabin door behind the latter as he entered.

Mainwaring was conscious that his shoes were sloshing as if he had waded over to *Burford* and he realized that gentlemanly elegance was a lost cause. He doffed the dripping tricorne and inclined his head in a simple short bow.

'Lieutenant Edward Mainwaring, His Britannic Majesty's Schooner *Athena*, sir.'

'Sit down, sir. No, don't concern yourself over the water. Damned stern lights make so much water m' feet are awash half the time anyway.'

Mainwaring felt a smile tug at his mouth. The voice of Edward Vernon, vice-admiral of the Blue at age fifty-five, and in command of the imposing force of ships riding at anchor at Port Royal this late October day, was at once warm and bluff. Vernon was dressed in the scarlet grandeur of what was generally recognized as an admiral's attire, although the stifling heat of the cabin must have made the stock, waistcoat, breeches and full-skirted coat purgatory to wear. He was seated behind a broad brass-mounted table which was lashed to ringbolts in the canvas-covered, checker-painted decking, and atop the table was a mass of charts, documents, and a few leather-bound books. Out of the corner of his eye Mainwaring noted with some surprise that the Admiral's great cabin was very sparsely fitted out, and looked largely like a more spacious version of his own in *Athena*. As his eyes adjusted to the gloom he saw that there were two eighteen-pound guns in the cabin, one to a side, snugged up to their breechings and tackles behind their closed gunports. 'Thank you, sir.'

'Where are you at anchor, Mainwaring?'

'About a half-cable off the inner battery, sir. Just inshore of *Worcester*.'

'You arrived this morning?'

'Last night, in fact, sir. Made the harbour mouth before sunset, but I kept off till dawn. Wind was fair, and we got in on the flood before the change of the morning watch.'

Vernon nodded. His face was round and forthright in a healthy-looking, country-squire sort of way, his eyes clear and direct in their gaze, with a look of vigour and intelligence in them. He wore a full-bottomed wig that just touched his shoulders, and the hands emerging from the mass of lace at his sleeve cuffs were brown, with an unexpected look of strength about them. Mainwaring had heard Vernon was a well-educated and even bookish man, extraordinary in a naval officer, but the man before him had as well the look of a seaman. He was using his hands in short, effective gestures as he spoke.

'*Athena*. Ah, yes,' he said. He paused a moment as a tiny man with a rodent cast to his features slid into the cabin, laid a dossier before the admiral, flashed a feral look at Mainwaring, and vanished silently. 'Armed schooner. American – no,

44

Bermudan built.' He opened the dossier and peered at it. 'What's her armament?' he said, abruptly.

'Six guns, sir. Three-pounders. And two swivels aft, one-pounders.'

Mainwaring moved in his stiff armchair. His hanger was pressing against one leg painfully, and he was conscious of water trickling down his temples into his neckcloth, while the wet wool and linen of his clothing was cloying and damned uncomfortable. The tricorne lay glistening with water in his lap. Behind Vernon, the angled glass was spattered and streaked by the rain which hung in curtains over the harbour beyond. The shape of a warship loomed like a black shadow some distance away. *Burford* moved ponderously under them, and the wind whistled in the wedged gunports.

'How well did the clerk of the cheque at Bermuda help you in storing her?'

'Moderately well, sir.'

'Which means?'

'I'm well stored, sir, as regards powder, shot, and material for upkeep of the ship: cordage, timber, and so on. It's in victualling that we received less than adequate stores, sir. I have no purser and relied on the dockyard staff to assist me.'

'What do you mean? The usual short casks of meat, that sort of thing?'

'Yes, sir.'

Vernon snorted. 'This is your first command, isn't it? And you were commissioned where?'

'Boston, sir. I was serving in *Athena* as master. She was a Provincial cruiser. Owned by the General Court of Massachusetts.'

Vernon glanced again at the dossier. 'Your record indicates that you took your Lieutenant's Board in Boston at the same time *Athena* was bought in. I am not clear how such consideration of you was authorized.'

Mainwaring felt his cheeks redden, but controlled the flicker of temper he felt within. 'By written agreement between Sir Charles Wager and my – the Governor of Massachusetts – sir; any Provincial officer serving in a Massachusetts vessel bought into the Royal Navy was to receive consideration for appointment to those vessels either by warrant or commission. I was called to a Lieutenant's Board in *Hampton Court* by virtue of my service in the Provincial Marine being accepted as – '

Vernon held up a hand. 'Very well, Mainwaring. I was not impugning your preparation. Nor the suitability of your receipt of a naval rank. It simply is extraordinary to have a Provincial warrant officer promoted to a lieutenancy in His Britannic Majesty's Navy.'

Mainwaring set his jaw and made the leap. The consequences be damned. 'No more so than selecting a post captain from halfway up the List and making him vice-admiral of the Blue, sir. With respect.'

For an instant the silence between the two men held, as did their eyes: Vernon's wide with surprise and some other emotion, and Mainwaring's with a simple, reckless determination that he would not look away.

And then Vernon rocked back in his chair, and let a burst of hearty laughter echo round the cabin. 'True! Damned true! Christ's guts, Mainwaring, you've pluck to say something like that! Davis! Where are you, you little weasel?'

At this roared summons the thin servant reappeared, a pained and patient look on his pinched features.

'Fetch out that bottle of Madeira I've been saving, Davis! And Lieutenant Mainwaring and I will have two glasses! Quickly, or you'll sit at the mainmast head for a week!'

Vernon grinned at the nonplussed American as Davis scuttled over to a corner locker and began fumbling in its interior. 'Not enough straight talk in this bloody service, to my mind. Damned valuable when you find it. Now, hitch your chair over here and look at this chart. I want you to know why I sent for you. And now that I think you may be the kind of man I hoped you'd be, we can talk business while we drink!'

The chart was a general one of the north coast of South America, stretching from Trinidad in the east to Darién in the west: the Spanish Main, haunt of freebooters' dreams in bygone days, and now the *terra firma* of the Spanish Empire in America. As Davis set down two brimming glasses of the Madeira, Vernon seized one, gestured for Mainwaring to take the other, and after a sizeable quaff waved the glass in a general direction at the chart.

'Know these waters at all, Mainwaring?'

'Only before the mast, sir. In Provincial ships. Leewards and windwards, for the most part. And I was master's mate in one cruise of the *William and Mary* scow to the Yucatan.'

'But you've not coasted the Main?'

'No, sir.'

'Pity. Still, for what I envisage for you, ignorance of the area may not be out of character. What do you know of my orders?'

Mainwaring swigged at the Madeira. 'Nothing, sir. Other than gundeck rumour.'

'You were told nothing? Given no orders?'

'Only to join you, or Commodore Brown pending your arrival, here at Port Royal, sir. For your disposition thenceforth.'

'Hm. When would you be ready for sea?'

Mainwaring bit his lip. He had hoped the juncture with Vernon's squadron might have given him time to make a number of rigging and stowage changes in *Athena*, for which he needed time either at anchor or alongside. 'I am essentially ready now, sir. But I had hoped – ?'

'Ready for a lengthy cruise? Such as in the waters – here, between the Gulf of Honduras and the Lesser Antilles?'

Mainwaring thought. A patrol along five hundred leagues of Spanish coastline, the home of *guardacostas* and brigands owing allegiance to no one. Changeable and treacherous winds. Uncharted soundings. And *Athena* manned with a toss-together crew of Massachusetts men and scavenged British merchant hands pressed from Boston harbour, that Mainwaring was only now managing to measure.

'If required, sir,' he said, after a moment.

'But clearly you're not pleased.'

'I had hoped for some time at anchor, sir. Stowage and rigging changes. And settling in my people – '

'Sea time will do that for you. And I regret I cannot afford the luxury of you not being at sea, Mainwaring. I intend to sail too soon for that. And you'd be wise to avoid too much time inshore, eh? Yellow Jack'll cut your people down before you know it.'

'Sir.' Mainwaring knew a lost argument when he saw it. At sea again without an interval to prepare. There would be much to do. Hooke would have to be told to shorten many of the tasks he and Aiken had set the men to. And as for the changes in the foremast rig –

'You are aware of the general situation that has led to this confounded war, are you not?' Vernon's voice broke in to Mainwaring's train of thought. The American cleared his throat and hitched at his hanger. He wished he had not worn the useless and damned annoying thing.

'Trade, sir. Into the Spanish Empire.'

Vernon took a mouthful of the Madeira. 'Quite. We are – or were – simply not obtaining sufficient access to Spanish markets for our goods and vessels. We tried to convince the Dons in a nasty little war fifteen years ago to open their gates somewhat. Treaty signed in 1728 was presumably the solution.' Vernon fumbled in a waistcoat pocket and produced a *chinoiserie* snuffbox, offered it to Mainwaring, was refused, snorted back an enormous pinch, sneezed, and continued. 'Damned thing failed, of course.'

'I'd thought the French were behind that, sir.'

'What? Indeed. Bloody compact between the thrones behind it all. It's an undeclared war on our trade by the damned Frogs, and using the Spanish as agents in the bargain. That young chap Pitt said it all, what? When trade is at stake, you must defend it or perish!'

Mainwaring nodded. He sipped at the Madeira, feeling its warmth now in his stomach. 'I thought the Spanish were amenable to pressure, sir. Was there not another treaty with 'em this past January?'

Vernon drained his glass and set it down with a ring atop the chart. 'Aye. At Pardo. Dons agreed to pay almost a hundred thousand pounds to repay English merchantmen ill-treated by the bloody *guardacostas*. But they've yet to pay tuppence of it. And damned unlikely to, either.' He shook his head. 'Force is the only answer, it would appear. Only force will make 'em let our ships and merchants trade freely in these waters.'

Mainwaring nodded. 'In Boston, sir, the word was that the government was reluctant to go to the extent of war.'

'*Reluctant?*' Vernon snorted. 'Damned fools have no sense of the matter. Walpole's a capable man, no denying, but by God, it took Pulteney and the Tories to make the Whigs see gunpowder was the answer! I told 'em the Dons can be beaten quickly here, eh? Take Porto Bello or Cartagena and they'd lose all. Ye'd break that circle of trade that takes home plunder year after year from the Caribbean and America, by just striking at the key links in the chain!'

Vernon was referring to the two ports which, along with

49

Veracruz in Mexico, were the principal gathering points for the vast plunder Spain shipped home each year from the Americas; ports where bullion and wealth in every conceivable form awaited the plodding fleets of ungainly, archaic galleons that would freight it back to Cádiz via Havana.

'Like pulling out a king block, Mainwaring. Never mind hovering off their convoy routes like some damned pirate. Give 'em nothing to convoy instead, and they'll sue for peace – and good terms – soon enough.'

'I understand, sir.' Mainwaring thought for a moment of the scale of the operation Vernon seemed to be suggesting. 'You'll forgive my impertinence, sir. But are six ships enough to – ?'

'My orders do not directly call on me to attack *any* point by name, Mainwaring. Neither Sir John Norris nor Sir Charles – with whom you seem to have some interest? – disagree with my views that one must avoid having to land and hold a place on these coasts. The people die of Yellow Jack too quickly and too soon. I am simply directed to commit all sorts of hostilities against the Spanish in such manner as I shall judge the most proper.'

Mainwaring thought for a moment. Vernon seemed prepared to discuss what was on his mind, a remarkable thing, given Mainwaring's lowly station in the naval scheme of things. 'Then – if I may ask – what *do* you intend to do, sir?' he asked.

'You may. Governor Trelawney here has proposed we lay siege to Cartagena. Poor Edward! Brown's press gangs have driven him to distraction, but b' God, he's standing behind us! He's given us two hundred of the garrison infantry under some zealous young bucko named Newton to use as a force to put ashore.' He shook his head. 'Haven't the heart to tell 'im that Cartagena is out of the question. We'd have to take *and* hold the damned place. The people would die like flies.' Vernon leaned forward and tapped the chart with one long forefinger. 'We need a target that naval power – *naval* power, Mainwaring – can render useless by simply destroying it, not occupying or holding it.'

Mainwaring looked at the spot where Vernon's finger tapped slowly.

'Porto Bello, Mainwaring. Porto Bello is our target.'

Mainwaring set aside his empty glass and studied the chart, seeing where Porto Bello lay on the top of the humpbacked curve of the Panama coast. He could feel the Madeira burning through his veins, and his head felt quite light. 'With just this squadron, sir?'

'It's all we require, Mainwaring. Commodore Brown is blockading Havana, but will return shortly. I'll add his vessels to mine. If we strike swiftly, we have adequate force to reduce the forts which guard the harbour and make the town ours. I know the place. And quick, decisive action will take it!'

The admiral's eyes were bright, full of conviction. Mainwaring thought of the stories he had heard of Porto Bello: a sleepy, fever-ridden collection of low buildings on the edge of hellish palmetto swamps, alive only for the few heady weeks that a kingdom's ransom was mule-trained into it to be loaded into the fat galleons of Spain.

'I intend to despatch the *Sheerness* frigate to watch Cartagena in the event that Pizarro or some other Don admiral comes out after us. As soon as we are victualled and stored, and I have Captain Newton's Jamaicans all aboard, I propose to sail for Porto Bello immediately. We must act quickly for, as I am all too aware, one's people begin to die after six weeks on these coasts.'

Vernon steepled his fingertips. 'And now, as to your orders,' he said. '*Athena* is fast, I take it?'

'Yes, sir. Fastest ship I've known.'

'Then she is ideal. I want you to play privateer with her.'

Mainwaring's eyebrow rose. 'Sir?'

'Not officially. But I want you to sail three days ahead of the squadron. Governor Trelawney will put a three-day embargo on shipping before we sail – so no damned spy can warn the Dons, eh?' Vernon went through the snuff ritual once more. 'I should like you, with such an American character to your ship and its company, to masquerade as a Massachusetts privateer just ahead of our track, which will be approximately,' and here he traced a line with his finger on the chart, 'thus, to Porto Bello. You are to look ahead of us, on an arc from here . . . to here. Should there be any vessel which seems likely to stumble on to us, and which might escape to warn the Dons in Cartagena or at sea, I will require you to take or destroy it. Should you come across sizeable quantities of shipping, I should like you to cause as great a diversion and disturbance among them as may distract them from what I am undertaking. At the very least you are to prevent them from seeing me.' He paused. 'Should you come across a major Spanish naval force obviously on the hunt for me – and evidently likely to find me because of the course it steers – I would appreciate being found by you before I am found by them. Is that quite clear?'

Mainwaring nodded. 'I understand, sir.'

'In the event you meet with no shipping, you will endeavour to join me at Porto Bello. I expect to sail on or about 5 November, and should arrive at Porto Bello no later than the 20th, God willing. You should therefore plan to sail by the 2nd.' Vernon opened a drawer before him and took out a thick, wax-sealed packet, which he handed across to Mainwaring. 'Here are your orders in writing. Study them carefully once at sea, as I have not said some things contained therein.'

Mainwaring felt the hazel eyes boring into him, seeming to

judge his reaction, alert for wavering or uncertainty. 'Very good, sir,' he said, as calmly as he could manage.

Vernon's expression eased. 'You may wonder why I choose to discuss these matters at so much length with you, Mainwaring. Let us just say that I am the type who thinks competent and intelligent people should be given the facts and the latitude to get on with the job. They usually come up trumps for you.' He paused. 'Don't prove me wrong in this instance.'

Mainwaring set his jaw. 'I shan't, sir. And neither shall *Athena*.'

Vernon stood up, a signal that the discussion was finished. As Mainwaring rose, Vernon extended a hand in a firm grip. 'I trust so. But I shall hold you to that promise.'

'Sir. May I – may I have – your permission – ' Mainwaring did not finish. He found the dizziness suddenly rushing in at him, and he reached for the back of the chair to steady himself.

Vernon was staring at him strangely. 'Steady, sir. Are you well, Mainwaring?'

Mainwaring peered at him. Vernon was hidden in shadows; shadows that rushed up now around Mainwaring and darkened the cabin until it seemed like night. His heart began to race.

'Sorry, sir . . . I . . . can't seem . . .' he mumbled. There was an intense roaring in his ears.

Vernon was saying something to him. For God's sake, would the man never stop? All Mainwaring needed was a breath of fresh air, a walk on deck . . .

'Gently, sir, gently.'

Mainwaring shook his head, and the pain in his temples brought him to the point of retching. He opened his eyes, but could see nothing but blackness. There were sounds: creaking timbers; sea noises, muffled; dripping water; and men's voices.

53

'Steady, sir,' said one of the voices. 'You're coming out of it. But lie still.'

'Stephen?' croaked Mainwaring. The voice had been by his shoulder, from a dark shape in the gloom. 'Is ... that you? Where in God's name – ?' He tried to sit up, but felt hands gently pushing him back. The pain roared through his head, and he sank back, conscious of the sodden, uneven and slime-coated mass of heavy cable on which he was sprawled. A seaman's jacket or shirt had been bundled under his head as a kind of pillow. The air was thick, and reeked horribly of bilge, and another indefinable smell that Mainwaring recognized after a moment as cooked garlic.

'Christ on a crutch. I feel terrible. Who – ?'

'Pellowe, sir. Try and lie still. You took a splinter in the head. Damned hard knock. Aiken, pass me that cup, will you?'

Mainwaring sensed other forms nearby, heard movement, the clink of a bottle against tin, and then his head was being lifted, and the sting of neat rum tingled his mouth. He took a great swallow and felt the fire race through his throat and explode up into his breathing passages. He hacked and spluttered.

'Good on 'ee, zur. Thought yew'd gone off th' account.'

'Hooke?' Mainwaring wheezed. The heat flash of the rum had eased the pain as if by magic. 'That you, Isaiah?'

'Aye, Cap'n. And damned glad ye're alive. But yew lie easy, loike Mr Pellowe says, zur. Ye've a nasty knock t' th' head.'

Beneath them, the mass of stinking cable heaved, and timbers creaked somewhere in the gloom.

'Where in the name of God is this, Stephen? A cable tier?'

Pellowe was dabbing at Mainwaring's head with a piece of cloth dipped in the rum. He waited until Mainwaring's furious oath was finished before answering. 'Aye, sir. In one

54

of the Spanish vessels of the squadron that was there to the south'ard, after all. We're in the *San Josefe*, I think. Didn't see the name too clearly. They had us lie down in the bottom of the boat.'

Mainwaring sat up, ignoring the pain. He found it easier to concentrate on the fiery impact of the rum on his stomach. 'Who is here with us?'

'Six others, besides you and me and Mr Hooke, sir. Burke and Abner, Winton and Aiken. Slade. Sawyer, too.'

Mainwaring was aware of a clutch of shapes moving closer to him. 'Six, only,' he breathed. 'And what of the others? And *Athena*? The last thing I remember is that whoreson Spaniard giving us his second broadside. What – ?'

Hooke, close at one shoulder, spat off into the gloom. 'That th' bugger did, zur. An' too damned well laid. Did for more'n a few o' the lads. An' took out the pinrail holdin' the main halliards. 'Twere the gaff what stretched yew out proper.'

Pellowe was fumbling with some sort of bandage on Mainwaring's head. 'Let me put this one on, sir. It's relatively clean. The bleeding's stopped, but it needs protection. *Athena*'s taken, sir. The Spaniards boarded us. Too many to resist.' He paused. 'I – I struck our colours to save the lads, sir.'

Mainwaring paused for a moment to let that sink in. It was evident Pellowe had made a painful admission, and it would do no good to berate him for it. 'Very well,' he said. 'Where is she now?'

'Think she's still wiv th' squadron o' Spanishers, zur,' said Hooke. 'But that's naught but a gut feelin'.'

'Did you see anything, Stephen?'

'Not a great deal, sir. I helped dig you out from under the wreckage of the gaff. Then a swarm of Dons came over the rail and I took a musket butt in the guts. When I woke up I

55

was in the bottom of a boat with the other lads here, and some very smelly feet holding us down. We were pulling away from *Athena*, and I caught a glimpse of some of the Dons aloft, trying to reeve new gear.'

'And you, Isaiah?'

'Oi think th' other lads were packed over the side into another boat, zur. None's aboard this 'un save us, far as Oi c'n tell, zur.'

There was a sudden scuffle of movement, the thwack of wet leather on wood, and a shrill, high, animal squeal. A voice Mainwaring recognized as Winton's echoed round the blackness of the cable tier. 'Hah! Done for another o' th' bastards! Biggest bloody rats I ever did see. Christ!'

Mainwaring bit a lip. 'What about the wounded men?'

There was a silence, broken only by the sound of water dripping and the creak of *San Josefe*'s timbers.

'What about the wounded lads?'

Hooke spat. ''Twere me that heard 'em, zur. The Spanishers knifed 'em an' chucked 'em overside, live or no. They be in Davey Jones' locker, now.'

'Sweet Jesus.' Mainwaring sank back on his pillow. 'How many?' he said, hoarsely.

'Five, maybe six, zur. Mr Pellowe saw three lads fall. I saw one – '

'An' I saw Harris get it, sir,' said Aiken's voice. 'Ball took 'is 'ead clean of.'

'An' Winton says he saw 'un,' said Hooke. 'That right, Billy?'

'Aye, sir. Were Martin, it was. Took a splinter or summat in the leg. But they likely heaved 'im over, too, sir.'

Mainwaring felt a cold, familiar anger rising in him, and it was whetted now by an uncomfortable feeling that, in misjudging the danger of the *guardacostas*, he had precipitated this tragedy.

'God damn their garlic-soaked greasy souls,' he whispered, finding some small solace in his ability to insult verbally those that he could not assault physically. 'The bastards will pay for that. By Christ they will!'

Beside him, Pellowe began to speak, and abruptly bit it off.

'Out with it, Stephen,' said Mainwaring. His voice was hoarse, and his throat hurt.

Pellowe sighed. 'Sorry, sir. But we're trapped down here in this cable tier, Christ knows how many feet below decks in a huge Don ship swarming with a pack o' cut-throat bastards. They were damned quick and good at doing for us and poor old *Athena* – ' He stopped, as if to control the break in his voice before it happened.

'And?'

'And – well – I don't see much hope of paying 'em back, sir. There's only nine of us that we know of, to begin with.'

Mainwaring thought for a moment. 'Stephen,' he said at length, 'the first step in making something take place is making the decision that it will take place. D'ye follow?'

A pause. 'Yes, sir. But – '

'Very well. Let us assume we are intent on taking some form of action. Christ knows *what* action, I grant you, but action none the less. Whether we are trapped in a bloody cable tier or not.'

Pellowe nodded. 'Aye, aye, sir.' His voice sounded a touch firmer, for which Mainwaring was glad. To have Pellowe lose his nerve now would be to lose a substantial degree of leadership. And Pellowe would lose far more in the eyes of the men.

'Good. And thank you for that whoreson rum wash. And the binding; I no longer feel as if I'm going to retch my guts out. Where in blazes did the rum come from?'

Hooke snorted. 'Mayhap all the Dons ain't horses' arses. One of 'em tossed in the bottle after we were set in 'ere.'

Mainwaring stood up, watching his footing on the uneven cable. The chamber was perhaps half the size of his cabin in *Athena*. Hooke, Pellowe and he were in one corner, and Winton and the others were sitting hunched with their backs to the other bulkheads. From the middle of the huge coil of slimy cable a column of wet, knobbly rope thicker than Mainwaring's leg rose to vanish overhead, where some kind of hatch arrangement was the only obvious entry.

'Damndest cable tier I've ever seen. And how did they get us *in* here?'

Sawyer's lank form rose beside him. He was a taciturn young man, another Yankee with whom Mainwaring had previously exchanged barely ten words.

'Through that hatch, sir. Reckon it ain't too hard effen y' slide away either side; that sort o' housin' round the cable. They slid it open an' jest chucked us in, keel over clappers.'

Mainwaring was peering up at the odd fitting. A quick look had shown that there were no other hatches or doors out of the compartment, unless they were not accessible from inside. That two-halved sliding housing that closed round the cable might possibly be something that could be opened from below – if someone could be lifted to it. How in God's name the Spanish put a working party into the tier without in effect imprisoning them –

'*Cuidado!*' There was a yell overhead, and feet sounded on the decking. The double hatchway was abruptly slid back, and lanterns were being held over the opening. The light was strong after the fetid blackness, but Mainwaring could see several faces peering down. As the other men scrambled to their feet around him, he dodged out of the way of a narrow rope Jacob's ladder that dropped down amongst them, snapped taut, and swung.

'*Inglés!* Capitán! Take heem an' climb!' The voice was harsh, and one of the figures above had poked a cutlass blade down into the arc of light from the lanterns and was pointing

58

with it at Mainwaring. The yellow light glinted on the smooth steel.

Hooke was at Mainwaring's elbow. 'Don't go, zur. They'll split us up, sartin!'

Mainwaring grasped the master's burly arm, feeling the bunched and ready muscle mass. 'Steady, Isaiah. It may be a chance to learn what's happened to the other – '

'*Hijo de puta*! Climb!' There was a sparkling pink flash and a thunderous report as a pistol was discharged down into the cable tier. The ball thumped into the soggy mass of the great anchor cable barely a palm-span away from Mainwaring's foot. The American's ears rang, and his eyes smarted in the thick, reeking smoke that filled the chamber.

'A clear enough message, Isaiah,' said Mainwaring. 'Up I go.'

The men were suddenly all around him, faces masks of grubby concern.

'Good luck, sir.'

'Don't tell the bastards a thing, zur.'

Mainwaring gripped the shaking ladder and put his foot on the first rung. 'Never you mind. Just don't forget *Athena*, lads. Aye?'

'Aye, aye, sir!' rang out the voices in ragged chorus.

'Good. Now let me climb this thing before those people shoot someone.'

Mainwaring swung awkwardly up the ladder, remembering only after a disastrous few moments to hook one leg round the opposite side of the ladder and catch the rungs with that heel. In a few moments he was head and shoulders through the opening and then rough hands seized him, dragging him over the hatch lip and on to his feet. He had a glimpse of several dark, glittery-eyed men in coarse seamen's clothing and cut-down hats, each one appearing to level an enormous pistol at Mainwaring's guts, before a blindfold was put across his eyes and tied tightly behind. He was propelled forward by the blow of a fist between the shoulder blades, fetched up against the coaming of a hatchway, and fell heavily through it, his knees and the palms of his hands slapping down hard on the deck. There was a burst of mocking laughter behind him.

Another kindness to repay, he found himself thinking, and then he was being hauled upright once more, to be thrust off on a seemingly interminable trek through skin-gouging doorways and hatches, thrust up narrow companionways or propelled along narrow passages. All around him, over the ship, noises, voices rang out in a ceaseless, high-pitched jabber. Could Spanish warships be *that* damned noisy?

His sense of smell was working hard as well. Soon, the mouldy reek of the cable tier had faded. But over the usual smells of a tar and wood ship, a pervasive odour of cooked – or cooking – garlic and onions swirled round him. The *San Josefe* was in a moderate seaway, for the decking rolled and heaved beneath him as he made his scuffling progress, the bare feet of his captors on either side slapping quickly along, the more solid sound of boots clopping behind. Whenever Mainwaring paused in the wild march, the hands round his upper arms tugged him forward roughly, supplemented by the firm and uncomfortable dig of a pistol barrel in the small of his back.

Abruptly, he was pulled to a halt. Orders were barked in Spanish by the man behind him, and somewhere in front a musket was slapped in salute. Then, without warning, Mainwaring was pitched headlong forward. His feet caught again on a hatchway coaming, and with a grunt he fell on his face on hard decking. 'Would you bloody mind putting an end to that?' he muttered, waiting for the hard kick in the ribs that had got him up the other times he had fallen.

'You are quite right, M'sieur. These Spanish are distressingly rude in their behaviour.'

The voice was smooth and calm, in almost unaccented English. Mainwaring found himself being lifted a good deal more gently to his feet. Feet moved beside him, and the blindfold was swiftly removed. He was squinting in the next instant into the glare of sunlight from an enormous bank of stern lights across the width of a very large and sumptuously furnished great cabin. The furniture was of beautifully enamelled *chinoiserie*; an intricate Levantine carpet covered the decking; and lanterns of glinting, spotless brass hung here and there under the heavy deckhead beams. The desk before the stern lights, and the chairs before and behind it, were Baroque masterpieces of gilt-escutcheoned ebony.

And behind the desk, gesturing to one of the chairs, was the elegant and immaculately dressed figure of a French naval officer. He was dark, with fine, almost chiselled features, and beneath curved black brows his brown eyes were watching Mainwaring with a cold intensity. The lace at his throat and cuffs was beautifully gathered, his small wig coiffed to perfection, and the cut of his blue *justaucorps* and scarlet small clothes, those that were visible, was seemingly without flaw. He was toying with a quill as he regarded the American, who found himself thinking, much to his surprise, that he must look a remarkably dirty and dishevelled sight.

The Frenchman inclined his head. 'Rigaud de la Roche-Bourbon, His Most Christian Majesty's Navy. At your service, M'sieur. I regret the rough treatment you may have been suffering.'

It occurred to Mainwaring that he should maintain the pose of Provincial privateer for the moment, although the intense intelligence behind those dark eyes might well have decided even before this moment as to the true identity of *Athena* and her people. He had a quick spasm of fear clutch

61

at his guts as he realized he had done nothing to hide or dispose of his orders from Vernon. They still lay in the locked small drawer of his desk in *Athena*, wherever she was. Or were they in that smooth dossier of papers that lay under Roche-Bourbon's brocaded coat cuffs? Mainwaring cursed himself for an incompetent fool, but thought that under the circumstances he might as well continue to bluff things out. He would learn soon enough if this icy Frenchman knew the reality of things.

He slumped into the chair, for the moment glad of it, and let his mind feel the flow of the Cape Ann speech.

'Ed'ard Mainwaring, Massachusetts privateer *Athena*, under a proper letter-o'-marque. An' where be my men?' It came to him that in his rough sea clothes there was very little of the officer in his appearance, and he accentuated the effect somewhat by sticking out ungainly legs and scratching a non-existent flea bite under his waistcoat.

'Indeed,' said Roche-Bourbon. 'You are a *bostonnais*.'

'Naught but a Christian seaman who fears 'is God an' 'onours his king.'

'A "Yankee", then.'

'Aye, if ye will. An' proud of it. Ye may lay t' that.'

The brown eyes narrowed. 'Of course. And doing your duty? Or were you merely playing pirate?'

'Hell, we be no pirates! Privateers, true as rain, letter-o'-marque an' all, like I said. An' where are my lads, eh?'

'Patience, M'sieur. You are, I should remind you, my – our – prisoner. And I shall ask the first questions.'

Mainwaring leaned forward, hands on his knees, and ignored Roche-Bourbon's comment. 'Ye're a Frenchman, eh?'

Roche-Bourbon's eyes glittered strangely, and he paused a moment before speaking over steepled fingertips, very slowly and distinctly. 'I am a French naval officer, yes. And although

62

full of admiration for your theatrical abilities, Mainwaring, you need not persist in your most realistic bumpkin drawl. I am quite aware that you are a British naval officer. So may we set aside this amusing charade?'

Mainwaring studied Roche-Bourbon carefully. The brown eyes were knowing and watchful. He sat up. 'Very well. I am Lieutenant Edward Mainwaring, Royal Navy. Commanding His Britannic Majesty's Schooner *Athena*. And I am a "Yankee", as you put it.'

Roche-Bourbon gave him the barest of smiles. 'Your servant, M'sieur.'

'And yours.'

Roche-Bourbon raised a finger. There was a whisper of shoe leather behind Mainwaring, as a small black manservant in scarlet small clothes appeared at the American's elbow. He was holding a choice of wine glasses on a silver tray.

'Some claret?' said Roche-Bourbon. 'It really is quite good.'

Mainwaring took a glass and sipped. It occurred to him that he must cut a ludicrous figure, sitting in the splendour of *San Josefe*'s great cabin with a meticulously elegant enemy officer, sipping at claret while wearing the ragamuffin clothes of a merchant seaman, daubed with slime and grease from the cable tier.

Roche-Bourbon had tasted the claret and set down his glass. He ran a finger around its rim. 'You are concerned about your people. Of course I am sympathetic.'

'We are nine in the lodgings we presently enjoy,' said Mainwaring, evenly. 'May I ask, where are the others?'

'They need not be worried about.'

'Perhaps. But where?'

'For the moment, I regret I cannot say.'

Mainwaring sipped at the claret, looking at the dark eyes,

trying to catch a flicker of meaning or hesitation. They were steady and unreadable. It was time to attack. 'Perhaps you choose not to. Should I have asked about my wounded people in *Athena*? And my ship itself?'

Roche-Bourbon's cheek twitched almost imperceptibly. 'Your ship is now part of this grand *flota*. But as to your wounded I cannot assist you.'

'Because you had them killed.'

Roche-Bourbon paled. 'That is not so.'

Mainwaring leaned forward and set down his glass on the edge of Roche-Bourbon's desk. 'As a gentleman to another, I ask you. *What happened to my wounded men?*'

Roche-Bourbon's eyes broke contact, flicked away for a moment. 'Things occur in war. And one cannot control, in some instances, the actions of one's allies – '

'Are you saying the Spanish murdered them?'

'Lieutenant Mainwaring – '

Mainwaring stood up. '*Were they killed?*'

Roche-Bourbon was studying his glass. His face was set as if of stone. 'I am deeply sorry,' he said at length. 'It would not have taken place in a French ship.'

Mainwaring's eyes narrowed into hard points. 'And the others who survived? My Christ, *are* there any others? Are we nine all that are left of – ?'

Roche-Bourbon seemed almost to be trembling. Suddenly he slammed a palm down on the *chinoiserie* table, jangling the glass. '*Sacristi*! It is *I* who will do any further questioning here! And you will sit down, and answer what I ask of you!'

There was a click behind Mainwaring. He turned to see the black servant levelling a huge-mouthed dragoon pistol at him. And behind the black, a muscular seaman, bare chested and darkly threatening, had stepped into the cabin as if on a hidden signal.

'Sit *down*, Lieutenant Mainwaring. I do not wish to have you shot here. But I shall, if you press me!'

Mainwaring sank back on to the chair. His eyes quickly scanned the brilliant scene outside the stern lights. There were at least four ships visible, apparently the end ships of two columns of which *San Josefe* formed part. The vessels looked to be at least sixty-fours, or possibly even –

'I have here your orders from Admiral Vernon,' said Roche-Bourbon, almost in a purr. His composure had returned, and his gaze was steady and triumphant. 'Your interest in the ships out there is purely academic for you now, I assure you.'

Mainwaring felt a cold chill move through his vitals as he saw Roche-Bourbon draw the manila packet from the dossier, the seal now broken. If Roche-Bourbon had read them carefully, Vernon's effort at surprise was finished. Roche-Bourbon and the Spanish could set a trap that would lead to a humiliating repulse of Vernon's effort. And all because Mainwaring, like some damned childish fool, had not made certain that the orders could not have been found, had not made provision for a lead-weighted bag to go over the side if defeat or capture threatened. He had been so sure, so damned cocky that *Athena* would take the *guardacostas*. But instead he had brought all but the men in the cable tier to their death. And now Vernon, and perhaps hundreds of men, would pay the penalty of defeat and even death for his stupidity. The realization made him sink into a pit of self-loathing and gloom. 'Indeed,' he said.

Roche-Bourbon smilingly opened the packet and read carefully. ' "You shall proceed at the agreed Interval before the Squadron in the manner ordered, and shall endeavour to disrupt, distract, or warn of Spanish vessels or Squadrons as may constitute a Threat to the enterprise upon which we are engaged, the ultimate identity of which we have discussed and which you shall proceed thereto in order to rejoin the Squadron when in your judgement . . ." Roche-Bourbon stopped. 'A very elegant paragraph. It is, however, the least explanatory of all. The other pages teem with detail, Mainwaring. I know virtually everything about you as this *rosbif* admiral's picket.' He paused. 'Except where you are going.'

Mainwaring kept his face a mask, trying to hide the sudden exultation within him. Vernon must have known, must have sensed that Mainwaring might be too impetuous, too ill-prepared to make provision for the disposal of vital papers in the event of defeat or capture. So he had deliberately not identified Porto Bello. There would be no way of guessing Vernon's target, for he had as well made no mention of the dates when he expected to make his landfall. Christ, what a fox!

'You are amused, Mainwaring?'

'Not at all.'

'It is not a humorous matter. You can appreciate I must know your admiral's destination.' Roche-Bourbon leaned forward. 'Much unpleasantness has taken place already, *hein*? Let us be gentlemen about all this. You may be certain of proper quarters, care and respect from me, and we might save us all a great deal of time and effort were you to provide me with the answer.'

Mainwaring smiled and paused for a moment. When he spoke, his voice was low and even. 'You and your Spanish are a pack of murdering swine. And with all due respect, you may go to hell, sir.'

Roche-Bourbon paled to the colour of chalk, and a muscle twitched at the side of his jaw. 'Very well,' he said, in a hoarse whisper. He looked at the huge seaman that had come into the cabin, and nodded.

There was a blur of movement, and the burly figure was in front of Mainwaring. Before the American could move, a

66

ham-like fist came out of somewhere to thump hard into his stomach as he sat there.

'Aaah ... God ...' Mainwaring felt the pain and nausea swirl up through him, and his eyes clouded over with a dark haze. He was unable to breathe and he felt himself slipping out of the chair to the deck. Twice, and then three times, a thick, open hand slapped him across the face, and on the third slap he felt blood well out and begin to run from his nose. Now he was on his side on the deck, his body full of incredible pain, trying to curl up with his knees to his elbows as the cloud stayed before his eyes, and the horrid, crushing blows of the great fists beat at his face, compounded by savage kicks at his back and ribs that drove involuntary cries from him. The huge shape of the seaman was sobbing with effort and some hideous kind of pleasure.

And through the wild pain and the cloud over his eyes, over the loathsome curses of the Spaniard and his own uncontrollable cries, Mainwaring heard Roche-Bourbon's voice, high and harsh, 'You will tell us where Vernon is sailing, Lieutenant. Even if it is necessary to beat you to death. You *will* tell us!'

3

The heat in the damp and slimy cable tier was becoming almost intolerable. From the roll of the ship and the muffled roar without, it was evident that the *San Josefe* was in a freshening wind and a building seaway.

From where he sat propped against one bulkhead, his feet braced against the dark coils, Isaiah Hooke watched Winton and Sawyer silently stalking an enormous rat which was nibbling greedily on a corner of ship's biscuit Winton had found in his shirt. As the master watched, each man froze for a moment, each hefting one of Winton's heavy shoes. Then, with a grunt and cry, both lunged and slapped wildly at the rat. The wretched animal shrieked and began threshing about in the shadows of the great cable coils.

'For Chris'sake, Winnie, do it in,' said Hooke. 'The bloody thing broke its back.'

Winton bared white teeth in a filthy face. He was watching the struggling rat with a look of avid satisfaction. 'Hate 'em,' he said. 'Hate 'em. An' a damned greaser rat in th' bargain. Hate 'em – '

Pellowe's voice rang out of the far side of the cable tier, in the deepest shadow, where he had been binding up a splinter wound Abner had taken. 'Kill the damned thing, Winton! We're not bloody Dons!'

'Amen t' that, sir,' said Winton. 'Aye, aye.' With a vicious whack he stilled the rat's struggles, and snatched back his other shoe from Sawyer.

Pellowe made his way over the greasy coils to Hooke and slumped down beside him. His face, like all the rest, was black with tarry slime, and the whites of his eyes gleamed in the gloom. 'Bloody hands are getting restless,' he whispered. 'Wish to God we knew what they've done to the captain.' He sighed and let his head sink back against the bulkhead.

'Dunno, zur,' said Hooke. He spat into an empty corner, wiping his mouth with the back of his hand. 'The Dons be fearsome cruel when ye ain't able t' fight back. Like not t' think wot's happenin', t' be truthful, zur.'

Pellowe looked at him. 'You think they've beaten him?'

'Aye. 'Twould be in character. Lessen they plan – '

There was a scuff of boots overhead, and the curious split hatch slid back. A blaze of lantern light flooded down into the cable tier, and the Athenas gathered instinctively round Pellowe and Hooke, looking up. Then, in the next instant, a limp figure was pushed over the lip of the hatch and fell with a thump at the feet of the English.

'Jesus Christ. They've killed 'im!' breathed Sawyer.

Mainwaring's face was streaked with blood, and a huge bruise was threatening to close his left eye. He moaned and suddenly tried to sit up, looking round as if uncertain where he was. There was a burst of laughter from above.

'Nah,' said Hooke. 'But they've coshed 'im proper!' He held Mainwaring's shoulders as the latter fell back, coughing, a dribble of blood coming from one corner of his mouth.

Pellowe stood and stared with infinite loathing up at the dark figures behind the lanterns. 'Filthy bastards!' he cried out. 'Try doing that to one of us fairly – !'

There was a curse from above, and the hatch slammed shut, the light winking out abruptly as the boots scuffed away. But not before a gob of spittle had struck Pellowe on the cheek. In disgust he cuffed it off, swearing through his teeth.

'Stephen,' croaked Mainwaring, still in Hooke's grip, 'you really must learn not to overreact . . .'

Pellowe was on his knees in an instant as Hooke helped

Mainwaring settle himself in a sitting position against the bulkhead. 'Christ, sir. You – you look – '

'Bloody terrible. I can imagine. Any of that rum left?' Mainwaring was fingering his mouth, checking for missing or loosened teeth.

To a man they scrambled round looking for the bottle until Hooke found it, unplugged it with his teeth, and pushed it into Mainwaring's hands. The latter took a huge swig, grimaced, coughed, and handed the bottle back. 'Thankee,' he said hoarsely. 'Thank Christ for rum.'

The men were clustered close round him now, and Hooke was peering at the damage the Spaniard's fists had caused. 'What'd th' bastards do t' ye, zur? Not that it ain't half obvious. Can ye – ?'

'What can I say? A gentlemanly enough beating. At least I can still walk. They had – damn, Stephen, none of your wetnursing now! – a burly boatswain or some such give me the back of his hand a few times.' He touched at his swollen eye and managed a grin at Aiken. 'Damned sight more vicious on a rope's end than you'd be, Aiken. To your credit,' he said. Aiken grinned.

Pellowe had been padding at Mainwaring's latest wounds with a wad of rag soaked in the rum. What with the blood, and filth, and Mainwaring's earlier head wound, the captain was looking like a very wild and desperate case indeed. As were they all. 'What *did* they want, sir?' he said.

'You mean what did *he* want. They've a Frenchman in real command, so it seems.'

There were grunts of surprise. 'A Frog, zur? Ye'd be sure o' that?' said Hooke.

Mainwaring grimaced as he tried to sit straighter. 'He was a Frenchman all right, Isaiah. Wanted to know Vernon's target.'

'And did ye – ?'

70

'Tell him?' Mainwaring managed a crooked grin. 'No bloody fear, Isaiah. At least, not yet!'

'D'ye think they've summat of an idea wot's up, zur?' said Aiken.

'You can be damned certain they know that it'll be somewhere on the Main, Aiken. From what I could gather they seem to think it'll be Cartagena.' He fingered a loose tooth. 'Damn.'

Slade had squatted down near Mainwaring's feet. 'Never yew mind th' losin' of a fang er two, zur. Hell, I ain't had 'em all since I were a sprog!' And he bared his yellowed, gaping smile.

Mainwaring laughed through his pain. He felt as if the hurt in his guts would never cease, but he was determined not to show it. Once he gave in to it altogether, he would be little more than a moaning heap in the corner . . . 'I've still a chance to lose them, Slade. They plan to haul me out again for another gentlemanly conversation.'

The men's faces fell solemn in the gloom, and there was a moment of silence.

'Christ, sir,' said Pellowe after a moment. 'You can't take much more of that.'

Mainwaring nodded at him. 'You don't need to tell me, Stephen. And I'm the last to guarantee I can die like some tight-lipped hero.'

Hooke stirred. 'Well, then, zur – '

'Exactly, Isaiah,' said Mainwaring. He sat up and touched at Pellowe's bandaging efforts. 'That is why I propose we get ourselves out of here,' he said quietly.

The men sat up, eyes suddenly brighter in their blackened faces.

'Gettin' *out*, zur?'

'T'ain't possible.'

'Cap'n, how're yew – '

71

'Quiet, damn ye!' Hooke's voice silenced them. 'Ye ain't a clutch o' jabberin' Dons! Hark, an' be still!'

'Thank you, Mr Hooke,' said Mainwaring. He looked round the shaggy heads and black faces. 'What have we got for weapons? Anything?'

The men shook their heads for the most part. Abner, the gunner, stirred.

'Yes, Abe?'

'Drawstrings o' breeches'd make a garrot, zur. If y' can figger a way t'hold yer breeches up at th' same time. Only thing I c'n think of, zur.'

'All right. Anyone else?'

Slade, now at Mainwaring's elbow, bared the grin again. 'The Dons thought they got all o' th' knives an' such, zur. But not quite, eh?' He reached behind his neck, into the edge of his shirt collar, and drew out a wicked-looking blade no more than a hand in length. 'Still got this.'

'Good man! We're likely to need it. Very well, anyone else? Nothing?'

Hooke spat. 'Our fists are still ours, too, zur.'

'Well said. Now listen. The Frenchman who was asking me the questions will likely send his swine back after me in less than a turn of the glass. And Christ knows what they would plan to do to *you* lads. That means we've got to move quickly.'

'But what can we do, sir?' said Pellowe, quietly. 'This bloody cable tier has damned near no way in or out.'

'One thing does come in or out, Stephen. Regularly.'

'What, the cable?'

'Exactly. If we were to get up and through that hatch, we'd still be three decks down in a Don sixty-gunner swarming with every whoreson version of a cut-throat you'd care to imagine. Against them we'd be nothing. Not with nine men, unless we could get to some weapons.' He paused. 'We need to get to the weatherdeck, lads. *Athena*'s a prize in this damned fleet. D'ye follow me?'

Hooke stared. 'Christ's guts, zur. D'ye mean – ?'

'Aye, Mr Hooke. I want our ship back!'

There was a murmur of excited assent from the other men, who were fidgeting now in excitement.

'But *how*, sir?' repeated Pellowe. 'If we're so far down in this ship, we – '

'Think about the construction of a line of battle ships, Stephen. The cables are hauled by a huge capstan, eh? Set for'rard or aft, and usually on the gundeck or lower. The cable comes in through the hawse and lies along the deck, usually so bloody thick a messenger line runs round the capstan and gets nipped to the cable in an endless loop. That's how ye haul it in. Follow?'

'Aye, sir. But – ?'

'But the point is, the cable in this ship is a huge piece of business indeed. Look at the coils we're sitting on. Damned near thick as your leg, or more.' He jerked a thumb upward. 'That odd sliding hatch and the space there lets the Dons see that the cable sits in here properly. But it doesn't just tumble down in here from the weatherdeck; not a mass of slime-covered and sodden cable like that, all afoul with bottom mud. She's rove through a leaden or wood box pipe that leads down here to the orlop, and the tierers can then flake down the cable as it pays through the pipe. Usually they put the large cables outboard in the tier, and hawsers and lighter line inside and between 'em. See, that's likely a cable there and here. Damned hard work.' He paused. 'But the key thing is that the box pipe leads right up *there* – '

'To the gundeck, at least,' breathed Hooke. 'O' course. Damn my eyes.'

'Can a man monkey up inside it, sir?' said Winton. He was

73

blond, and in the gloom his hair glowed with a ghostly aura, albeit darkened with the cable slime.

'That's the question. Is it big enough? And if it's got footholds? They'd want it slick inside, but if it's cast lead, there'll be joints. To make sure the cables don't foul, the pipe's more'n a foot on a side, usually. That'd give a cross-corner opening that *might* be enough for a man.'

'Even Mr Hooke's line-o'-battle hull, zur?' cackled Slade, to a general burst of good-natured laughter.

'Yew mind yer tongue, Jonas Slade,' growled Hooke, not unkindly.

'The problem is,' went on Mainwaring, 'that there is a cable in the damned thing now. I think it means only *one* man can get into it. And a small one at that.'

Abner piped up. 'That'd be Jonas, zur. Any way out o' a tight spot be his trade, ye may lay t' that!'

'Think you could do it, Slade?' said Mainwaring. 'The mouth of the pipe'd be just above that hatch, I reckon, if we can open it.'

Slade sucked a tooth. 'Willin' t' try, zur. But ain't that hatch openin' on to some companionway or chamber or some such, zur? Like where them Dons pitched yew down from?'

Mainwaring nodded. 'You're right. And if we got ourselves out through it we'd be on the lower gundeck at least. But I'm damned sure they'd keep it locked or barred. That pipe is the best chance of getting a man out of here.'

'If ye don't mind me askin', zur – ?'

'Go on.'

'Well, zur, I ain't certain what ye'd want me t' *do*, once I gits free up on the gundeck, or wherever.'

Mainwaring grinned. 'Good point. It wouldn't be to sample all that garlic cooking. The main thing would be simple – and bloody difficult, at the same time – work your way down and free us from the outside. And do it quickly and quietly.'

'That calls fer us all t' monkey up that cable if he gits th' thing open, then, zur?' said Hooke.

Mainwaring steadied himself as the *San Josefe* lurched over a swell, and wiped sweat from his brow with his sleeve. 'Never fear, Mr Hooke. You'll make it.'

'T ain't that, zur. What if that slidin' hatch be barred?'

'I don't think it is. But now's the time to find out. Up you go, Slade.'

'Lord lummee . . .' muttered Slade. With the other men clustering around him, he reached up, trying for a grip on the great rope. 'Too damned greasy, zur. Why'n hell is it rove up through th' pipe anyhow?'

'The Dons may be holding a bower anchor ready to let go in a hurry. Can't manage it?'

Slade scrabbled at the cable and then slid back to stand on the coils. 'Nah. No good, zur. Too slimy. Christ, what a stink!'

'Come on,' said Mainwaring, briskly. 'We'll try something different. Isaiah, Stephen, stand either side o' that cable. Face in and get a good hold on each other's shoulders. Winton and Sawyer, climb on their shoulders and take the same position. Quickly, now!'

Grunting and balancing, the men struggled until Hooke and Pellowe, arms locked, were standing spread-legged in a kind of embrace facing the slimed column of hempen cable. Winton and Sawyer were teetering, feet on the shoulders of the lower men, clutching at each other the same way.

Winton and Sawyer sniggered. 'Bloody tumblers at Rane-lagh, eh, Mr Hooke?' said Winton.

'Just you damned well stay still,' grunted Hooke.

Pellowe nodded at Mainwaring. 'I think we've got the balance, sir.'

'Right.' Mainwaring nodded at Slade. 'Up you go, and

slide back that hatch. But gently. Make as little noise as possible.'

'Aye, aye, zur.' With a deep breath, Slade scrabbled his way up Hooke's and Winton's backs, with not a little cursing in accompaniment as his hard toes dug into softer spots. Finally, he was holding on to the cable, his head no more than a few inches from the hatch.

'Steady,' said Mainwaring, as the *San Josefe* heaved beneath them again. 'Now. Slide it back.'

Slade pressed his palm flat on the hatch and tried to move it. After a straining, trembling moment, he slumped against the cable, shaking his head. 'No good, zur. Christ on a crutch!'

'Hold steady there, Winton. Don't let him drop, for God's sake. Slade, try again. Get your fingers in the opening.'

'Don't look like I can, zur – '

'*Try!*'

Slade arched backwards and hooked his fingers into the seam between the two hatch halves. He strained and swore. For a moment, nothing. Then, abruptly, the wooden slab rumbled back. Slade, losing balance, clutched at the cable while Winton and the others struggled to hold him in cursing effort.

There was nothing visible except the mouth of a square-sided pipe, up which the great column of the cable disappeared. On all four sides the space above the hatch was boxed in by partitions, leaving only a small lip a foot or so wide around the hatch. On one side, hinges and a latch showed an access door had been cut in one partition. It was through it, Mainwaring knew, he had been dragged, and the Spaniards came and went. 'Good man. Can you get yourself up over the hatch lip?'

'Tryin', zur.' With a sudden movement that almost toppled his human ladder, Slade leaped, squirrel-fashion, for the lip.

76

His legs flailed the air wildly for a few brief moments, and then he scrambled over the edge.

'The doorway. Is it barred?' called up Mainwaring, trying to keep as much volume out of his voice as possible.

After a moment Slade peered over the lip. 'Tight as a nut, zur. No greaser guard outside. But,' he said in a hoarse whisper, 'I c'n see a half-dozen hands workin' at some lines just along the deck, under a lantern. Ain't no other way out, zur.'

'I thought as much.' Mainwaring peered at the gaping mouth of the pipe. 'Can you get into the pipe mouth?'

Hooke and Pellowe had waited while Winton and Sawyer had scrambled down, and now were beside Mainwaring, looking up.

'Sawyer might make it up the pipe too, sir,' said Pellowe.

Mainwaring looked at the Massachusetts youth. 'Think you're small enough, Sawyer?'

Sawyer sniffed. 'Reckon I could be, sir. Ain't hardly been much I ain't been able t' squeeze out of. Or through.'

There was a low whistle from above, over the sea noise.

'Slade?' said Mainwaring.

'The pipe's cast lead, right enough, zur! A joinin' lip every two feet or so. Ain't much of a toehold. But I c'n git in, sure!'

'Right. Stand fast for a moment. I'm sending Sawyer up with you.'

In a moment the human ladder was in place again, with the gunner, Abner, the sweating replacement for Sawyer. A minute later, both small men were crouched on the hatchway lip, craning to peer up the pipe.

'Yew go first, Jonathan,' said Slade, ''n I'll catch ye, sure, if ye fall!'

Sawyer answered with a grin and a surprisingly knowing obscenity, reached out for the cable, and then for a few heart-stopping seconds clung to the slimy column largely with his

77

feet while he scrabbled with his hands for a grip inside the pipe. Then he had it, and, turning himself to fit up the narrow space, he pressed his chest to the cable, splayed his toes against the sides of the pipe, and began to vanish upward.

'Christ, it's filthy in here!' came his muffled voice.

'Slade, keep the lad from talking too much,' said Mainwaring. 'And don't lose him to the Dons.'

'No fear, zur,' said Slade. With a lick of his lips, he was in turn scrabbling at the pipe walls, his fingers scraping painfully on metal, and then he vanished in sweaty effort up the pipe. For some moments their struggling upward progress could be heard, until finally there was nothing but the slight thrum of the cable to mark their efforts.

Abruptly, Mainwaring cursed himself for a fool. He had let Slade and Sawyer climb on without pulling the sliding hatch back into place. It would have to be put back, or the first Spaniard with a glimmer of intelligence who came upon it would see that something was out of order.

'Abner. Can you hold weight with that leg? Good. You and Winton stand ready to climb. Aiken, you and Burke form the base legs, as the others did. Quickly, now.' Mainwaring nodded at Pellowe. 'Stephen, you'll climb and close the hatch.'

'Aye, aye, sir.' In an instant, the midshipman was up, balancing precariously on Winton's shoulders. He lifted the hatch halves and slid them shut.

'Hold on, there,' said Mainwaring, as *San Josefe* rolled heavily beneath them. Then, 'Good work. Down quickly, now.'

Pellowe dropped lightly on to the coils beside him. 'Sir, d'ye think the lads are – ?' he began.

There was a sudden thumping of boots overhead, and the rattle of a key in a padlock. Voices sounded, and at a barked

78

order the hatch was thrust aside, a shaft of lantern light painfully piercing the gloom.

'Just in the bloody nick o' time,' breathed Hooke.

The Jacob's ladder dangled again. A cutlass blade appeared again. And again its point was centred on Mainwaring's chest.

'*El capitán! Vamos!*'

Pellowe was suddenly holding Mainwaring's elbow, distance and formality forgotten. 'We're with you, sir!' he said quietly. 'Don't forget.'

Mainwaring rose, seeing the faces of his men, their eyes white in the dirty faces, the looks full of concern. He tried to ignore the sick feeling in the pit of his stomach, and forced his voice to be low and level. 'Don't concern yourself, Mr Pellowe.' He glanced upwards at the mouth of the cable pipe. 'Think only of help and guidance from above.'

Pellowe nodded, a grin breaking the solemn, worried cast of his grease-smeared features.

'Aye, aye, sir.' There was a murmur of support from the men. And then in the next instant Mainwaring was swinging up the ladder, seeing again the lanterns and ready pistols, the mixture of bare and booted feet, and was hauled roughly up over the hatch lip by numerous hands that grabbed roughly at him.

The moment he was on his feet, the blindfold came out of nowhere again, this time a reeking rag that smelled of fish oil and human sweat. Even as he felt the gag rise in his throat, he was thrust into the painful, sprawling and stumbling frog-march once more, until with a jerk on his collar he was halted before what he was sure was Roche-Bourbon's cabin door. He tried to anticipate the doorway coaming, but in the event caught one toe and thumped down hard on one knee as he was thrust in. The blindfold was ripped away, the cabin door slammed, and he squinted against the painful flood of light. As his sight adjusted, he was looking at Roche-Bourbon, all smooth elegance and watchfulness, seemingly in exactly the pose he had last remembered behind the desk. The heaving face of a sunset-hour sea, tracked over by *San Josefe*'s wake, was visible outside the stern lights. Lanterns swung on several hooks against the coming darkness, and the pale orange light also shone off the sweat-glistened torso of the ape-like Spanish seaman who had beaten Mainwaring before. He was looming with a slit-eyed leer of anticipation, to one side of Roche-Bourbon's chair, his back to the stern lights.

Mainwaring met the man's porcine gaze and could not control an inward shudder. He looked away to the cold, set features of Roche-Bourbon.

'My word, M'sieur,' said the Frenchman smoothly. 'You are quite as filthy as a chimney sweep, *hein?*'

'Our quarters permit nothing else,' said Mainwaring. 'As you no doubt intend.'

'But they permit you to have leisure time. To think, for example.'

'On what?'

'Shall we say, the indignity of being beaten by someone so obviously your mental and social inferior. A humiliation, in fact. One so easily avoided.'

Mainwaring met the cold gaze evenly. 'Indeed,' he said. 'By your observance of the simple ethics of a gentlemen towards an enemy. But you seem by the look of things to be no gentleman.'

The muscle moved in Roche-Bourbon's jaw. He made an almost indiscernible gesture, and before Mainwaring could react, the seaman had stepped forward several paces and given him a vicious backhand slap across the face. Mainwaring staggered back a pace, and caught at the back of the chair near him to keep from falling. Blood welled from inside his mouth, warm and salty, and ran out at the corner. The ape-like sailor hovered, grinning expectantly, eager to do more.

'Your propensity to lecture bores me, M'sieur,' said Roche-Bourbon, as Mainwaring levelled a furious look at him. He picked up a slim flintlock pistol that had been lying atop a stack of papers to one side, and toyed with it. Mainwaring noticed that the pan was closed and the hammer set at half cock. 'But Diego here does so enjoy the opportunities it provides for him to – '

'What is it you want?' said Mainwaring. 'Or need I ask?'

Roche-Bourbon laid the cool steel of the pistol barrel along his cheek and sat back in the chair. 'The same answer you so unwisely wished to conceal the last time we spoke. Vernon's destination.'

Mainwaring tried to keep a stony and unchanging look on his features. He had glanced at the great stern lights and the dark indigo sea, whitecaps touched by the peach tones of the setting sun. At the moment he had looked there, a movement in one corner had caught his attention. When he flicked his eyes back he was looking with a barely bitten-back gasp of astonishment at the inverted features of Jonas Slade, whose face appeared for an instant, his queue hanging down like a rat-tail, and then pulled back upwards out of sight. It reappeared at Mainwaring's next glance, grinned ludicrously at him, pointed with a look and thrust of his chin at the starboard side gallery, and ducked up again out of sight.

Mainwaring shot a glance at the sweaty, anticipating hulk of Diego, hoping it seemed a fearful and exhausted one. From where the brute stood, he could not have seen Slade.

Mainwaring licked his lips. He had to gain time. He looked again fearfully at Diego, tried to smooth back his dirty, matted hair, and sank against the back of the chair.

'All – all right,' he sighed, putting a tremor into his voice. 'I – have no wish for any further beatings. No more. Please.'

Roche-Bourbon sat up, setting down the pistol. His face had a look of triumph on its thin features. Triumph, and the hint of contempt. 'A very wise decision. I was beginning to think you were prepared to suffer on rather than tell me. The usual English mettle we come to expect, *hein?*'

Mainwaring nodded, every inch the beaten man. 'I'll tell you – what you want. Only for God's sake keep him – keep him from – '

'Of course, of course.' Roche-Bourbon indicated the chair Mainwaring was gripping. 'Sit down.' His eyes fairly brimmed with disdain.

Mainwaring slumped into it, careful to throw another fearful look at Diego and gingerly touch his own facial cuts and bruises.

'Now,' said Roche-Bourbon, briskly. 'You will tell me the target for which Admiral Vernon and his fleet are sail – '

To the left, level with Roche-Bourbon and just behind the sweat-greased shoulders of the hulking Diego, a small door was visible, and led, Mainwaring had presumed, out on to the quarter gallery where, hidden under the overhang of the ship's stern carvings and rail, Roche-Bourbon had the luxury of access to his own personal 'seat of ease'. As Roche-Bourbon was in mid-sentence, that door suddenly splintered inwards with a crack and a blaze of sunlight, the sea roar suddenly loud. And with the flying pieces of door came the small, hurtling body of Jonathan Sawyer, arms bunched to smash through it, sprawling and tumbling in a black, ragged heap across the cabin deck, and scything Diego's legs out from under him. The giant grunted and fell in a ponderous sprawl to the deck.

'*Sacristi*!' cried Roche-Bourbon, and with snake-like speed he snatched up the pistol, pulled it to full cock, and levelled it at Sawyer's figure as the latter fetched up against the far bulkhead of the cabin.

But Mainwaring had been far quicker. He launched himself in a dive across the desk, and cannoned with his shoulders into Roche-Bourbon. They fell back with a crash to the deck, but even before they hit, Mainwaring felt Roche-Bourbon's wiry frame twist with astonishing strength, trying to fight free of the bearhug the American had closed around him. Mainwaring grunted as the Frenchman brought his knee up hard into his groin, and in the instant of relaxation that brought in the wrestler's hug, Roche-Bourbon slithered free, sprung to his feet, and levelled the pistol at Mainwaring. As he rose, a red mist behind his eyes, the wild-eyed Frenchman aimed the pistol at Mainwaring's forehead and pulled the trigger. The pan flashed pink, the smoke puff billowing up. But no other report shook the room. The pistol had misfired.

'*Merde*!' breathed Roche-Bourbon, and flung the weapon at Mainwaring's face. But he ducked it easily, and moved swiftly in.

'One chance is all you receive, sir. And now the turn is mine!' said Mainwaring, through a mirthless grin.

Roche-Bourbon aimed a vicious kick once more for Mainwaring's groin. But this time the American was ready for it, and twisted away so that the shoe toe struck only the hard muscle of his thigh. And then in the next instant, even before Roche-Bourbon recovered his balance, Mainwaring drove two short, popping punches into the Frenchman's face that snapped his head back, the carefully coiled coiffure of his wig flying awry. A third low swinging punch to the chest bent the Frenchman forward, gasping for breath, and with infinite relish Mainwaring delivered a savage right hand that snapped Roche-Bourbon back like a rag doll against one of the stern lights. Eyes glassy, he slid in a rumple of silk and bloody linen to the deck.

There was a splintering crash behind Mainwaring, and he spun to see the slumping huge form of Diego slide down the bulkhead, releasing his strangling death-grip on the throat of a white-faced Sawyer, the splinters of the chair Slade had smashed over the lout's head rattling to the deck. Mainwaring found he was breathing in great gasps, and his knuckles hurt where he had struck Roche-Bourbon.

'Good on 'ee, Jonas. But damned near 't weren't soon enough,' said Sawyer, his thin, Nantucket features still pale under the black of the cable tier slime. 'That bastard liked t' choked me half t' death.'

'Oh, damnation, Jacko,' replied the Briton, 'Ye'd uv lived. Why 'twere naught but a love hug he were a-given' of yew, eh?'

Mainwaring put his hands on his hips and stared at the two grubby little men, scarcely able to conceal his own grin as they beamed at one another. 'Where in the name of hell – ?' he began.

Slade winked at him and poked the inert mass of Diego with one toe. 'Strike me, zur, that pipe did what yew said, right enough. We went up 'er, smart as paint, seemed like a league or two – '

'Damned smelly hole it is, too, sir, I c'n tell ye,' put in Sawyer.

Mainwaring put up a quieting hand. He moved noiselessly to the cabin door, and pressed his ear against it. Outside he could hear the sentry scuffling his shoes and whistling tonelessly. ''E's whistlin',' said Slade in his ear. 'Hell, he be no sailor, that 'un.'

'No,' whispered Mainwaring. 'But he didn't hear all that. Or thinks it was more of our Froggy friend's games. Go on.'

Slade wiped his mouth with the back of his hand as he and Mainwaring padded back to the middle of the cabin. 'Well, zur, after a bit we fetched up at th' open end uv it. 'Twere on the gundeck, just for'rard o' th' main companionway. Hell, there were a hunnert jabberin' Dons all around, muckin' about wiv their seabags and slingin' hammocks an' what not. I figured sure they'd spy us. Eh, Jacko?'

84

'Jonas's right, sir,' said Sawyer, sniffing. 'Reckon it were th' change of thc watch, mayhap the first. Don't know how thcy ain't seen us, sir.'

'Aye,' went on Slade, 'but it were damned dark in th' gundeck, an' they had a few glims lit over the guns, eh, but when they got more o' their 'micks slung, it shadowed it all, like. So when a mob o' the greasers went jawin' and jabberin' -off down the gundeck, we nipped out o' that pipe, sharp-like, an' fell in wiv' 'em, wiv the shadows hidin' us, like – '

'An' then we saw an open gunport, and squeezed out past the gun,' Sawyer grinned. 'An old privateer trick, sir. We worked our way along the wales, sir. Along th' outside o' the hull. 'Nough tumble-home to do it. 'Twere then we saw you, sir.'

'Eh? You did what?' Mainwaring found himself staring.

'Aye, zur,' said Slade, baring the sharp teeth. 'Look'd in one port an' saw yew bein' dragged past, aft. So we worked along aft wiv ye.'

Mainwaring glanced out at the darkened sea face. *San Josefe* was moving under them heavily, and a substantial swell under a fresh breeze was running. For Sawyer and Slade to inch from handhold to handhold along the *outside* of the hull, at gunport level with only the narrow lip of a projecting wale for a toehold and God knew what for a handhold was an incredible feat, even given the extreme tumble-home of the archaic Spanish hull design.

'Well done, both of you,' Mainwaring said quietly. 'Well done. But I think we'd best secure these two gentlemen before we make our next move.'

Out of nowhere the knife was gleaming in Slade's hand. 'Shall I gut 'em, zur?' It was a matter-of-fact question.

'No. I won't play Frenchman's games with 'em, Slade. You keep your knife. We'll need it soon enough, I'll warrant!' He looked round. 'Strip those coverlets off that box bunk. We'll rip 'em into strips and lash these two down where they'll stay out of action. And we'll gag 'em as well. Quickly, now.'

In fifteen minutes Roche-Bourbon's box bunk held his still unconscious form with a gag bound securely over his mouth, and his hands and feet lashed by the effective and energetic knotwork of the three men. The bulk of Diego had been dragged over behind the desk, where a look in through the cabin door would not readily see him.

Sawyer, sweating with the effort of hauling the huge Spaniard across the deck, shook his head in wonder as Slade briskly finished up a welter of lashings on the unconscious giant. 'Sink me, Jonas, he'd have to be a bloody shark t' chew through them lashin's.'

Slade grinned. 'That be th' idea, me lad. Where's the captin?'

'Out on the quarter gallery. He's spotted *Athena*!'

Mainwaring was at that instant crouched behind the low, ornately carved rail of the quarter gallery, pressed back against the ship in case anyone aloft or on deck above ventured to peer down. But the potential danger of being seen was not the cause of his suddenly increased heartbeat, and an odd catch in his throat. 'My Christ,' he murmured. '*Athena*!'

San Josefe was rolling and heaving along through the dusky light towards the orange and scarlet riot of the sunset, last in a long column of fat-bodied warships. A second column, perhaps a quarter league away, ploughed along in loose-canvased, overweight splendour off to larboard. But in the interval between the two columns, her square topsail just now losing the last rays of the vanishing sun, the slim and inexpressibly beautiful form of *Athena* rode. With only the fore tops'l, the jib and a badly reefed mains'l drawing, the low and graceful schooner still kept easy pace with the two lines of her wallowing captors, and as the dark shape lifted and fell along, the sea foam gleaming rhythmically under her bows, it seemed to Mainwaring that it was one of the most moving sights he had ever seen.

'Christ. Ain't she a sight, sir?' said Sawyer at his elbow. He spat off into the sea for punctuation.

'Yes. A sight indeed. And by God, I'll have her back!' He looked round. 'Where's Slade?'

'Checkin' the riggin' of our friends in there, sir.'

Mainwaring squinted at *Athena*. There was some kind of movement at her rail. No, on the other side of the ship. Then it became clear. He pointed. 'Look there. A lugger. Longboat, perhaps. Putting out from her.'

Slade had joined them. He narrowed his eyes. 'Sink me, but ye'd be right, zur. An' I think she's trackin' over to us!'

Mainwaring stared. Sawyer was right. The boat, clearly a longboat now under loosefooted main and fore lugsails, was heeling along, bouncing over the swells on a course that clearly would bring it to *San Josefe*. It could be anything, of course: the prize crew exchanging with new men in *San Josefe*, the prize commander coming over to speak to the Spanish vessel's captain – God grant that Roche-Bourbon was only a passenger, and not her captain – or even some plunder from the Athenas' possessions being brought over to scatter among *San Josefe*'s crew.

'Fast,' muttered Slade. 'She'll hook on in ten minues.'

Mainwaring's mind began to work quickly. The opportunity was being handed to him on a platter. He would have to grab for it *now*, or they all were lost. 'Quickly, lads. Can you lead me for'rard, back along the ship? To where we can get at the hatchway to the cable tier?'

Slade looked at Sawyer. 'Well – er – I reckon we can, sir,' said the latter. 'We figured the hatchway they dug yew out o' might be two decks down from where we fetched up. But – '

'But what? Quickly, now!'

Slade wiped his nose on one greasy, tattered sleeve. 'Ain't no way back, Cap'n, 'ceptin' how we came. Along th' ship's side.'

'I can see that. Have you still got your knife?'

'Aye, zur, but – '

'Very well.' Mainwaring kicked off his heavy shoes and stripped off the remains of his tattered hose. 'Lead on, then. We've not a moment to spare!'

Slade and Sawyer exchanged a quick glance, and then nodded. 'Aye, sir. Watch yer footholds an' handholds is all, sir!'

'Fine. I've no wish to swim. Go!'

Swiftly, the three figures moved round the great carved stern, pressing against the ship until they were on the starboard side, away from the sight of the approaching lugger and the other column of ships. They halted at the forward end of the quarter gallery, where Sawyer, who was leading, looked quickly upwards to see if any eyes were peering down, and then leaned out, pointing for Mainwaring's sake at the broad gilt-and-red face of *San Josefe*'s flank, roaring along like some great rolling wall, the sea hissing and leaping as it rushed past the hull. The entire effect was one that made Mainwaring think suddenly that he had badly underestimated the motion of *San Josefe*, the roughness of the sea, and these wiry little men's achievement in working like squirrels along that fearsome perch virtually the length of the ship. But it had to be done.

'Christ save us,' he muttered. 'Right then. You first, Sawyer.'

Slade was speaking in his ear as Sawyer threw a leg over the quarter rail and groped for his first hand- and foothold.

'Watch 'im, zur,' he said. 'Flatten yerself right out, like a crab, zur. Keep yer eye on th' mizzen chains an' make fer 'em.'

Sawyer was clinging for an instant to the gallery rail, reaching with his feet. Then in the next instant he was standing on the four-inch footing of the mid-hull wale which began virtually at the end of the quarter gallery. He was pressed flat to the ship's side, fingers hooked to cling to any projection, and finally digging into the caulking-stuffed gap between the hull planking. Carefully, staying motionless as the ship rolled toward him, he inched toward the mizzen chains, some twenty feet away. Then Slade was over the rail and following behind.

Then it was Mainwaring's turn. He went over the rail, feeling the trembling in his knees and cursing it, cursing his fear. The sea was suddenly roaring and hissing, it seemed just inches below his heels, and he clung in a spasm of terror to the slick planking, sure that in the next instant the great wall would roll towards him and he would topple backwards. But then he saw Slade eyeing him, and he made his feet move.

Dear God, thought Mainwaring, as he inched along. The sea roar was sounding like thunder in his ears, and each roll of *San Josefe*'s hull sent a spasm of fear through him, certain the great oaken wall would cant over him, making a grip impossible, and he would plunge away backwards into the hissing wash under the counter, and death . . .

'Almost there, sir.' It was Sawyer's low call over the sea noise, and at its sound Mainwaring tightened his resolve. The sun was sinking now, a pale medallion behind riotous cloud tumbling over an ink-blue sea. Darkness was settling in, shadowing the great hull along which they crept like flies. Ahead now, Slade was at the mizzen channel, vanishing in under the shadows there on to the chain plates. It was only a few feet more. Mainwaring gritted his teeth and made his feet move, inching along the slippery wood. His fingers dug into the seams, and an ache began to spread up from his wrists. Would he never be there . . .

Then in the next instant Mainwaring was clutching at the tar-smeared irons that angled out from the hull, and he wrestled himself breathlessly in under the channel, until all three men were hidden in the shadow, crouched together like caged monkeys, their eyes white in the dark as they looked at one another.

'Sweet Christ!' breathed Mainwaring. 'How in the name of God you made the length of the ship, I should like to know, Sawyer.'

The Vineyarder's teeth flashed in a grin. 'Jes' more o' th' same, sir, exceptin' – '

Mainwaring put up a quieting hand. A boatswain's pipe was sounding above them on *San Josefe*'s deck, keening high over the hiss of the sea rushing by below their perched toes. Then another pipe, and a third, and now a wild babble of oaths and cried orders rose overhead.

'Callin 'all 'ands, zur?' ventured Slade.

Mainwaring nodded, smiling wryly. 'Or waking the dead. I think we'll know if we hear – '

As if in completion of his sentence, there was a sudden rush of hundreds of feet from within *San Josefe*, bare and booted feet thundering on decking and companionways.

'D'ye think they've found the Frenchman, sir?' said Sawyer, eyes white.

Mainwaring's lips were white. 'Perhaps. I pray to God not.'

There was a sudden babble of voices clearer, closer, and the three men instinctively shrank in under their precarious perch as the irons under their feet began to shake and vibrate.

'Goin' aloft on th' mizzen, zur!' hissed Slade.

Mainwaring motioned for silence. Above them the ratlines squeaked as the feet of a throng of seamen rushed up them. The irons trembled, and the men's voices rose in a continuous stream of noise, joining with the din elsewhere in the ship.

'Sink me. Sounds like ol' Boston fishmarket, sir,' said Sawyer, shaking his head in wonderment.

Beneath them, the ship was slowing, turning. From high above came the squeal of block sheaves. 'Clewing up. They're taking in sail,' Mainwaring murmured. He stretched to peer cautiously up past the edge of the channel at *San Josefe*'s yardarms, then ducked quickly back in. 'Men aloft on all three masts. I think they're heaving to.'

'Pardon, sir?'

'Heaving to, Sawyer. She's turning into the wind. They're going to lie to for the night, by God!'

'Cap'n?' Slade was pointing. 'T' other column o' ships is comin' into view, zur. Hell, if she turns 'er 'ead eastward, anyone on th' decks o' one o' thcm bastards'd see us, easy . . .'

Mainwaring looked quickly around. Under the pressure of her helm, and the efforts of the enormous numbers of men at the braces, clewlines and sheets, *San Josefe* had swung off her westward course and was wallowing round slowly to put her head to wind, into the south-easterly Trades. Already Mainwaring could hear the great foretopsail thump as it went hard aback on the foretopmast. As the ship turned, the three hidden men were presented with a view of the other long column of similarly manoeuvring ships, all apparently turning to lie to as well.

And in the gap between the two columns, riding serenely as a gull even under a sloppily reefed and sheeted foretopmast staysail, was the dark, lovely shape of *Athena*.

Mainwaring scanned quickly to either side. Of the longboat there was no sign. Possibly it had crossed *San Josefe*'s bows as the ship turned, and was even now hooking on below an entry port on the far side. There was no time to lose.

He craned out, peering along the hull. A bare six feet

ahead of them a gunport gaped open, its red lid held open by its tackle, the red-muzzled black hulk of the gun lurking in the run-back position in the shadow's within.

'That gunport. Make for it. There's only a moment or two for us, while the Dons are aloft!'

'Aye, zur!' Sawyer and Slade gave quick nods as one man, and in the next instant both were out, pressed flat like squirrels on a wall, inching along the wale towards the gunport. They were there in a matter of seconds, peered quickly in, and then vanished headfirst into it.

With a prayer that the men on the mainyard aloft would not see him, Mainwaring twisted awkwardly out from his perch, got a precarious footing on the wale, tried to ignore the sea hissing and licking below him, and in several heart-stopping moments had inched his way to the port. Leaning in, he lost his balance, and then half plunged and was half dragged into the gloom within. He banged down painfully hard on decking, and found himself sprawled with Slade and Sawyer between two long guns on a vast, low-beamed gundeck lit weakly by the light of several smoky glims hung randomly over the guns. Cautiously, as his eyes accustomed themselves to the murk, Mainwaring raised himself and peered round. The gundeck appeared deserted.

Slade was whispering urgently at him. 'Lummee, zur, I was wrong. This be it! This be the deck where the hatch opens into th' cable tier!' He pointed forward into the gloom.

Mainwaring rose, thumped his head painfully on a beam, cursed, and nodded. 'Then lead on. Find it, and quickly!'

In a crouch, the three men moved out from behind the guns and made off down the gundeck, dodging round pillars, gratings, and companionways as they ran on noiseless bare feet. Mainwaring knew that in their ragged and dirty state, a quick look in the darkness of the 'tween decks would mistake them for Spaniards off on some task. But even with that

92

thought, Mainwaring's neck was tingling with tension as they ducked swiftly past the long rows of guns, the mess tables, scattered bales and tumbrils lashed against bulkheads, and every so often a tiny, partitioned box set up as a cabin for one of the plethora of officers which inhabited *San Josefe*. Now they were past the main companionway, having pressed to the side around it to stay out of view from the jabbering throng on *San Josefe*'s weatherdeck. It seemed the gundeck would go on for ever.

Then, 'Here it is, sir!' and Slade and Sawyer were crouching before a crudely partitioned box that had materialized before them in the centre of the gundeck, a box with a small, splintery door fastened with a padlock. Mainwaring looked round quickly to see that they were still alone. That state of affairs, in a man of war crewed by several hundred men, would vanish in moments. 'How strong is that lock?'

Sawyer hefted the padlock. 'Damned heavy, sir. Need a bar to break it.'

Something made Mainwaring look up.

'Perhaps something simpler will do,' he said, and lifted a heavy key and ring off a nail that had been driven into a beam.

'Well, I'm buggered,' grinned Slade.

Mainwaring thrust the key into the padlock. With a twist of his wrist the lock snapped open. 'Keep a good watch, now. If we're seen, we're finished!'

Slade and Sawyer nodded, white-eyed, and turned to watch fore and aft as Mainwaring wrestled the lock off and pulled open the door. Before him, in the gloom, was the lip of the box pipe, the column of slimed cable, and the sliding half-hatch. With a thrust, the hatch slid back easily as Mainwaring put his strength against it. He peered below. 'Below, there. Any interest in a turn on deck?'

There was a burst of exclamations and movement in the darkness. 'Sir! It's you! Thank Christ!'

'Strewth, Winnie, I told ye they'd do 'er!'

'Good on 'ee, zur!'

Mainwaring stopped the chatter with a bark. 'Silence, all of you! Mr Hooke? Mr Pellowe? Where are you?'

'Here, sir!'

'An' 'ere, zur!'

'Good! Form that tumbler's pile and climb out of there. Mr Hooke, you'll be first out. Mr Pellowe, you'll come last. Quickly, now!'

There was quick movement again, and heads and shoulders were visible now as the men grunted with effort to form the human ladder. But it was done, and in a few moments Mainwaring was looking into the sooty, jubilant face of Isaiah Hooke as the latter heaved himself out over the hatchway lip. 'Whoreson glad to see ye, zur,' he growled.

'And I you. Dear God, Isaiah, you're even blacker than we are. Quick as the lads come up, get them down low between that set of guns. Slade and Sawyer are watching for the Dons.'

'Zur!' Hooke turned back, and heaved the second and third bodies up through the hatchway. Within a few minutes only Pellowe and Winton still remained in the tier. The others were crouched, ready, in an expectant knot on the larboard side of the gundeck. It took a few moments of desperate scrambling, and Hooke's muscular strength at a key moment, but at last both Winton and Pellowe were up, the last being hauled out bodily by his arms after managing to slither partway up the column of the cable.

Pellowe, his face now black as ink, guffawed with startling white teeth at Mainwaring. 'Thank you, sir. We all were beginning to think – ' He did not finish.

'Yes. Fortunately not the case, Stephen.' Mainwaring closed the door and replaced the padlock. 'No need to announce our departure. Slade, Sawyer. All clear?'

Slade nodded. 'Still aloft furlin', zur. A petty officer or some such came down the companionway, but went on below, zur. Didn't look this way.'

'All right. Now listen, all of you.' Mainwaring crouched down among the men. The flicker of the candle flame in a nearby glim cast the features of his face in deep relief. 'We've got to move fast, and we'll get but one chance. We've left the Frenchman bound and gagged, but he'll be found in a moment as soon as the Dons finish snugging down for the night and wonder where in hell he is. And when they find him, all hell will break loose. *Athena* is heaving to about two or three cables off the starboard side now – '

'*Athena*! The ship, sir?'

'Yes. But you'll never see her again unless you let me finish. She's likely got a prize crew. There's a longboat from her alongside *San Josefe* here right now.' He looked up. 'Slade. Can you see the longboat?'

'Aye, zur!' Slade hissed after a moment. 'Hooked on at the main chains! Canvas's brailed up, an' there's only one man in 'er!'

'Good! That's our one chance, lads. And here's what we do. The Dons will be sending down the watch below any moment. So we're going to move along to the closest gunport over the longboat and drop into it. Follow?'

The men stared, suddenly too excited to speak. Pellowe spoke for them. 'Aye, aye, sir!'

'Good. Now follow me. And not a damned squeak from anyone! Slade, lead us for'rard. Sawyer? Watch astern!'

The tumult overhead was easing. Mainwaring knew it would only be a matter of moments before the gundeck was alive again with Spaniards. Slade leading, they ran in crouching stages down the gundeck, sheltering for a moment in the shadows of the guns, then rising to sprint on.

Mainwaring and Slade arrived together at a gun that the

latter had pointed at. Slade ducked in behind it, moved to the gunport, peered out quickly, and nodded. Outside the port Mainwaring could see the longboat's foremast swaying, the dipping lugsail brailed against it, a corner luffing in the wind.

He was beside Slade in an instant, the rush of bare feet behind him indicating the others were crouched in behind. Slade's face was shining with sweat over the black grease.

Mainwaring threw a quick look out of the gunport. 'That man, Slade.'

'Zur?'

'You'll have to use your knife on that man in the boat. Do it the first time. And no noise.'

Slade bared his teeth, reaching for the knife in his shirt collar. 'Smooth as Poll's arse, zur,' he breathed.

'Damn your foul mouth. And for God's sake be careful. Go!'

Slade fitted the knife between his yellowed teeth and eased out through the gunport. Mainwaring thanked a watchful providence for making the dusk come on so rapidly. Slade might make it into the boat without being seen by someone on the decks or yards above . . .

Almost at the moment Slade vanished into the gathering dark there was a slap of feet on the companionway aft down the gundeck, and twenty to thirty seamen came thumping along it, voices at full pitch.

'Oh Christ!' moaned Pellowe at Mainwaring's ear. 'Now we're for it!'

'Stay low, all of you!' rasped Mainwaring. 'Don't let 'em see you over the guns!' He crawled back to the gunport and risked a look out. He saw the longboat riding below in the heavy shadows below *San Josefe*'s main chains, a seaman in a red Portuguese stocking cap slumped in the sternsheets, at ease against a lashed tiller. For a brief, alarming instant Mainwaring thought Slade had missed his footing and fallen to a silent death in the water under the longboat. Then he saw the seaman look watchfully up, and show a familiar, gap-toothed smile. His feet were resting on a crumpled form that was almost, but not quite, thrust out of sight under the stroke thwart.

Mainwaring craned to look up. The yardarms were empty, and no men were aloft. The clutch of Spaniards who had come down to the gundeck had continued on down, off on some task in the bowels of the ship. They had been given a moment or two more, but only that. He held out his hand to Slade, and made a quick cutting motion. Slade understood, reversed the knife, and threw it with frightening accuracy at Mainwaring's face. Mainwaring caught it somewhat wildly and dropped back into the gundeck. Another party of Span-iards was thundering down the companionway, and Hooke and Pellowe had the men lying flat in the space between the two guns.

'Isaiah! Help me with this tackle!' Mainwaring hissed. He sprang to the nearer gun. Its side tackles were set up, tied off to ringbolts on either side of the gunport, the after blocks hooked to eyes on the cheek of the carriage. Feverishly, Mainwaring sliced through the mousing holding the after block's hook to the gun and, as he did so, Hooke hauled in on the fall with furious hand-over-hand energy, until the blocks were snug together, achock against the ringbolt beside the gunport. Behind him, Mainwaring gathered up the loose coils of the fall, wrestled them to the gunport, and dropped them out. They fell noiselessly down the wall of *San Josefe*'s side into the floorboards of the longboat, where Slade was gesturing frantically for them to come down.

Mainwaring swung back to the men. 'Right, lads! Out you go. Mr Pellowe, you'll lead, if you please. Quickly, now!'

One by one the sweating, wide-eyed men pressed them-selves out through the gunport, gripped the line, and vanished into the darkness. Mainwaring glanced out at *Athena*. There was a small, amber-tinted lantern glowing at her transom. He would need that mark.

'Your turn, zur!' Hooke was looking at him.

Mainwaring looked round and saw that he and the burly master were the only two left. 'No, after you – ' Mainwaring began, and then froze. There was sudden noise behind them. The thunder of boots on planking. Voices raised in alarm and fury, and among them a French voice. Roche-Bourbon. 'They've found them. Damn your eyes, Isaiah, you'd better get out that port, or we're dead men!'

Hooke hesitated. 'But, zur – ' he began.

'*Go!*'

Hooke flung himself out through the port, vanishing out and down. Mainwaring swung round. The tide of men had rushed aft from the companionway, all but one thick-set seaman in baggy, short-legged trousers and a stained red wool jacket, open to show a naked chest. His hair was lank and black under a tattered little tricorne, and he was hefting a cutlass. He turned forward, towards Mainwaring, and moved swiftly along the line of guns, the expression on his swarthy face like that of a man who had heard a rat in the pantry and was out to find it. In a moment he would be there and would see him, and already it was too late to try and wriggle out of the gunport in time –

Mainwaring rose to his feet in a low crouch. With a growl in his throat he launched himself around the gun in an accelerating sprint, his feet digging hard for traction on the worn planking. He had a momentary vision of the man's eyes widening in surprise, his mouth opening to shriek a warning, the cutlass lifting, and then his shoulder cannoned into the man's belly, and the two thumped back hard to the deck, locked in a kicking, struggling embrace. The Spaniard had lost his breath, and was making wheezing yelps as he tried to take in enough air to call out.

Mainwaring found a wild, savage energy coursing through him, and he fought clear of the man's grip, rolling away from the vicious downward cut of the cutlass that sank with a *thungg* into the decking inches from where his head had been. Spinning to his feet, Mainwaring just had his balance as the Spaniard rolled to his knees and wrenched the blade free, to cut a vicious backhand arc at Mainwaring's legs. But Mainwaring was already airborne, diving at the man with hands outstretched. Even as he struck him, Mainwaring's left hand was closing in a vice around the man's throat, throttling back the call for help, and his other hand, a balled fist, was driving once, twice, three times into the man's face. There was a hideous feel of snapping gristle under his knuckles, and blood jetted in a dark flood from the Spaniard's nose. The man was on his back now, his free hand clawing at Mainwaring's face, the other thumping the hilt of the cutlass hard against the side of Mainwaring's head. The blow sent a haze over the American's eyes, and with a snarling, incoherent cry, he wrenched the cutlass out of the Spaniard's grip with both hands, rolled to his knees, and then with both hands on the hilt, drove it to the deck through the centre of the man's chest. The Spaniard goggled, his face a bloody rictus, and then slumped back.

His breath coming in burning gasps, his body shaking as if with fever, Mainwaring stumbled in a daze over to the gunport. Then, in the next instant, he had launched himself out recklessly into the dark, feeling the rope come into his hands, and he was swinging down it like a chimney sweep on a steep tiled roof towards the waiting longboat in the gloom below. The dark was so intense that he thought for a moment that the boat was not there, and suddenly he would slip into the sea and be gone . . .

Abruptly, his feet thumped down on the thwart of a boat, and a half-dozen hands were clutching to steady him. 'Mr Hooke!' he croaked, trying to see where he was. 'Get for'rard and shake out the brails on the fores'l.' Now he could see. He was in the sternsheets, inches from the tiller bar. 'Mr Pellowe?'

'Here, sir!'

'Shake out the main! Quickly, lads! Aiken?'

'Here in the bows, sir!' came a voice out of the gloom.

'Cut away that painter for'rard! Is she tied on aft?'

Burke had appeared beside him, grabbing at the tiller bar. 'No, sir,' he said. 'They were lettin' 'er stream alongside.'

'Sir, I need a – !' came Aiken's cry.

'Abner! Pass Slade's knife for'rard to Aiken!' barked Mainwaring. 'Slade?'

'Zur!'

'Where's your man?'

'Here, zur, under th' thwart. I cut 'is throat, zur.'

Mainwaring could not repress a shudder. 'Well done. Throw the bastard over the side. Aiken!'

'Painter's cut, sir!'

Mainwaring looked up. The thundering feet were moving along the gundeck now. Voices were rising in fury. And faces were appearing at the rail, faces that gazed down in astonishment, and behind them, other figures that stepped forward, musket barels gleaming in the light of lanterns held high.

'*Alto*! *Alto*!' There was a pink flash overhead, brilliant in the darkness, and as the sharp report of a pistol stung his ears Mainwaring felt a ball thump into the gunwale inches from his hand. 'Sheet home! Christ save us, *move*!' he roared.

Figures in the boat dived for the sheets of the wildly luffing lugsails and hauled them taut in furious work. Mainwaring thrust the tiller bar over, pushing Burke away with one hand

100

as he crouched to see under the foot of the sails. 'Sorry, Burke, but I shall do this! But stand ready to take it if I fall!'

'Aye, aye, sir!' There was discipline and acceptance in Burke's voice, and in a sudden burst of feeling that he just as quickly crushed out of his mind, Mainwaring was glad of it. The wind caught in the bellies of the big, loosefooted lugsails with a thump, and the boat heeled alarmingly over, accelerating away in a rush from the side of the Spanish ship.

'Trim her, lads! Some of you to wind'ard!' Mainwaring barked. There was a welter of scrambling arms and legs as the men threw themselves up along the windward gunwale to keep the little craft as upright as possible. There was another ripple of brilliant pink flashes, sharp reports, and more balls struck the boat in odd pinging and thumping sounds. But there were no cries of pain.

'Down, lads!' called Mainwaring, his voice cracking. 'On the floorboards, not the thwarts! Give 'em no target!' He spat vigorously off to leeward. 'Mr Pellowe?'

'Sir!'

'Ease the main! She's too flat, and not drawing!'

The boat plunged over a swell, the thump of the bows sending a rinse of spray back to patter on the sails and drench the men. Mainwaring clutched at the tiller bar and crouched, cursing the sail foot for blocking his view.

'Damnation! Aiken, where does *Athena* lie?'

'A touch to loo'ard, sir! But I'd hold this course, t' weather her an' run down!'

Hooke was at the mainmast foot, snugging down the mainsail brails out of the way. He was staring aft. 'Them Dons are stirrin' well enough now, zur! Christ, if they gets a *gun* to workin' – '

Mainwaring twisted round to look. *San Josefe*'s rail was alive with figures, lanterns waving and rushing to and fro, the light glinting on musket barrels. And in the next instant there

101

was another ripple of flashes as a ragged volley of musket fire burst from the rail. The shot spattered into the water all about the plunging, hurrying longboat, and a sharp *thwock* aloft and a look up showed a neat round hole in the mainsail barely inches above Hooke's head. 'They will. It'll be a matter of minutes, no more!' said Mainwaring through clenched teeth. 'Aiken! How far off are we?'

'Hunnert yards, zur! She's dead ahead!'

Mainwaring put the helm up. With the water boiling and foaming under her transom, the boat heeled off on a reach, slicing across the top of a steeving dark swell. From behind the screen of the longboat's sails *Athena*'s dark shape, suddenly close and huge, loomed before them. In a quick glance, Mainwaring's eyes took in every detail possible. The hull lying to in the long, rolling swells; two figures on deck, aft, one rushing forward towards the main companionway, the other pointing toward the onrushing longboat; the glow of the amber lantern above the transom rail; the rippling face of the slowly luffing staysail. Christ, she was beautiful!

'Ready y'selves, lads!' Mainwaring cried over the wind and sea noise. 'We'll bang in, bows to wind, on this side of her! Aiken, try to hook on at the main chains, and hold her while we board her! Go up her side, best as you can, and get those two aboard! Burke?'

'Sir?'

'You'll make for her helm. Keep her hove to but ready to move on my orders. Clear?'

'Aye, aye, sir!'

'Cap'n, sir?' called Winton, forward. He had been down digging through the longboat's gear, which was loosely stowed under the thwarts. 'Sir? There's a boathook here, an' two grapnels, an' line. Should I – ?'

'Good man! Pass 'em aft! The grapnels, I mean. Aiken, you take that hook! Isaiah, you'll take one grapnel and

Stephen the other. Hook on fast, and tie 'em off! Slade, Sawyer?'

'Here, sir!'

'Slade, you'll use Mr Hooke's line to board. Better get your knife back from Aiken. Sawyer, you'll go up Mr Pellowe's. The rest of you, follow 'em. Clear?'

'Aye, aye, sir!' chorused several voices at once. Eyes gleamed whitely in excitement through the gloom.

Athena towered over them. Mainwaring threw one look back at *San Josefe* and could see figures working frantically on the gundeck, framed in the dim orange squares of the gunports.

He spun back. The longboat sped in. They were fifty yards off the dark hull. Now thirty. The grapnels were ready, poised. The men crouched on the floorboards. Would there be *no* resistance from the prize crew? It seemed impossible.

As if to answer Mainwaring's thought, a flashing report erupted aft by the schooner's helm. There was the deep *ftoom* of a musket's report. But not before Aiken, crouched in the bows with the boathook, had snapped back against the gunwale, the boathook clattering out of his grip into the bottom of the boat. His head lolled back, and his legs twitched briefly. Even in the gloom Mainwaring could see the dark, thumb-sized hole in his forehead, a few inches above his wide, sightless eyes.

'Goddamn them! Damn them!' barked Mainwaring. 'Winton! Get for'rard on that hook!'

'Aye, sir!' Winton scrambled forward. As the longboat heaved up and then knifed through the flank of a swell, he reached Aiken's body, and wrestled it over the gunwale to splash into the sea. It went past Mainwaring, the water washing over Aiken's face, still staring up with a ghastly astonishment. In the bows, Winton was hefting the hook, ready.

Ten yards. Then five.

Now!

Mainwaring thrust the longboat's helm hard over, and the sails began a sharp rippling and thumping as it moved in a swooping turn under the shadow of *Athena*'s hull. With a splintery thud, the boat drove against the schooner, the impact sharp and violent. The grapnels flashed up, Winton was hooking at the main chains with wild curses coming from his lips, and the men were on the gunwales, and then leaping upwards, scrabbling for a handhold on *Athena*'s side. Now Mainwaring was looking up, seeing the rail above him, and leaping for the main channel irons, clawing his way up past them, wild with fear that he would slip, equally wild with joy that he could feel the schooner under his hands again. There were roaring, baying voices all around him, and then he realized that one of them was his own. A musket blasted, ear-splittingly close, and a shriek sounded. And then the rail was there, and he was tumbling over it to sprawl awkwardly on the deck, rising to see Slade and Hooke overwhelm the Spaniard with a musket, the flash of Slade's knife cutting off the wretch's frenzied shriek, and turning to see the other Spaniard, at the top of the main companionway, stare in horror at the baying black apparitions rushing at him, and turn and throw himself with a wail over the far rail.

Hooke was seizing the wheel with a wild cry of triumph, and Mainwaring saw Pellowe, brandishing the Spanish musket, take one man and plunge down the companionway to check below. The others were rushing about the deck like starving men in a bakery, touching the ship, drinking it in, feeling the wood and the lines, their eyes alight.

'Burke?' called Mainwaring. 'Can you take the helm?'

'Burke's dead, sir,' said a voice.

'Goddamn and blast. Winton, then! Relieve Mr Hooke at the helm! To me, Mr Hooke!'

Pellowe was appearing up the companionway.

'Clear below, sir! No Dons. Those two were all. And she's in fair enough nick, sir. They didn't gut her!'

Mainwaring threw a look at *San Josefe*. There was rhythmic action at the gunports. Shouted orders. And the squeal of gun trucks. *Oh God*, he thought. *They're running out.*

Hooke and Pellowe, two black-faced frightening shapes, were before him. 'Orders, zur?' growled Hooke.

'Stephen, you'll take the headsails and foremast. Isaiah, the main. Take Slade and Sawyer with you, Stephen. Abner'll help you, Isaiah. *Make sail*!'

In the next instant the two men were sprinting forward, pulling their men with them. Mainwaring stepped quickly to the wheel.

'Winton, get for'rard there with Mr Hooke. I'll take the helm.' He braced the helm with his body as Winton raced off forward, and cupped his hands.

'Can you raise the main alone, Mr Hooke?'

'No, zur!' came a grunt-filled reply. 'Needs – us all – !'

'Mr Pellowe! Come aft and tail on to the main throat and peak halliards! We'll have to hoist 'em one at a time! Main first, the fore, then headsails! Follow?'

Pellowe and his men pelted aft. 'Aye, aye, sir!'

With curses and grunts, the six men threw their weight and strength against the halliards, swinging off to get slack and then laying out almost flat on the deck to haul taut, their bare feet scrabbling for footing on the deck planking. The Spanish had left the gaskets off – Mainwaring had completely forgotten about them – and the great sail rose to their efforts, a vast, glowing face of canvas that suddenly shone with the ivory light of the moon, rising like a pale orb above a bank of horizon cloud. Behind Mainwaring, the main sheet tackle creaked and moved as the rippling canvas rose.

'High – 'nough, zur!' gasped Hooke. 'She'll not sit any higher!'

'Right! Belay and turns, then! Winton, come aft and stand by the mainsheet. Mr Hooke, can you hoist the fore with five of you?'

Hooke was loping off forward, the others a pack at his heels. 'Aye, zur! Jes' keep 'er 'ead t 'win'ard, zur!'

Suddenly, the moonlight was outshone by a lurid row of flashes along *San Josefe*'s side. A wall of blue smoke rolled out from her and a deep, blasting thunder punched into Mainwaring and the other men with the force of a physical blow.

Broadside, he had time to think, and then there was a sound like wood being slapped hard on a calm water surface, and a half-dozen huge, shimmering shot splashes geysered up a few yards off *Athena*'s side, enormous columns of spray as high as *Athena*'s crosstrees, which collapsed in hissing clouds of rain down over the schooner's deck and the furiously working knot of men at the foremast foot.

'Under! They'll range up, next shot, sartin, sir!' cried Winton, who was feverishly throwing off the sheet coils and readying the lines to run.

'Not if we aren't here to hit, Winton!' said Mainwaring. 'Mr Hooke! For God's sake, are you – !'

Then he saw. The foresail was up, luffing in long, booming slaps while Abner scrabbled at the larboard and starboard sheet tackles of the big, loosefooted sail. And the staysail was luffing, too, its sheets free, the outer headsails rising now like pale triangles in rhythmic lifts, dark waves rippling over their faces as they rose.

'They're up, zur!' came Hooke's bellow. 'Stays'l, jibs an' fores'l!'

'Thank Christ!' Mainwaring threw a wild look around the scene. *Athena* lay between the two columns of hove-to

Spanish warships. Only *San Josefe* was to windward of her. But if he pointed *Athena* up high enough . . .

'Stand by the heads'ls, Mr Hooke! Flat the jibs out to larboard! We'll take the larboard tack out of this trap!'

'Aye, aye, zur!'

With the triangular faces of the two sails held flat over to windward, *Athena*'s bowsprit dipped and curtseyed slowly, then with increasing speed, round to leeward. Mainwaring waited, his skin acrawl with anticipation, feeling the muzzles of *San Josefe*'s guns boring into his back, hearing the faint clamour on the other Spanish ships as the response to the escape spread. Damn, would she *never* come around!

'Off the wind, Cap'n!'

Mainwaring felt the catch of excitement in his throat. 'Jibs! Let go an' haul! Stand by your sheets, there! Slade, come aft and help Winton with the main! *Move*, you sons of – !'

Athena paused, as if uncertain of her freedom. Then the wind took its full grip of her arching, ready canvas. In a rush that took Mainwaring's breath away, the schooner leaped ahead under his feet, the rigging and hull suddenly alive with the creak and roar of movement. The sea gurgled and hissed under her counter. Under his hands the helm trembled, the life pulsing through it, and he had steerageway. They were free! *Athena* and her men, the so pitifully, damnably irretrievably few that remained, were free!

Athena lay over and thundered through a swell, her speed building by the instant. Astern, another thunderclap of gunnery sounded, the flashes bright against the schooner's sails. But this time the great columns of water jetted up at least a cable astern. Already *Athena* was knifing across to windward of the bows of the leading ship of the far column, a portly seventy-gunner whose foredeck was packed with gesticulating, shrieking figures. A few muskets popped, the flashes soundless winks, the balls flying wide and harmless, and *Athena* was lifting her skirts and running away from their helpless wrath.

An involuntary, formless cry burst out of Mainwaring, and he could not choke it back in time, wondering if it had been heard over the sea and rigging noise, over the whistling wind. He exulted in the arching canvas, so still and powerful in the moonlight; in the fat hulks of the Spanish, lying impotently astern; in *San Josefe*, uselessly thumping out ragged broadsides that fell far astern now; and in the lift and surge of the hypnotic, ecstatically beautiful ship under his feet.

And now the sheets had been hauled and jam-cleated, and Hooke, Pellowe and the others were back before him, laughing and staring incredulously back at the Spanish and up at the curving wings of sail that were bearing them off into the inexpressibly bewitching night.

'Mr Pellowe,' said Mainwaring, his eye on the leech of the great sail above him, 'we'll go watch and watch. Please decide who will form yours and Mr Hooke's. You'll take the first watch, so I would appreciate a man on the wheel. Our course is,' and here he thought for a moment, glancing at the compass box, 'sou' west by south, for the present.'

'Sir.'

'Man only helm and lookout, if that is all you can. Lookout to be in the foretop.'

'Sir.'

'Mr Hooke? When you've got your watches determined – I shall join the short-handed one – send a man below to see if the Dons left any food and drink in the ship. Water, particularly. We shall be needing it.'

'Aye, aye, zur.' Pellowe and Hooke spent a few moments in quick conversation, and Mainwaring was glad to be free to think of nothing for the moment beyond the feel of the schooner's helm in his hands as she forged along, the sweetness of the night wind, and the ivory beauty of the moonlight tracing a silvery path across the sea face to light *Athena*'s canvas in special beauty.

The two men had evidently decided. Winton arrived at the wheel, knuckled his forehead, and took the helm from Mainwaring.

'Slade!' barked Hooke. 'Yew git below an' see what the Dons 'ave left us. Biscuit an' breadbags, particular. An' see if the galley fire can be lit.'

As Slade vanished in barefooted nimbleness down the companionway, the master moved to where Mainwaring stood at the weather rail. 'Beggin' yer pardon, Cap'n. T' tell yew truly, zur, I never thought t' see 'er again. That were a hopper-arsed do in that Spanisher, right enough!'

A wave of fatigue had settled over Mainwaring, making his head swim. But he still managed a laugh at the incredulous look on the beefy master's face that gave him the air of a startled bear. 'True enough, Isaiah. I just wish there had been more of us to see her back in our hands.' He pushed the dark wave back once more from his mind. 'What have you decided on your watches?'

'Winton an' Slade wiv me, zur. Abner an' Sawyer wiv Mr Pellowe. An' wiv yer permission, zur, I exchanged wiv 'im for th' first watch, zur, so's mayhap he might see t' feedin' us, zur, bein' as how he's good wiv cookin', an' all.'

'Mr Pellowe? A cook? Sink me, Isaiah, I find new talents in this ship's company all the time. Very well.' He raised his voice. 'Mr Pellowe!'

'Sir?'

'Get down to my cabin and see what might still be there, if you please. Most importantly, see if the chart folio was left in her. And then I gather you're going to feed us?'

Pellowe stared. His mouth popped open and then shut, like a grouper watching a school of fish. 'Oh. Ah. Well, sir, I shall be *looking* below. But as to *cooking* below – ?'

109

Mainwaring kept a straight face. 'Ah, a confusion of terms. I see. Very well then, Mr Pellowe, carry on. But I am disappointed.'

Pellowe looked deadly serious. 'Your pardon, sir, but I'm not.' And as Hooke and Mainwaring burst out laughing, he vanished down the companionway.

Hooke turned back to Mainwaring. 'May I ask what is it ye plan t'do, zur?'

Mainwaring stared back at the distant Spanish. 'That lot will be blundering on in pursuit of our squadron, Isaiah. So we've an admiral to meet and warn. And likely we'll help him take Porto Bello, if we manage to get there, short-handed like this.'

Hooke was beaming at him. 'We all want to say thank you, zur. We're damned glad t' be out o' that greaser scow, zur.' There was an unhidden admiration in his voice.

'Thank you, Isaiah. But no more than I,' he said. 'And as you now have the watch, could your lads strike a few buckets of sea water up here to the quarterdeck?' he said, starting to peel off the ragged, greasy clothing. 'I'm filthy, and have had quite enough of looking like a damned black rat!'

4

The dawn was barely beginning off to the east on the morning of 21 November 1739, and its pink glow warmed the dark shapes of the six line-of-battle ships, two cutters and the schooner *Athena* that rode at anchor. The squadron was three leagues along the dark, palm-clad coast from the narrow harbour mouth of Porto Bello. The winds were light and westerly, with no hint of the usual blustery south-east Trade. Off the bowsprits, the coast led towards the target, a target the collective minds of Admiral Edward Vernon's captains were about to consider over final instructions in the great cabin of His Britannic Majesty's Ship *Burford*. Vernon had called a conference of captains for two bells in the morning watch, and on all the ships people were about, lanterns moving, blocks squealing as boats were swung out. But the first boats would not arrive for fifteen minutes, and Edward Vernon was taking those minutes to consider the report – and the events – which had brought Edward Mainwaring to stand before him again in *Burford*'s great cabin.

Vernon was looking at the tall American with a searching expression. 'Let me be quite clear in understanding your report, Mainwaring. You say you did not reveal anything of our descent upon this coast to this Frenchman – er . . .'

'Roche-Bourbon, sir. No, I did not.'

'I see. And apparently in spite of improper treatment, for which I commend you. But you did lose your ship.'

'And I recovered her, sir.'

Vernon leaned forward and studied the carefully penned

words again. 'Yes. An extraordinary thing. And you say here that you brought her here without sighting any other vessels?'

Mainwaring shook his head. He was gaunt and, if such a thing can be imagined, seemed pale under the mahogany suntan. He was still dressed in the now quite ragged seaman's clothing, albeit cleansed of the cable grease through much scrubbing. *Athena* had startled the anchored squadron, appearing out of the nor' east as the sun had set the evening before. With the fluky winds and damnably unpredictable current that set at three knots or more along the coast, it had taken until an hour ago, in the glare of a brilliant moon, for the schooner to work up to the squadron's anchorage. Mainwaring had left a pale but determined Pellowe and Winton on anchor watch, the others slumped in sleep about the deck, except for the indefatigable Slade and Sawyer, who had rowed the jolly boat over to *Burford* with a last reserve of energy originating not a little in their own pride. As *Athena* had worked up to the anchorage, Mainwaring had found time to go below and blearily scribble his report. It had been a painful experience recounting the loss of *Athena*'s men – a loss Mainwaring dwelt on inwardly as a product of his own stupidity and recklessness more than the viciousness of the Spanish. As he stood, barefoot and hatless, waiting while Vernon read the last paragraphs, he felt little more than an overwhelming sense of failure.

'No, sir,' he said, pulling himself out of the pit of gloom. 'When we had Roncador abeam we saw tops'ls to the nor' west, but it was one vessel, and bound away to the north.'

'And the Spanish force which took you?'

Mainwaring rubbed his brow. It was all there in his report. 'Two columns of line-o'-battle ships, sir. About twelve sail all told, fifty guns or more. Badly manned, I'd say, with the exception of the *guardacostas* that took us. I gathered that they had no idea of our true destination, but thought Cartagena

112

was likely. They intend to put in there. But they should search us out quickly enough, sir.'

Vernon frowned. 'By God, with these currents and winds they'll have a difficult time enough making Cartagena. And the *Sheerness* frigate I've set off there should give us warning, eh? At least I trust it shall. A good deal will depend on our success ashore here if we are to escape the clutches of your Roche-Bourbon.'

'Yes, sir.'

'Mainwaring, you've done bloody well. I had very little faith in our ability to keep this enterprise secret, so you should not chastise yourself too greatly for falling into the Dons' hands. I value far more the resourcefulness you have demonstrated in recovering your ship and returning here to warn me.'

Mainwaring's face was wooden. He knew the truth of the matter. 'Thank you, sir,' he said.

'I can see that you are an exhausted man, Mainwaring,' Vernon went on. 'But I cannot release you yet, I am afraid, to return to your ship. I will have a conference of captains in a few moments on what I intend we shall do today. And I shall want you here.' He stood up. 'But my servant makes a palatable Spanish coffee, and I've sent him to the galley fire to warm some for you. It may restore you somewhat.'

Ther was a hint of warmth and concern in Vernon's bluff manner, and Mainwaring felt a pulse of gratitude towards him. 'You're most kind, sir.'

'Nonsense, Mainwaring. I need intelligent and active officers with initiative if we are to succeed in this enterprise, and I need their minds now. You are one of those, and I am simply looking after my resources.' He paused. 'You've something else on your mind, eh? Well, what is it?'

'My ship's company, sir. I have a midshipman, a master, my gunner and three seamen, sir. Is there a possibility of a draft of additional men?'

113

'What is your normal complement?'

'I can sail and fight her with twenty, sir.'

'That isn't what I asked,' said Vernon. 'Oh, very well. Were you manned entirely with Provincials?'

'No, sir. About half, sir.'

'Hmmm. Very well, Commodore Brown will be asked if Captain Dent can spare a draft of fifteen hands out of *Hampton Court* to you. She's best manned. I'll ask that they be sent to you before the watch changes. You'll have to take what he offers, I'm afraid.'

Mainwaring nodded. 'Thank you, sir.'

'Yes, yes,' said Vernon impatiently. 'Now see to that coffee and return here. I hear the first boat alongside now, if I'm not mistaken.'

In the welter of activity that took place in *Burford* in the next minutes, Mainwaring managed to find – or be found by – Vernon's servant, who put into his hands an enormous china mug of hot, sugary, black syrup which Mainwaring had drunk greedily, feeling the warmth course through his body. He had gone to the rail to see about Slade and Sawyer, but arrived in time to see a solicitous boatswain's mate handing down a half-bag of biscuit and an earthenware jug to the two men as they lay in a kind of stupor in the boat. What might be in that jug was a question for the moment best unasked. He wondered if Pellowe and Hooke had managed to get the galley fire lit, but then found himself watching the due process of ceremony which greeted the arrival of Vernon's captains aboard *Burford*.

As each boat approached through the dusky light, the ritual hail of 'Boat ahoy!' brought the bellowed name of the ship whose captain was being borne in it. In orderly turn, the boats tossed their oars and hooked on at the forechains, the elegantly dressed gentlemen in their sternsheets scrambling with varying degrees of agility up the battens to *Burford*'s

114

entry port, the boat dropping astern to lie at the quarterbooms until called.

Vernon's flag captain, Watson, had seen to it that a half-company of Newton's Jamaica regiment was formed up on the broad expanse of deck, and the port flanked by sideboys and a party of boatswain's mates, who launched into long, twittering calls, as each figure appeared at the port. The gaitered infantrymen, streaming already with sweat, ponderously presented their firelocks, their officer dipping his spontoon and sweeping off his hat in a graceful bow, and the captains lifted their hats to the great ensign curling at the staff above *Burford*'s quarterdeck before being led off below to Vernon's cabin.

From his place on the far side of the waist, where he stood feeling the effects of the coffee and receiving odd stares from seamen in *Burford* who were better dressed than he, Mainwaring reflected that the entire scene lacked one thing. The uniformity of the dress of the Spanish and French officers marked clearly their profession as king's sea officers. For all the stirring ritual of the little ceremony on *Burford*'s deck, the welcome might well have been extended to a clutch of successful merchants coming aboard, so varied had been the dress of each captain. Then Mainwaring remembered the state of his own ragged dress, and the far more important fact that he was to take part in the meeting. He managed to find Vernon's servant and return the cup, then slipped into Vernon's cabin just as he was about to begin. Chairs and a table on trestles had been set up, and Mainwaring slid self-consciously into the last one when Vernon pointed to it. The captains turned frowns or amused smiles at him, and the self-consciousness over the ragged clothing returned. His face burned, but he fixed his eyes on Vernon and waited.

The admiral had his back to the cabin's stern lights, out through which a much brighter picture of the breezy sea face could be seen than when Mainwaring had been here minutes earlier. Down either flank of the table, their lace and buttons bright under the row of lanterns that hung from hooks in the beams, the commanders of Vernon's squadron were ranged. On his right sat Brown, the tall, handsome commodore at Jamaica, and beside him, his captain in *Hampton Court*, Dent, who was small and swarthy. On Vernon's other hand was a gaunt-looking officer with fever-yellowed skin in the facings of the Jamaica regiment, who was evidently Captain Newton, the land forces commander. The other captains Mainwaring had met in Jamaica: Watson of the *Burford*, taciturn; Main of the *Worcester*, florid and voluble; Waterhouse of *Princess Louisa*, dark and watchful; Trevor of *Strafford*, elegantly handsome, with pale blue eyes seemingly devoid of expression; and Herbert of the *Norwich*, a square-faced, shovel-handed man with the look of coming to rank 'through the hawse hole', as promotion from the lower decks was described.

'My reason for calling this conference, gentlemen,' began Vernon briskly, 'is to review what I intend us to do. Commodore Brown, will you be so kind as to lay out the chart of the place.'

The chart which was unrolled down the table and held down by odds and ends that materialized from Vernon's desk showed a deep, rectangular bay, some two miles in depth by perhaps a mile in width. With the upward bulge in the Darién coastline, the entrance was in fact facing south-*west*ward, so that a vessel beating straight into the harbour would steer to the north-east. The land to either side was evidently much like what could be glimpsed from the present anchorage: rising steeply from the shore to high hills, and thickly wooded with palm and palmetto. On the left hand, or northern point of land at the harbour mouth, a formidable-looking fortification was shown, the Castillo de Todofierro, or Iron Castle. A little more than halfway in along the right, or southern shore, a second, bastioned fortification was shown, marked as the Castillo de Gloria, or the Gloria Castle. Finally, at the end of the southern coast, the small town of Porto Bello stood, protected before it by a square fortification that sat out in shoal water, joined to the town by a narrow causeway. This last work was named the San Geronimo Castle. Altogether it appeared to be a substantially defended place, to Mainwaring's eye.

Vernon picked up a wooden pointer from his desk and stood. He followed his words with slow, deliberate indications of the pointer on the chart 'The wind, gentlemen, is unfortunately westerly only by fits and starts, and we shall have to make the best of it. But if it sets fair enough, I propose the following. All of you, gentlemen, will stream your boats, with your landing parties told off an' armed, astern, when we slip. Captain Newton, as you and the body of your people are in *Hampton Court*, I'll ask that you have your first party in Captain Dent's boats, ready to be directed ashore when it appears to me the moment is ripe. All other boats are to follow yours, on my hoisting a green pennant to the foremast head in *Burford*.'

Newton nodded. 'Very good, sir,' he said.

'These "castles" must be reduced, gentlemen, if we are to take the damn'd place with any hope at all. The Iron Castle has seventy-eight guns, with its lower battery mounting thirty-two. The Gloria has no less than ninety-eight. I propose we take them in detail.'

He looked at Brown. 'Commodore Brown, in *Hampton Court*, shall lead us in a close line o' battle as close in to the Iron Castle as possible. Therefore, in slipping, see that you man your larboard batteries first. In succession, as your guns bear, broadside the place. But I want no hurry, no waste of shot. Ensure your gun captains know that.'

Trevor of the *Strafford* leaned forward. 'Will Commodore

117

Brown lead regardless of the wind, sir?' he said languidly. 'Perchance it may veer. The *Fighting Instructions* – '

'I am altering the *Instructions*, Captain Trevor. He is to lead regardless of wind. I shall hoist a red colour at the maintopm'st head, and as long as that flies you shall steer to follow Commodore Brown.'

He paused and looked round the table. 'On passing the Iron Castle, Commodore Brown is to take *Hampton Court* in and anchor as closely as possible to the eastern bastion of the Gloria; *Worcester*, which shall sail second in formation, shall anchor off the western bastion. You are to bombard the place forthwith. The *Norwich* shall enter third, and upon discharging its broadside at the Iron Castle, will pass up the harbour and engage San Geronimo Castle.' Vernon glanced at the remaining captains. 'I shall sail fourth, in *Burford*, with *Strafford* and *Princess Louisa* in that order after me. We shall anchor off the Iron Castle and continue its bombardment. As Captain Rentone, who has experience in these waters, will be in *Hampton Court* as a pilot, we should find our way to good holding ground with little difficulty – or so I intend.'

'And my soldiery, sir?' said Newton.

'Patience, Captain. I'll be obliged if, when in the boats, you proceed into whichever target I shall indicate to you by message, carried in one of *Burford*'s boats. But simply be ready in your craft.'

He looked round the table. 'I cannot predict the likelihood of capitulation, gentlemen. But I offer to you that vigorous force resolutely put to the Dons is the surest way of shaking their resolve. In all events, our objective shall be to secure the fortified places, and then take possession of the town.' His eyes finally fell on the shabby figure of Edward Mainwaring. '*Athena* will stand in astern of *Princess Louisa*, in company with the two tenders, Mr Mainwaring. Your task will be to intercept any of the Spanish small craft which may attempt to escape to seaward, and in any other way support me as I so direct. A boat will be sent to you with orders as the situation may require.'

Mainwaring was too tired to care greatly that *Athena* was being virtually excluded from the action. There was little enough that the schooner, with its ludicrous armament and handful of men, could do against fortifications. The coffee's brief effect was wearing off, and he felt unutterably tired. All he felt now was a concern for Hooke, Pellowe and the others, and the wish to get back and see that they had been fed, and catch whatever moments of rest they could . . .

'Is that clear, Mr Mainwaring?'

Mainwaring sat up, realizing the table was staring at him.

'Ah – yes. Aye, aye, sir.'

'Very well,' said Vernon, briskly. 'Are there any questions, gentlemen? No? Then we shall weigh anchor in one hour in succession and begin working ourselves to windward. We shall steer to weather the Salmadinas rocks and then stand in for the harbour mouth.' He paused. 'Good luck to you all, and do remember that a disciplined fire will always have a superior effect to a restless one.' Vernon rose, and the conference was at an end.

Sawyer and Slade were ready for him as he came down *Burford*'s battens; the twitter of the single boatswain's pipe choked off abruptly as Mainwaring's head sank below weatherdeck level. As he thumped down into the sternsheets sheets, Slade was bearing off with the boathook, and in a moment they were pulling back for *Athena*.

'Sir?' said Slade, disturbing Mainwaring's train of thought.

'Yes?'

'We were a-watchin' *Athena*, sir, an' saw the galley stack puff a bit o' smoke. C'd be a decent meal waitin', sir. Better'n two days o' biscuit, sir.'

Mainwaring was about to tell Sawyer curtly to keep his

mouth shut and tend to his rowing when he realized that both men were looking at him in a worried and almost solicitous way. He bit back the sharp words. 'Be a find prospect if true. Damn'd evident we'll need strength soon enough.'

'Th' attack, zur?' said Slade.

'Mind your oar. When we muster everyone you'll learn then.'

When Mainwaring regained *Athena*'s deck, Hooke grinned at him in welcome. But it was not the master's expression that startled Mainwaring. Hooke was dressed in an outlandish welter of bright-coloured clothing: baggy yellow breeches; a scarlet shirt; and a brocaded gentleman's coat of pale green with enormous skirts. The contrast with his broad, bare feet and beaming face was so extraordinary that even though he was almost faint with fatigue Mainwaring could not restrain a burst of laughter. 'In the name of God, Isaiah. You look like a Spanish mother's nightmare. Where in hell – ?'

'Struck down in th' forepeak, zur. The Dons had their chests in there. Good-sized ones, like a gennulman's. Hell, there be enough buntin' t' dress us all like lords!'

Mainwaring stared forward. Abner was appearing up the forward companionway stuffing the voluminous tail of an elegant ruffed shirt into pale blue velvet breeches. 'We've a proper suit for ye, zur!' the gunner cried. ''Tweren't proper, yew havin' t' go t' th' captin's meetin', in naught but slops, an' them rags at that. We put 'em in yer cabin, zur!'

Pellowe and Winton emerged up the after companion. Both were attired in a rainbow selection of full-sleeved, baggy-kneed Spanish styles that gave them an indescribably raffish air.

'Well, sink me for a newt. It's a bloody *parade* of foppery!' breathed Mainwaring, to Hooke's vast amusement. 'Mr Pellowe! Blinded by your elegance as I may be, may I alert you that you will be receiving a draft of fifteen men from the

120

Hampton Court presently. See that you alter the Watch and Quarter Bill for 'em after you've entered 'em in the books.'

'Aye, aye, sir,' said the young man, and his face grew serious. Mainwaring could almost see his mind working over the blank spaces in the list Mainwaring had carefully drawn up, which gave every man in the ship a place and duty for any one of a number of situations, whether gun action or coming to anchor, or the other innumerable tasks of a vessel at sea.

'Mr Hooke?'

'Zur?'

'I really cannot compliment your tailor enough. Please be sure to parcel out the new hands carefully. Who knows how familiar they'll be with schooner rig? Rate Slade boatswain, and Winton as boatswain's mate to help him. The squadron will begin weighing in succession in one hour, and we are to take station on the *Princess Louisa*. She'll be last in to attack the forts, and we shall likely have to tack and wear back and forth in front of the harbour mouth. We're to stop any Dons from escaping and do whatever else we're told. Clear?'

'Aye, aye, zur.'

'I hear you've managed to get the galley fire lit?'

'Aye, zur! An' in them stores the Dons struck into 'er we found some fresh casks o' beef, zur. Winton's been fryin' it up. And we found about fifty breadbags, all fresh.'

The thought of the taste of beef and bread was so overpowering that Mainwaring could scarcely speak for a moment. 'I – I'd like some in my cabin, if I might.'

'Aye, sir! Right away!' Winton had heard him and was vanishing down the companion once more.

Mainwaring looked with tired eyes to the eastward, where a blood-red dawn was flooding across the sea, a promise of stifling heat. The fatigue was close to mastering him. 'I'm going below, Mr Hooke. Tell Mr Pellowe I should be called as soon as the squadron weighs.'

'Aye, aye, zur.'

Mainwaring stumbled down to his cabin. On his table a steaming plate of thick beef chunks lay, with a half-loaf of sweet, soft bread beside it, and a pewter mug brimming with some kind of pale beer. In numb joy he wolfed the food, washing it down with great swigs of the beer. Then, with the fatigue rolling over him like a great wave, he fell face forward on the rumpled blankets of the box bunk, and was asleep in a few seconds. And as he slept he suffered under a repeating dream of the faces of the men he had lost in the *guardcostas'* attack, and with them Aiken and Burke; faces that gathered and looked at him in mute, pale appeal, asking a question with their unblinking eyes that he could not answer, asking until he was crying out to them at the top of his lungs, a cry that was silent, for no sound could be made by his voice in the dream, no matter how much he would try.

'Sir? Captain? Please, sir, wake up.'

Mainwaring sat up. For a moment he was unable to recognize his surroundings. Then the cabin came into focus, the sun brilliantly slanting in through the windows and backlighting the skinny form of Sawyer. His lank hair was wisping out from under an enormous cocked hat that dripped with egret feathers – an incongruous sight above the Nantucket youth's thin, rustic features.

'Mr Pellowe say he's sorry, sir, but he felt yew should know, sir. The rest o' the squadron's weighed, but with the wind at nor' nor' west they've not been able t' beat up t' th' harbour mouth till now, it bein' fluky an' foul. He says t' tell yew th' *Hampton Court*'s likely to make it on this board, though, an' the hands in *Princess Louisa* are bein' piped to th' capstan. She'll be liftin' 'er hook presently.'

Mainwaring shook his head, trying to clear the foggy

122

feeling. 'Ah – yes. Very well, Sawyer. Thank you. What – what time is it?'

'Time, sir? Turn o' th' glass fer th' last hour of th' forenoon watch, sir?'

'*What?*' Mainwaring swung his legs over the edge of the box bunk and stood up, remembering only at the last moment to avoid the low beams.

'Mr Pellowe and Mr Hooke figured ye needed sleep, sir, an' they thought we'd not be liftin' the hook till 'bout now – '

'For Christ's – !' Mainwaring bit it off. 'Very well. Thank you, Sawyer. Tell Mr Pellowe I'll be on deck directly.'

'Aye, sir.' Sawyer made off out of the cabin door.

Mainwaring ran his fingers through his hair, and then paused as his eye was caught by the display on the settee. Laid out carefully on it were a pair of scarlet velvet breeches, a fine linen shirt and a waistcoat and coat of the same rich velvet. A neatly cocked hat lay atop a pair of white hose, and on the deck sat a gleaming pair of boots.

'Damn my eyes,' he muttered. He flung off his rags and drew on the breeches and shirt, leaving aside the waistcoat and coat for the moment. Next on were the hose, and then, with scant hope, he tried the boots. But they slid on as if made for him.

'A gentleman, by God!' He laughed at the polished steel mirror behind his door, and jamming the hat down over his eyes, made for the upper deck.

When he emerged up the companionway, the blaze of the sun and the intense heat struck him like a wall, the sweat beading him in an instant. *Athena* was riding with her head to the weak, fitful nor' east breeze, and off to starboard, along the coast towards the mouth of Porto Bello harbour, he could see the pale pyramids of sail that marked the ships of the squadron. They were strung out, tacking on or off, barely moving pale images in the shimmering heat haze. One vessel, the furthest away, which Mainwaring saw was Brown's *Hampton Court*, appeared to be passing inshore of a low islet the chart showed as Drake's Isle. That meant Brown had succeeded in weathering it, and would make the Iron Castle on the next board if he held this one long enough. But, ghosting along as he was, Brown was still an hour or more from making his attack.

He swung round. Two cables or so away, *Princess Louisa* loomed, and he could see the hands working on the fo'c'sle, saw the hawser move up and down, the pawls clinking on the capstan as she broke out her anchor. The wind was barely toying with the great, hanging sheets of her canvas.

Hooke appeared at his side. 'She'll not move quick in this wind, zur. Ye've time t' get more biscuit into ye.'

Mainwaring eyed him. 'Isaiah, all this care after my welfare is very comforting. But what in heaven's name went on while you left me snoring like a dog down there?'

Hooke pointed upwards. 'We got the ship back t' rights, zur. The Dons foul'd some o' th' gear an' left garlic in the bilges, but otherwise she's smart as a new scraped carrot. The greasers must've been plannin' t' use 'er as a picket ship or th' loike, 'cause she's vittled an' watered t' th' deckhead, an' a lot wiv good English stores the *guardacostas* must've took from English ships. Pity of it is, there ain't no rum, zur. Left naught but bottles o' foul greaser wine. Footwash, th' hands say, but Mr Pellowe put it under a lock t' be safe, zur, if ye get my meanin'.'

Mainwaring nodded, watching *Princess Louisa*. The great anchor had been catted, dripping slime, and was being fished out of the way. The ship was virtually motionless, the canvas hanging slack still, and over the flat, shimmering water came the muffled clump of movement and voices.

'Damn near a dead calm,' said Mainwaring. Then, 'What of the arms? Those cutlass casks?'

Hooke beamed. 'Forget 'em, zur. We've three chests o' Spanish stands of arms! Infantry kit. Cartridge boxes, bayonets, the lot. An' a dozen good cutlasses, a clutch o' boardin' pikes, an' four casks o' powder.'

Mainwaring's eyebrows rose. 'And powder and shot for the three-pounders?'

'Same as before, zur.'

'Armed to the bloody teeth, are we?'

Hooke spat. 'In a manner o' speakin', zur, that we be.'

Mainwaring shook his head. 'We should be taken by the Dons more often. What of the draft of hands out of *Hampton Court*? Did they – ?'

Hooke pointed forward. 'Mr Pellowe's takin' down their particulars in th' waist, zur. Not as rum a lot as I expected. An' we're t' keep th' cutter they pulled over in for th' attack, if we need it.'

Mainwaring strode forward, enjoying the feel of the boots, Hooke at his heels, and nodded to Winton's chuckle as he passed the wheel. In a ragged line across *Athena*'s waist, somewhat more than a dozen men were standing. They were dressed in the usual odds and ends of worn civilian clothing and ship's slops, their chests or seabags on the deck before them, as Pellowe – resplendent in a great-cuffed coat of canary yellow and a vast, feathered hat – went down the line, a seaman with him bearing ledger and inkpot. Hooke was right. The men were not the nightmarish collection of physical refuse, invalids and cripples Mainwaring had been expecting. Most were sturdy, well-built men, with only one or two having the pallid, wracked look of fever or consumption; it was too soon for Yellow Jack to strike. Not a few had the big-boned, tarry pigtailed look of the best kind of seaman, and they were eyeing Mainwaring alertly as he approached. Their expressions were guarded, however, and it was difficult to tell if the draft into *Athena*, away from *Hampton Court* and her attack, had been received well or ill.

Pellowe came up, sending the seaman beside him padding off below with the ledger and ink. He doffed the huge hat with considerable style.

'An extraordinary hat, Stephen,' said Mainwaring drily.

'Thank you, sir. Not as extraordinary as this fine lot of men they sent us,' the youth beamed.

Mainwaring looked along the line. 'Where are they from?'

'Usual mix, sir. Mostly English, a few Scots, a Welshman. A Dutchman. And even a Spaniard.'

Mainwaring's eyebrow rose. 'Indeed? Run from the Dons?'

'No, sir. Raised by his English mother in Cádiz, sir. Joined the first English ship he could. Spanish Protestant.'

'A rare one, then. May prove useful. And the others?'

Pellowe grinned. 'Near half are like you, sir. Provincials: Boston, Philadelphia, three out of Nantucket, another Vine-yarder, and two Kennebec men. And they know schooner rig, sir, or most of 'em do. A prime lot.'

Mainwaring pursed his lips. Dent, in *Hampton Court*, with all he had to prepare for, had taken time to send them men *Athena* could use, and use well. It was a gesture Mainwaring knew he would have to repay in some way. 'Very well. I'll speak to them, Stephen.'

He moved forward, took off his hat, and looked along the line of attentive, sunburned faces, seeing the mix of readiness and wariness that was there. Lives in his hands again. Lives like those he had lost. Would he lose these too?

'Pay attention this way,' he said, briskly. 'You've been drafted into a good ship. And you're replacing good men, who did their duty to the end. I'll expect – this ship will expect – that you will do as much. You'll find me fair, and the officers as well. You know the Articles, so I'll not repeat 'em. Stand by your ship, and I'll stand by you. Let her – and yourselves – down, and God help you. Mr Pellowe?'

Mainwaring had turned, about to order Pellowe to carry on with getting the men squared away below, when a voice stopped him. 'Sir? Beggin' yer pardon, sir?'

Mainwaring swung back. A blond, heavily built seaman with thick shoulders and a look of competence had stepped forward and knuckled his forehead.

'Yes?'

'An' it please you, sir. Isaac Jewett, topman, sir, an' spokesman, like, for us. May I speak, sir?'

'Go on.'

Jewett's gaze was clear and unwavering. Here was a man to fist in the bunt of a topsail in a freezing gale and think nothing of it. 'We'll do our duty, right as new paint, sir, and you'll have our davvy on that. But we wanted you t' know, sir, that it ain't on account o' bein' drafted into this 'ere wing-sailed ship that our glims are doused, sir. Not by a point.'

'Haul your wind, Jewett,' said Mainwaring. 'What are you trying to say?'

'Fightin', sir,' said Jewett, 'wiv Cap'n Dent an' the commodore, sir, we'd always be sure of a good scrap. An' for Porto Bello, sir, we were countin' on a good tussle wiv the Dons, an' prizes, an' a hope o' pieces o' eight, or dollars, sir. But it's knowin' ye're to sit tender off the port, sir, as has our stays'ls doused.'

Mainwaring could not think for a moment what to say. By the expression on the other men's faces, Jewett had voiced their opinions as well. Dent had certainly sent him anything but 'king's hard bargains', as the expression for slack or weak men went.

'Listen to me, Jewett,' Mainwaring said after a moment's thought. 'And the rest of you as well. We have our orders, and those orders shall be carried out. Do your duty as they require,' and here he looked meaningfully ashore, 'and I promise you, you'll have more than enough action to suit you.'

Jewett nodded, the knuckle coming up again. 'Thankee, sir. We just wanted you to know, sir.'

'And now I do. Fall in, there. Mr Pellowe! Mr Hooke!'

'Sir?' chorused both men.

Mainwaring raised his voice deliberately higher in volume. 'We've a wildcat crew o' Don-eating sea dogs, now, it seems!' he said. 'So I shall trouble you to make known to them their duties, their parts of ship, and their station at Quarters before I unleash them on the poor bloody Dons!'

There was a roar of appreciative laughter from the line of new recruits, and Mainwaring caught the beam of pleasure on Hooke's face. It was evident the burly master felt he had been given a gift from the gods with this pack of prime men.

'Mr Pellowe. I'll trouble you to join me at the rail when you're finished.'

'Sir.' Pellowe turned back to his dispensing of orders to Hooke and Slade, whose pride in his new role as *Athena*'s boatswain had him positively swaggering about the deck.

Mainwaring took off his hat and wiped his streaming brow with one sleeve. The heat was awesome as he squinted against the shimmering, hazy glare off the oily sea face. He could see *Hampton Court*, far ahead, inching in towards the point that marked the closer headland of Porto Bello harbour. That low, grey shape on the headland with a speck of flag shimmering above it was the Iron Castle, and it would take a good hour before her guns would bear. The rest of the squadron, painfully tacking up through the still heat to get past Drake's Island, would be hours getting into position, and with the faint wind in this quarter – almost nor' east – – the ships would be lucky to make it into firing position before the Iron Castle, let alone the inner harbour fortifications. The

Hampton Court would be passing damnably close to the Iron Castle, by the look of her heading, and Mainwaring pondered the grim thought that, if Brown and Dent obeyed their orders, they would drift with aching slowness past the almost point-blank battery of the Iron Castle's seventy-eight guns, and the thirty-two guns of the battery at the water's edge below the Castle. That meant a broadside of one hundred and ten guns against *Hampton Court*'s larboard battery of thirty-five guns.

Mainwaring sucked a tooth. The odds were insane. *Hampton Court*'s five hundred men would be slaughtered in the wreckage of their ship. Brown and Dent would die obeying their orders to the letter, and the wind would do the rest to ensure the attack would fail.

His eyes sought out *Burford*, closer, inching along under slack canvas. With the damnably inadequate signalling systems – each admiral virtually devised his own, or did without – Vernon could alter the plan only by boat-delivered message. But no small shape was pulling away from the flagship. Vernon was adhering to his plan, a plan that could only succeed if the wind set fair enough for a swift attack, and penetration of the harbour. *Hampton Court* was two turns of the glass away from destruction under those one hundred and ten guns.

Unless . . .

Mainwaring stepped quickly to the helm and took the great telescope from its leather sheath. He pulled the glass open to its full extension and trained it on the Iron Castle. The image shifted and danced in the heat, but he could make out a low, walled shape, with featureless curtain walls facing inland and along the coast away from the harbour, with the crenellated ramparts bearing gun embrasures just visible where they curved away overlooking the harbour mouth. There were the

129

roofs of some buildings visible within the walls: red tile, shaking in the heat like squares of flame. There was a trace of dust rising from what looked like a track leading away from the Castle, along the coast bluff or back round the harbour to the town. He lowered the glass slowly. Bluffs, tree-clad and dark, falling almost vertically – that could be the glass foreshortening – to a palm and mangrove-snarled shoreline beyond a line of breaking rocks lying in a semi-circle a musket-shot offshore, the pale green of a narrow lagoon showing within the white flicker of the low swells, but inshore of the lagoon there was a beach. Small and almost invisible. But a beach.

'Sir?' Pellowe was at his side.

'Stephen, I'm leaving you in command of this ship. With ten men you should manage her well enough. And you know the duty required of us.'

'*What*?' Pellowe stared. 'But, sir – !'

'Damn your eyes, Mr Pellowe, I'll thank you to listen to your orders when they are being given to you!'

Pellowe's lips tightened, his face burning. 'Aye, aye, sir. Sorry, sir.'

Mainwaring sighed. 'Oh, for Christ's sake. Look, Stephen. You are at once my friend, and a midshipman in this ship. I am addressing the latter.'

The hurt look left Pellowe's eyes. 'My fault, sir. I'm sorry. Just – just a little anxious not to miss a fight, sir.'

'I understand. But I need your skills where they best serve us.'

'I understand, sir.'

'Very good. You'll select ten men to man *Athena*. Keep Abner so that you can work a gun. And Winton as your boatswain. Sawyer'll help to break in those new hands on her lines, so rate him boatswain's mate.'

He paused while *Athena*'s bell rang out its double-beat chime, eight strokes in all. Eight bells, or noon. It struck

Mainwaring that it was one of the few times he had consciously noted the striking of the bell. Now, in the heat, the notes seemed clear and sweet. Almost too precise. He shuddered slightly and went on. 'Weigh and stand along the shore as *Princess Louisa* tacks in. You know our task is to interdict any Spanish vessel trying to slip out. Not that a dugout Carib canoe would make it past Dent's rabid gunners, to my mind. Keep station there until the admiral sends new orders to you. Or till I return.'

'Aye, aye, sir.'

'I'm taking Hooke, Slade, and the remaining men in the longboat ashore. And I shall attempt to even the odds somewhat for Commodore Brown and his people.'

Pellowe's eyes widened as he peered ashore. 'You – you're going to attack the *Iron Castle*, sir?'

'I shall act as opportunities arise, would be the best description. If you are asked where I am, remember the phrase, and add that I am assisting Commodore Brown.'

Pellowe swallowed. 'Yes – aye, aye, sir.'

'Now listen carefully. The important papers of the ship are in the left front locked drawer of the desk in my cabin. The key is on that hook behind the door, where I showed you. I'll give you the magazine key before we leave. If some damned Don hundred-gunner comes bucketing up over the horizon and you fling yourself in front of her for death or glory, for God's sake put those papers and the weighted bag over the side.'

'Aye, aye, sir.'

'Now please be good enough to stop staring at me like a hungry gannet and get me Mr Hooke.'

Twenty minutes later, Mainwaring was standing in the schooner's waist as the landing party fell in, the excitement making them jabber until Hooke's snarl silenced them. Around Mainwaring's waist he had wound a scarlet net sash, into which a heavy Spanish pistol with its odd Miquelet lock was thrust. Suspended from the American's left shoulder to his right hip was a Spanish infantry cartridge box, holding thirty rounds for the slim, three-banded flintlock musket with its sling that he cradled in one arm like a New England huntsman. A small 'breadbag' or haversack with a half-dozen ship's biscuits and one of the gourd-like Spanish canteens full of tepid water were slung to complete the picture from his right shoulder to his left hip. Mainwaring's shirt was ripped open halfway to his waist, and was sodden with sweat. It would be hellish marching through that dark mass ashore, but that could not be helped.

Before him, Hooke was moving along the line of men, all armed and equipped much as Mainwaring was. A few had bayonets or small boarding axes thrust into waistbelts, and Hooke himself was packing an enormous bell-mouthed musketoon that would detonate, Mainwaring was quite sure, like gunpowder. It had reassured Mainwaring to see the men testing their flints, springing their ramrods and fitting bayonets with the ease of infantrymen; it was obvious that Dent had made small arms training an important part of *Hampton Court*'s routine. Now, with bandanas knotted round their heads against the sun, they underwent Hooke's inspection quietly, but stood shifting their weight from one leg to the other as they leaned on the long muskets, spat accurate jets of tobacco over the side, and looked with hard, appraising eyes at the distant shape of the Iron Castle.

Pellowe appeared at Mainwaring's side. '*Princess Louisa*'s hove short, sir. I'll have to make sail presently.'

Mainwaring nodded. 'So you will. Mr Hooke! Call away the party into the longboat, if you please!'

'Aye, aye, zur!' growled Hooke. 'Right, lads. Over yew go. Careful o' them arms.'

Orderly and quietly, the men slung their muskets and

clambered over the rail, dropping into the longboat after a step or two down the battens. Under Slade's oath-strewn orders, the oars were readied at their thole pins until it was time for Mainwaring to board. The latter paused at the rail and fixed a look at Pellowe's concerned expression. 'Keep our *Athena* well, Stephen,' Mainwaring said. 'Rely on your common sense in addition to your orders.'

'Sir. How will I know if I can help you, sir?'

'Recover us if you see a boat floundering out in your direction. In all other respects, you must not forget that you are to stand by the *Louisa*.'

Mainwaring slung his musket and swung a boot over the rail. 'It will serve no one if these lads are slaughtered wholesale, Stephen. I shall think of that ashore. Please think of these lads and the ship the same way, as far as duty allows.'

'Aye, aye, sir. And – good luck, sir.'

Before Pellowe could blurt out something that would prove an embarrassment for both, Mainwaring footed down the battens to the boat and dropped into his place in the sternsheets.

Hooke grasped the tiller with one broad paw, lanced a jet of tobacco juice into the sea, and nodded. 'Let go, bows,' he rumbled. 'Out oars. Give way together. Handsomely, there, yew wiv the red shirt. We ain't a-towin' of anyone.'

The boat pulled away from *Athena* over the oily sea, its surface so still that Mainwaring could see the white underhull of the schooner, the waving weed growth slowly beginning to form on it, floating over the green abyss. The schooner looked rakish and powerful, and he felt a tug in his chest as they drew away. Already Pellowe had Winton barking orders in a manner that would have made Hooke proud, and the windlass bars were being fitted to hoist the schooner's anchor – *Athena* was too small to carry a true capstan. The schooner turned slowly to her cable as the longboat drew away, and

Mainwaring wondered if any ship would ever look quite as beautiful to him.

He turned back to the boat, looking at the sunburned, slit-eyed faces as the men lay back in unison at the long oars. The sweat was already streaming from their faces, glistening on their bared chests, but they were holding Hooke's rhythm beautifully. They were moving swiftly away towards the shore, which already was looming larger.

Mainwaring stood to peer ahead. 'Starboard a point, Mr Hooke. That'll take us through the middle gap in the rocks.'

'Starb'd a point 'tis, zur.'

The boat moved on, the lift and splash of the oars a hypnotic sound under the searing sun. The deep green of the shoreline seemed cool and inviting, even though Mainwaring was sure the heat ashore would be equally hellish. Already from the dark, billowy wall of forest he could hear bird calls and other strange hoots and cries, echoing in the depths.

Abruptly they were gliding through a scattering of rocks that protruded, guano-coated and slimy, from the sea, the water heaving in oily eddies round them as gulls and ugly, heavy-clawed crabs vied for standing room on their slick surfaces. Expertly, Hooke steered them through the gap, and they moved into the pale green water of the lagoon, the boat floating above its shadow on the white, rippled sand some twenty feet below. The high wall of the jungle face loomed ahead over them, the thin silver of beach dead ahead.

'A dozen strokes more will do it, Mr Hooke.'

'Zur,' said Hooke. He stood for a clearer view. 'Steady pull now, lads, less 'n half-cable more. Bows.'

The seaman in the eyes of the boat expertly tossed his red oar and laid it fore and aft down the thwarts. Then he gathered up the painter coils and stood, ready to leap ashore.

The dark jungle mass, menacing, shadowed, full now of raucous cries of all kinds, rose over them like a giant rogue wave. The boat sped in towards the beach.

134

'Stroke,' intoned Hooke, then, 'way enough! Boat yer oars! Get yer line ashore, bows!'

With a thump and clatter of oars, and the gritty scrape of the keel on the bottom, the longboat slid into the shallows of the beach and stopped.

'Ashore, lads! Quickly, now!' said Mainwaring, and threw his legs over the side of the boat. His feet landed in six inches of water and a gelatinous ooze below it that welled up around his ankles. With a curse he joined the other floundering, splashing men who were pushing the boat further up the beach. So low and close overhead was the canopy of leaf and branch that they could not stand upright, but had to crouch.

'That'll do, Mr Hooke,' said Mainwaring. 'She'll not be visible unless someone falls over her. 'Swain?'

Slade, beaming at the title, moved quickly to Mainwaring's side. 'Zur?'

'Likely you're as able as you are afloat. Pick two men to go with you. I'll want you to be our picket.'

'Aye, zur. I'll take Quintal, zur. An' Valero. He's quick, 'n speaks the lingo.'

'Very good. Mr Hooke?'

'Zur?'

'We'll move in single file. Check to see each man keeps his muzzle clear of mud and away from someone's head, and his hammerstall on. Slade and his two will lead, then myself, then the lads. You'll bring up the rear. Clear?'

Hooke nodded and shifted his plug. 'Aye, zur.'

'Good.' Mainwaring looked at the faces of the men. Their eyes were white and watchful in the gloom, and their fingers moved to take better grips of their muskets. Mainwaring hefted his own musket and wiped the sweat from his face again with a sleeve. A cloud of mosquitos was hanging in whining annoyance round their heads.

135

'We'll strike up through there, Slade. There should be a coastal path of some sort at the top. Away you go, 'swain.'

And with a last look back at *Athena* the men tugged at their kit straps, hefted their firelocks, and ducked after Slade into the dark green mass of the jungle.

'Lopez! Where in the name of Christ's guts are you?'

The Chevalier de la Roche-Bourbon slammed his hands down on the waistdeck rail of *Aguerra*'s quarterdeck, his voice piercing the gale like a pistol shot. The ship's gilt and scarlet hull gleamed wetly in the brilliant sun as the *guardacostas* plunged into the back of another blue swell, punching up a cloud of glittering spray. The vessel was driving furiously before a howling easterly squall that had come up without cloud, and the press of canvas was powering the ship through the seas with an urgent brutality that matched the mood of the hard-eyed Frenchman on her quarterdeck. With topsails, t' gallants and courses all set and straining, headsails and spanker winging out to add their power to the small ship's rush, *Aguerra* thundered through the spume-tracked Caribbean under hard blue skies, her bowsprit thrusting like a lance south-west towards the unseen coast of Darién, a day and a half's sail away.

'Here, señor!' cried a worried voice from amidships. '*Madre de Dios*, she will not be able to stand much more of this!' *Aguerra*'s captain, a short, muscular man in sweat-stained velvet, wiped the spray from his face with one hand and stared uneasily aloft. Around him a crowd of the ship's hands was also looking up with fearful expressions at the straining canvas and bar-taut lines of the rigging and the plunging masts that creaked and groaned against their wedges.

'She will take it, Lopez,' snarled Roche-Bourbon over the sea roar, 'if the men driving her can do so! Now I'll trouble you to set the mizzen topsail!'

136

Lopez stared up, lurching as *Aguerra* lifted and crunched down over a breaking swell.

'*Qué*? Señor, you must be mad! She cannot – !' he stopped abruptly, his eyes wide and fixed on the muzzle of the heavy flintlock pistol which had appeared in Roche-Bourbon's hand. The Frenchman's arm was fully extended, and the weapon was levelled at Lopez' head.

'Either you will set all canvas, you grease-fingered son of slime, or by the mother that bore me I will shoot you down where you stand. *Set the topsail!*'

Lopez turned round with a wild look of despair. He was no coward, and had driven his ship hard before. But the groans and popping of the hull and the building strain overhead were warnings only a fool – or a madman – would ignore. But as he looked up at the contorted mask of fury that was Roche-Bourbon's face, Lopez was sure he was dealing with insanity. 'Señor,' he cried, almost in a sob. 'The wind is building. You will not let us take in a reef. You will not let us shorten sail. The hull is working, and she makes water almost as much as the pumps can manage. If we set the mizzen tops'l, it's certain she'll carry away something – !'

'Lopez, hear me!' barked Roche-Bourbon, freshening his grip on the pistol. 'If there is one thing I am going to do, and one thing that *you* will do with me, it will be to track down that pink-faced English admiral and his squadron. And in it I will find that damnable schooner, and the *bostonnais* who sails her. And, hear me, Lopez, when I find him, I will kill him. With my bare hands, if need be. D'ye hear? D'ye understand, cretin? *I will kill him!*'

Lopez stared up, the heave of the ship forgotten in his awe of the expression on Roche-Bourbon's face. Dully, he touched the front cock of his hat. '*Aye, si*! *Ya lo creo*! As – as you command, señor . . .' He turned forward, and a

137

rapid-fire stream of orders sent a clutch of hands swinging up the mizzen shrouds.

The Frenchman's eyes kept their wild, hunting look as he thrust the heavy pistol back into the broad sash about his waist. With a snarl to the man struggling at *Aguerra*'s wheel to lose his course at his peril, he leaped off the quarterdeck and vanished down the after companionway. A moment later, he was standing straddle-legged before a broad table in the *guardacostas*' great cabin, staring at a chart of the Caribbean, an evil-looking stiletto that had been holding down one corner of the chart turning in his hands.

'Soon, my barefooted Royal Yankee,' he whispered hoarsely, his fingers tightening round the knife, 'I shall give you full measure for what you dared do to me. *Full* measure. And let that damned fool Pizarro poke into Cartagena and drag his hulks from port to port. *I* know where you will be. And there, *bostonnais* bastard, I shall have my revenge. *There*!'

And with a grunt of effort through clenched teeth, he drove the stiletto into the table top through the chart, cutting in half the carefully penned outline of the harbour of Porto Bello.

Within a few yards of starting up the steep shore slope, it was evident to Mainwaring that their progress would be slow and difficult. The thick growth closed in so densely round them that they were forced to stay within arm's length of one another to avoid losing touch. It was a dark, shadowed, insect-ridden trap; ahead, Slade and his two pickets ducked and pushed with curses through the tangle, their feet slipping and slithering on the sodden mat of rotting vegetation of the slope, and the slick, clay-like red soil underneath. Again and again their toes caught on hidden roots or loops of vine, and they fell to their knees, struggling to keep the musket locks out of the wet humus. Very soon it became a process of fixing eyes on the sweat-soaked back of the man ahead, listening to one's own laboured breathing, feeling sweat stinging the eyes, trying to pick footing carefully while not falling behind.

The heat was almost overpowering, with no sea wind to ease it, and it was not only the humid air that caused each man to be dripping wet, but also the water that hung in drops on the packed, cloying vegetation. As they pushed through, hidden thorns snagged on sleeves and trouser legs, or cut into exposed flesh. Insects of incredible size and frightening appearance were everywhere, and spiders' webs with the consistency of cheesecloth hooked over faces or wrapped round musket barrels, often with their alarming occupants along for the ride. The light was low, as they were beneath the great canopy of trees, lost in the thick lower growth, and in the dim half-light enormous clouds of mosquitos and stinging midges hung, falling on the exposed necks and faces of the seamen until they slapped in blasphemous futility at them, and soon had red welts and running pinpricks of blood appearing everywhere.

As he fought his way upwards, eyes fixed on the sheath knife in the middle of Quintal's broad waistbelt, Mainwaring listened to the hoarse gasps of his own breathing and began to think that he had made another incalculable blunder. If this horrendous green tangle was all they would meet, the men would be exhausted before they went a half-mile. And the Iron Fort was a good mile's distance from the beach where they had landed . . .

Suddenly, Quintal stopped, and Mainwaring caught himself just in time to keep from thumping into him. A few muffled oaths behind him indicated others had not been as watchful. There was a crashing through undergrowth, and Slade was standing before him, sodden shirt torn by thorns, face swollen with midge bites and marked by dirt where he had cuffed at the bites. 'Clearin', zur,' he panted. 'Trail. Leads off left and right.'

'Thank Christ!' breathed Mainwaring. He shook his head, a cloud of midges hovering infuriatingly before his eyes. 'Must be the coastal path. Knew it had to be there. Anyone – or anything – on it?'

'No, zur. 'Bout two men wide. Looks like they cut it back often, zur.'

'Right. Let's get out on it and form up.'

With exhausted relief the men emerged on to the trail, which was wide and hard-packed, as if from constant use. The men leaned on their muskets and stared at one another, panting with the effort of the climb, eyeing how sodden and mud-streaked each was.

'Stand to, lads,' growled Hooke. 'Check yer firelocks. Wipe th' locks wiv yer shirt-tails.'

'Water, sir?' puffed a short, powerfully-built seaman with a thick black queue. Mainwaring remembered his name was Evans.

'Yes. Take some water, all of you. But just a mouthful or two. You'll need the rest. Mr Hooke? Look at each man's kit and see he has nothing adrift. 'Swain?'

'Zur?'

'Put Quintal aft of us there, a hundred yards or so. We'll be going to the right. You and Valero station yourselves ahead of us, same distance. Clear?'

'Aye, aye, zur. Now, zur?'

Mainwaring looked round the men's faces in the gloom. A bird's shrill cry echoed, far overhead. 'In a clock's tick. When all this blowing and wheezing dies down. Quintal? For Christ's sake don't be left behind.'

Quintal grinned. 'No fear, sir. Ain't no monkey.'

Mainwaring answered the grin. Hooke had finished the inspection, and Mainwaring stood back a bit so that each man could see him. 'Listen. We'll prime and load now. But you're not to trail or shoulder your firelocks like good bloodybacks. You'll carry it like this.' Mainwaring demonstrated, laying the long flintlock cradled in his left arm across the body. 'Keeps you from blowing the head off the poor bastard ahead. Pull it more vertical if the trail narrows. And keep those bloody hammerstalls *on*. Clear?'

'Aye, zur,' said a wiry, quick-eyed man with a Cornish accent. 'Like true Yankees all, zur.'

'What's your name?' said Mainwaring.

'Starkey, zur. Meant no disrespect – '

'No, no, Starkey. That's quite all right. You keep thinking you're backwoods marksmen. Just be sure to bag a brace o' Dons each!'

There was a ripple of laughter at that. Swiftly, the men drew cartridges from the heavy leather boxes on their hips and primed and loaded the long muskets. Slade and his consorts had finished first, and were padding off down the trail to their station. Soon the last rammer thumped back into its pipes, and Mainwaring moved to the head of the little column, looked back to see them all eyeing him with expectant expressions, and nodded. 'Right. Move off, then.'

The path was easily trod, and although the heat was still stifling, and the clouds of mosquitos and midges just as infuriating, the marching was nothing like the torment of the climb. Now, too, the sun shafted down at intervals into the gloom, providing pools of brilliance below angling columns of golden light up which teeming insects hovered and circled. Somewhere ahead lay the Iron Castle, and out to their right, Mainwaring knew, the squadron would have been visible, and *Athena*, all inching along under slack canvas over the calm sea to the attack.

As they marched, the openness of the path allowed the men to see the lush wonder of the forest which before had gripped and blinded them. They stared as wildly coloured birds winged over them in the murk, cries echoing as if in a cathedral, and gaped at the beautiful colours of the blossoms that hung amidst the green. And once, with nimble feet, they stepped around a huge, brown-haired spider that was tugging the body of a mouse across the path. They marched silently, the seamen's bare feet noiseless on the packed earth, needing no word from Mainwaring or Hooke that at any moment they might stumble across the Spanish.

Abruptly Valero was visible ahead. He was at a bend in the trail, crouched, looking ahead, motioning for a stop with one hand. Mainwaring held up a hand and sank to a squat, the line of men behind him following suit. After a moment the slim, dark-haired figure rose, and in a swift, noiseless run was crouching at Mainwaring's side. 'The trail breaks just ahead, señor,' he panted. 'An' you can see the walls of the *castillo* and the sea beyond. The land, she is cleared back to it.'

'Anything else?'

'*Si*, señor. The 'swain says to say there is a log barricade just ahead of us, in the open ground outside the edge of the trees. Like a re – like a re – ' He struggled with the word.

'A redoubt. Small fort. Christ. What else?'

'He says to say he saw soldiers in it, señor.'

Mainwaring spat. 'All right. Go back up and watch it. Tell the 'swain I'm coming up.'

'Aye, aye, señor!' Valero scampered away.

'Mr Hooke?' Mainwaring kept his voice barely above a whisper. It was almost lost against the insect buzz and the bird cries.

Hooke was at his side, surprisingly light-footed. Mainwaring saw that the brocaded coat was streaked with mud and torn from thorns. 'Zur?' he rumbled.

'Keep the lads here. Low and off to either side of the track.

142

Wait till I come back. I'm going up to look at this redoubt of Slade's.'

'Aye, aye, zur.'

With his musket at the trail, Mainwaring sprinted forward along the trail, keeping low. For a moment flashes of memory came back to him: flashes of a pine-needle trail in the towering evergreen forest of the Upper Connecticut, his mocassined feet padding swiftly along it, the hair on his neck prickling in anticipation of an Ottawa war shriek behind him. And then he was at a bend in the trail, and Slade and Valero were crouched to either side of it, half hidden in the growth, peering out at the scene. Keeping low, Mainwaring moved to where Slade squatted on his heels and stared out himself. 'Well, I'm damned!' he breathed.

'See, zur?' whispered Slade. 'It's a bloody fort isself, 't's wot it is!'

Beginning barely a yard or two from where the three men were hidden, a rough, stump-cluttered clearing opened before them. It was the beginning of cut-over land that stretched all the way to the imposing grey mass of the Iron Castle, hulking on the harbour mouth edge. The view was breathtaking: off to the left, at the head of the harbour, the squat, whitewashed buildings of the town sat burning in the heat, the humped fortifications of the Gloria Castle and the San Geronimo a contrast to their low, red-roofed blocks. The harbour gleamed in the sunlight, and the same bright light turned the ghosting, almost motionless shapes of Vernon's squadron into haze-wrapped wraiths. All save the heavy bulk of *Hampton Court*, which was drawing in towards the harbour mouth – and the deadly guns of the Iron Castle – in stately dignity.

And set astride the rough track leading from the forest edge towards the Iron Castle there sat the splintery-looking

143

mass of a rough, log-palisade fort, over which a ragged Spanish ensign fitfully drifted.

Mainwaring narrowed his eyes. The wall facing them might be a hundred feet in length. Certainly no more. There were no bastions, and then it might simply be a square structure, which would mean less difficulty in –

'Fair nut t' crack, zur,' said Slade, and spat through a gap between his teeth. 'But if we goes round it, I'd lay they c'd sally out an' take us from astern.'

'How high are those walls, d'ye think?' said Mainwaring.

Slade scratched at the stubble on his chin. 'Fourteen, maybe fifteen feet, zur.'

'There'd be a firing step on the inside face.'

'Likely, zur. Saw a man pace by a minute ago, wiv 'is firelock shouldered. 'Ee was watchin' *Hampton Court*.'

Mainwaring nodded. That would explain the apparent lack of activity. The men in the rough fort were likely on its far side, watching the approaching English ships. If a move was going to be made, it would have to be made now, and quickly. 'Valero! Get back to Mr Hooke, at a run. Tell him to bring the lads for'rard here, quickly as you can!'

Valero nodded and sprinted off, his cartridge box rattling and thumping at his hip.

'Mark carefully, now, 'swain. D'ye see any sort of port or door, this side?'

Slade shook his head. 'No, zur. Nowt. Been lookin' for it.'

Mainwaring stood up and pushed his cartridge box back behind his hip. 'Right. We vault the walls, then.' He spun round, hearing the rush of feet, seeing the eager, wide-eyed faces in surprise at the scene. He threw a last look at the log walls. Still no sentry pacing back.

'Listen carefully!' he said, in a low, penetrating voice. 'We're going to rush that place. Not a man fires till we're over the walls. When you get to the wall, the first two lads

144

make a step of a musket between you, and hoist the following ones up. We'll go in two groups. I'll lead one, on the left. Mr Hooke, the other, on the right. Starkey, McComb, Jewett, you're with Mr Hooke. 'Swain, Adams, Quintal, Valero and Evans, you're with me. Clear? Good. And once over the wall, no holding back till we've taken it!'

There was a growl of readiness. Lips were licked, grips on muskets tightened. Hooke nodded at him, eyes kindling.

'Right. Come on, then!' hissed Mainwaring, and burst out of the growth into the clear ground. He pounded down the long slope at a dead run, musket held high, his kit banging about him as he leaped over logs and branches. Behind him he heard the rush of running men, the clink and rattle of equipment, and out of the corner of his eye he could see Hooke's ursine form moving in a rapid shamble, the ragged yellow coat-tails flying behind him down the branch-littered slope, the huge bell mouth of the musketoon gleaming like gold in the sun. Mainwaring felt his throat burning. He seemed to have a haze closing in round his vision as he rushed towards the rough log wall, the pack of men gasping with effort now behind him. His heart thumped in his ears. God, they would be shot down like wingless pigeons if so much as one slack Spaniard in there took his eyes off the approaching *Hampton Court* to look back, and saw them . . .

And then he was there, thumping against the rough bark as Slade and the others stumbled up behind him, pressing flat against the crude walls, staring up and panting like midsummer dogs. 'No rest now!' croaked Mainwaring. 'Slade! Valero! Hold that firelock! And lift me hard and fast!' Mainwaring threw his musket-sling over his head so that the weapon hung across his chest, clutched at Slade's shoulder and stood on the trembling musket.

'Now!'

With a grunt the men heaved Mainwaring upwards. He

145

scrabbled furiously at the rough, sharp bark, and then with a flailing grab had a grip on the crude, axe-cut point at the top of one log. The wood was sticky with resin. With a surge of fear he dug at the bark with his boots, and then levered himself over the points, feeling them tear at his breeches, feeling the shirt front rip away and a sear of pain cut across his chest, and then with a half-sob and last spasm of energy he was toppling over, headfirst, to thump down hard and awkwardly on one shoulder on the narrow, splintered surface of a firing step. He struggled to his knees, teetered frighteningly for an instant out over the empty space to one side, and then was tugging to free his musket as he looked up.

A Spanish soldier in a dirty white linen coat, unshaven and wearing a dog-eared tricorne, was staring at him from ten feet away along the rickety, shaking platform, wide-eyed in astonishment, his fingers slack about his musket. In a kind of frenzy Mainwaring yanked the Miquelet from his waist, levelled it, and fired. The big pistol bucked in his hand with an ear-splitting report, and beyond the sudden gout of smoke the Spaniard shrieked, clawing at the bloody ruin of his destroyed jaw, and fell with his next step backwards off into space.

Mainwaring thrust himself to his feet, wrenching the musket free, feeling the sling leather snap, looking wildly around. His ears were full of shrieks, musket blasts, and hoarse, bellowing yells. He was conscious of being above a low, muddy courtyard with three crude log cabins grouped in a horseshoe shape, the open side facing an open gate that led off to a beaten earth cart track that wound away towards the bastions of the Iron Castle. The firing step shook under his feet as Slade and the others came falling and cursing over the palisade, Hooke and his men beginning to appear over on the right. Out of the corner of his eye Mainwaring saw the muscular Welshman, Evans, fling a leg over the palisade and

146

vault almost effortlessly over, to land upright on the firing step, unlimbering his musket as he came. Almost as he touched down he threw up the piece and fired, the round taking down a running Spaniard below as if a punch had levelled the man.

Now the musketry blasts were ringing all around him, in a painful, staccato fusillade. Below, more Spanish were tumbling out of the crude cabins, staring up at the men who continued to pour over the walls. On the far side, a clutch of white-coated figures who had been watching *Hampton Court*'s approach from the firing step over the gate crouched and spread out along the step, staring agog. Here and there a musket flashed and thumped, and balls began to thwack into the logs near Mainwaring.

The American jerked his weapon to full cock, and threw it to his shoulder. He aimed it at a knot of men rushing towards the gate as if to close it, and fired. The musket bucked against him, and through the belch of smoke Mainwaring saw a man go down kicking into the muck.

Now the Spanish were firing back with a will, and beside him Mainwaring heard a man gasp and slump back against the palisading. They had to get off the step!

A ladder led down a few feet off to the left from the step. In a rush Mainwaring was at it and half climbing, half falling down it to the ground, the Athenas crowding behind him. Already the interior of the miserable little fort was thick with choking gunsmoke, filled with running figures and the pink flashes of gun shots, and the sprawled, still forms of dead and wounded men. Overhead on the step, Hooke's musketoon sounded with an ear-splitting blast, dropping two Spaniards who had been rushing with fixed bayonets towards the men fumbling their way down the ladder.

Mainwaring landed hard, his boots slithering on the wet, clay ground. A dead Spaniard lay in a grotesque sprawl a few feet before him, eyes staring upwards, a huge red hole in the chest of his linen coat. A cutlass lay on the ground near one flung-out arm.

'The buildings! Take 'em, lads!' cried Mainwaring, and he flung down his musket and stooped to scoop up the cutlass before stumbling through the smoke and slop towards the nearest hut. He sensed several men running at his heels. The smoke swirled round him, and he coughed uncontrollably, feeling the pain now from the cut across his chest. Musket blasts were almost a steady, deafening roar, shrieks and oaths sounding above them, and the noise and tumult were producing a crazed kind of battle fever in Mainwaring that he found difficult to control. Somewhere he could hear Hooke roaring incoherently over the din.

In the next moment a swirl of the smoky murk curled away and Mainwaring was fetching up against the rough, crudely planked door of a hut. With an effort of bull strength he bodied into it and smashed it open. Some unknown instinct threw him down into an immediate crouch, and a vicious roundhouse cut from a heavy sword whistled out of the dark within to clang against the iron fittings of the door. There was a curse of pain and the sword fell, thumping off Mainwaring's back to the dirt. The American lunged forward and up, arrowing his cutlass at the dim shape before him. He felt it strike home, heard him make a horrid, gibbering sound, and wrenched the weapon out as the man, a fat and bewigged form in bloodied shirtsleeves, fell heavily past him. Mainwaring threw a fast look round the room, seeing Slade, his eyes wide and staring, beside him with a levelled bayonet. The hut was empty, only some furniture and chests littering its dark interior.

'Outside!' barked Mainwaring. He plunged back out of the door, vaulting over the still twitching form of the fat Spaniard, and then stopped. The shooting had ceased, a pall of gunsmoke lying in chest-high bands in the air. In the centre of the muddy courtyard Hooke and the others were herding together a dozen or so unarmed Spanish soldiers, pathetic-looking thin creatures in dirty coats, with frightened or glowering black eyes set in sallow, fever-yellowed faces. A litter of muskets and accoutrements lay at their feet.

Mainwaring looked round. The firing steps were empty, save for slumped white-coated bodies here and there. By the crude pole of the flagstaff, Quintal, his brown face bloody from a cutlass wound, was gleefully hauling down the tattered Spanish ensign.

Hooke was before him, huge and dirty, breath coming in great heaves. His lips were black from biting cartridges. 'We've done it, zur. Taken it.'

Mainwaring was suddenly conscious of the burning in his own chest, and of trembling knees. 'Well done,' he said. 'Well done. Casualties?'

'Jes' Valero, zur. An' nowt but a touch o' ball in th' arm. He'll do.'

Mainwaring peered round, feeling the sweat slip, stinging, into the corners of his eyes. 'I managed to get into one building. What's in the others?'

'That one's a sort o' barracks, zur. We got into 't an' did fer a few Dons what were inside.'

'And the other?' Mainwaring was looking at the third hut, a roughly whitewashed structure just to one side of the gateway. Its lone window was covered by a shutter, centred by a heart-shaped musket loophole.

'Dunno, zur. No response from it. Christ, d'ye think – ?'

Mainwaring pointed to two men who were standing nearby, leaning on their muskets, cheeks bulging with hurriedly snatched bread. 'Evans. Starkey. Swallow that tucker and flank me, either side. We'll examine that hut. Mr Hooke? Get these prisoners locked into their barracks. But take their

149

breeches and shoes off 'em first. And see they've no weapons or a way to get out easily.'

Hooke grinned. 'Aye, aye, zur.'

'Prime and load, you lads,' said Mainwaring. He hefted his cutlass and moved watchfully towards the remaining hut.

'Think it's empty, sir?' said the man called Starkey at his side. He tore the head off a cartridge with his teeth and spat out the paper, briskly loading his musket as he padded beside Mainwaring. ''T ain't been a peep from it.'

'We'll see soon enough. Take the left. Evans, the right.' In the next minute they were before the plank door. There was still no sound of movement within, no musket muzzle suddenly appearing in that heart-shaped opening.

'Sir?' whispered Evans. The Welshman pointed at the door. 'Bolted. From outside, look you.'

'Aye. A storehouse, likely. Stand ready, now . . .' When both men were ready at either side of the door, backs pressed flat to the rough walls, muskets at full cock, Mainwaring nodded to them, and eased the bolt back from the door. He took a deep breath. Then, taking a fresh grip on his cutlass, he kicked in the door with a blow of one boot heel, and sprang inside.

But he froze in the crouched position he had assumed as he leaped in. His eyes were fixed, not on the dark interior, but on the muzzle of the English Sea Service pistol which was levelled between his eyes, barely inches away.

'Make another move and, by God, there'll be one less freebooting bastard alive in the world!'

Mainwaring stared back along the barrel to the slim hand that held it, and along an extended arm to a man's shirt front, torn and ragged, and wrapped over a disturbingly rounded fullness, and then up to a dark, beautiful face framed in tumbling black hair; a face with high cheekbones and a flush of colour under suntanned cheeks, a pretty, curved mouth set now in hard and determined lines. And the eyes: long-lashed, hypnotically pale green eyes, fixed on Mainwaring with a furious, intent look. The voice had been warm and throaty, and even with its hard-edged threat had sent a kind of shiver up Mainwaring's spine. 'Dear Christ. Are you *English*?' he breathed.

The girl tossed back her hair, fixing both hands now on the pistol. The muzzle had not moved from Mainwaring's forehead. 'Put the cutlass down. Put it down, damn you!' she said, through her teeth. 'You two outside! In here, and on the deck, on your bellies! Lively! And twitch just one wrong muscle – !'

Evans and Starkey stared in, seeing the pistol held to Mainwaring's head. For a moment they wavered, the muskets turned on the girl, their eyes moving from her to Mainwaring. 'Do as she says,' said Mainwaring evenly. Slowly, the men lowered their muskets and then lay face down on the earth.

Mainwaring's eyes were able to see more in the darkness. Behind the girl there was a wall; a wall against which six black men in tattered seamen's clothing were chained to ringbolts driven into the logs. There was a place for a seventh, where the chains hung loose. And below it, on the packed dirt floor, there lay the body of a pot-bellied Spanish soldier, a length of chain wound tight around his neck, the eyes in his bulging face goggling in strangled death.

'Who in hell's name are you – ,' began Mainwaring. He started to straighten, but stopped when he saw the girl's fingers whiten on the pistol. 'Shut your mouth!' snapped the girl. 'Adam!' she said over her shoulder to one of the chained men. 'Can you see the keys?'

'Aye,' said one black, a huge, hulking shape. 'Half under his body. Fell on them when you gave him the necktie, missy.' The deep *basso* voice had the same Caribbean lilt as the girl's.

151

'Right. I'll cover these while you get them out with your foot. Can you reach – ?' she began.

'Please. For God's sake,' said Mainwaring. 'We're not here to harm you. We're English. Royal Navy, damn it!'

The girl's eyes flickered, full of mistrust. Christ, she was *beautiful*!

'What ship, then?' she said.

'*Athena*. Armed schooner. And out there is *Hampton Court*, Admiral Vernon, and a whole damned squadron. We're attacking this place!'

Through the door the girl could see Hooke standing with his hands on his hips, eyeing the cabin door with a worried look. Behind him the Athenas were herding the disarmed – and breechless – Spanish into one of the other cabins. Her eyes flicked back to Mainwaring, their expression softening by a small degree.

'You're – you're not buccaneers? In the pay o' the Spanish?'

Mainwaring shook his head. The girl was not tall, perhaps a few inches over five feet, with slim, rounded hips in corduroy breeches tucked into stained seaboots. Her hair fell in lustrous waves to the middle of her back, and the coarse and torn seaman's shirt could not conceal the heavy, rounded beauty of her breasts. The high-cheekboned cast to her face seemed to indicate that Carib or African blood was mixed with European. But it was her eyes and their incredible intensity that held him and compelled him to meet their penetrating clarity.

'No! King's men. On my mother's grave, I swear. Are you prisoners of the Dons?'

The pistol slowly lowered. 'I – yes. We're plantation folk, off San Andrés. My father and I run sugar cane there, and trade in to Cartagena. The Spaniards were content to leave us in peace until – The governor o' this damned hellhole Porto Bello, Martinez, has got my father in some prison, back

152

there in the town. We – we were lured here to talk over new "trading licences", the swine said, but what he wanted to trade for was half the crop and his filthy hands on me. I – I tried to sail the *Black Gull* out at night, but – '

'Your father's vessel?'

The girl's eyes flashed. '*Mine. I* command her! A topsail cutter that'll beat any bag-sailed Port Royal barge!'

Mainwaring nodded. This was clearly no ordinary island doxie. 'Go on.'

'They've got 'im in some horrible cell. And they sent us up here to help defend this place. If we didn't, Martinez said he'd – my father – would die.'

Mainwaring sucked a tooth. Evans and Starkey were on their feet now, collecting their weapons. Outside, he could hear Hooke bellowing for some men to move in on the cabin.

'But why the chains? If you were supposed to fight – ?'

'We – tried to sabotage the place. Blow up the magazine and make it seem an accident. The pig of a commander found out, and – '

Mainwaring remembered the shriek, the heavy body falling in the other cabin as he wrenched out his cutlass. 'Yes?'

The girl shuddered. 'He had us chained in here. He was – going to rape me. This,' and here she gave the corpse at her feet a vicious kick, 'was taking me over to him. When he unlocked me – '

'You killed him.'

The girl's gaze was level. 'Yes.'

Mainwaring nodded, meeting her eyes. He felt admiration swelling up inside him as well as that other disturbing reaction to the green eyes. 'May I ask your name?'

'Brixham. Anne Brixham.'

Mainwaring made a slight bow, and smiled warmly at her. 'Lieutenant Edward Mainwaring. His Britannic Majesty's Armed Schooner *Athena*.'

153

The girl could not resist a smile in return, and it seemed to Mainwaring to be all warmth and joy, lighting the dirty, death-filled room like a beacon.

'Look,' he said, 'in scarcely a clock's tick the leading ship, *Hampton Court*, is going to be under the guns of the Iron Castle. I've got to attack the Castle from the rear with some hope of evening the odds, if the squadron's attack on the place is to have any chance of success.' He flicked a glance at the chained men. 'Will you and these lads of yours join us?'

The girl stared at him, questions in her eyes. And an igniting spark of hope. 'We're not your damned "hearts of oak". We fight as we wish.'

'You'll be on your own. Just *with* us.'

The girl looked at the crew of the *Black Gull*, whose eyes were dark points of fire in the gloom. 'That sit fair with you, Adam? Jesse?'

Teeth flashed in broad grins. 'Aye, missy! Take these slave chains off!' boomed the one named Adam.

Mainwaring nodded to Evans. 'Get the key and free 'em!' He turned to the door and bellowed out at the approaching, suspicious Hooke.

'Isaiah! Get me six stands of arms from that Spanish lot! We've six – !'

'*Seven*!' barked the girl.

'Seven new recruits!' Mainwaring grinned. He turned away from Hooke's astonished stare to see the girl looking down at her muddy boot toes, all at once forlorn and small. 'What is it?' said Mainwaring. 'Your father?'

'Aye.' The girl nodded. 'He'll die now,' she said bitterly. 'God damn the Dons!'

A thought began to form in Mainwaring's mind, a thought at once outrageous and attractive. 'Where exactly *is* your father?'

154

'As – as far as I know, in the governor's house. He uses one room as a sort of prison. In the town.'

'Then we'll find him.'

'*What*?' The girl's head snapped up.

'We'll find him,' Mainwaring repeated. 'Help us disrupt this Iron Castle, and we'll slip into the town – wherever this Martinez is – and we'll find your father.' Mainwaring's lips lifted in a mirthless smile. 'And in the process perhaps we can raise sufficient hell in there to hasten a surrender!'

Behind the girl the powerful-looking blacks were chafing their wrists, exchanging jokes with Starkey and Evans. Now they had heard Mainwaring, and clustered round the girl, a huge wall of support and loyalty.

'Do it, missy! Do it! An' we'll get the *Black Gull* back in the bargain! Aye, that we will!'

The girl's eyes filled momentarily with tears. But with a grimace she willed them back, and again the thrill stirred inside Mainwaring. The girl uncocked the great pistol, thrust it into her belt, and stepped towards him. For a moment all Mainwaring was conscious of was the fall of her hair around her face, the push of her breasts against the rough shirt, and the sea-green flash of her eyes.

She met his gaze, an ironic light kindling in her own as if she was reading his thoughts. A corner of her mouth lifted. 'Very well, Lieutenant Mainwaring. Shall we take your damned fort?' she said.

Within minutes the remainder of the Athenas were clustering round the door of the hut, and as the San Andrés men spilled out, blinking in the searing sunlight, there were tentative handshakes and then warmer greetings as their tough, seagoing natures perceived kindred spirits. At Hooke's orders, flintlocks and cartridge boxes had been brought over from the pile the wretched Spanish had thrown down, and now the powerful, muscled blacks were taking them up – as well as wolfing down vast chunks of the bread the Athenas dug out of their own haversacks. The black named Adam hefted a musket over his head and let out a whoop. 'Hot times comin' for the Spanish bastards! Yes! Hot times, man!' he roared, even, white teeth bared in a fierce grin.

The girl was chewing on a bit of the half-loaf Mainwaring had carried in his own haversack. 'Ah, that's sweet!' she said, between swallows, her cheeks abulge.

'Water?' Mainwaring offered his canteen.

'Rather rum, thanks very much. Suppose you've none of that?'

Mainwaring grinned at her as she leaned back against the cabin wall, eating the bread with all the relaxed gusto of a countryman after a day's plowing. 'No. These men have got to *make* the attack, not besot themselves.'

'All right,' the girl said. She wiped her hands on her breeches and stood looking inquisitively up at him. 'How do we go about this, then?'

Mainwaring gestured to the wall. 'Come up on the firing step.' They clambered together up the ladder beside the gateway and peered over the wall. 'Christ!' muttered Mainwaring.

'What is it?'

'Look there. *Hampton Court* – the ship close in, there – is only a cable or so off her gunnery position. Damn me, we may be too late already! Miss Brixham, can you tell me – ?'

'Quarterdeck niceties aren't necessary. Anne will do.'

'Thank you. How do I – we – get into that damned Iron Castle down there? Do you know?'

The girl peered under a shading hand at the bulk of the squarish fort. 'You'll not leap-frog over *those* walls, Lieutenant. My God, your ship *is* close. If the waterfront battery starts using its guns – '

'I know it's too close. But is there a way in?'

156

She was pointing. 'Yes, yes. Look. See low down, over by the first angle of the left-hand bastion, or whatever. That smudge, low on the wall?'

'Half hidden by the lip of the dry ditch. Yes, I see it.'

'Sallyport, I think they call it. Low, small door that leads to a tunnel through the walls. They dragged us out through it to bring us up here.'

'But isn't it barred?'

She shrugged, her breasts shaking gently inside the shirt.

'Barred or not, Lieutenant, that's the one way in. The main gate's on the far side, above the track leading down to that shoreline place where they've got many more guns – '

'The waterfront battery.' Mainwaring raised his gaze. *Hampton Court* was almost in line now with the front face of the Iron Castle, her topsails translucent and luffing gently as she glided in behind the stone mass. If he made no move, in the next few minutes she would begin dying under a storm of shot. 'Let's do it!' he said, briskly, heading for the ladder.

'What are you – what are we doing?' said Anne. She loped to catch up.

'We're going to get down there and have a go at that bloody sallyport, is what! Mr Hooke!' He was bellowing as his boots hit the ground. 'Have the lads stand to! Prime and load! And see the new buckos know what they're about!'

Anne landed lightly from the ladder beside him. 'You *silly* bastard,' she murmured.

Mainwaring stared. 'Sorry?'

'D'ye think they're children? They know powder and ball well enough. And as bloody well as your mob of footpads!'

Chastened, Mainwaring found himself staring into the green fire of her eyes. A thin trickle of sweat ran from her throat to vanish into the valley between her breasts.

'I'll take your word for it. But is that clumping great horsepistol of yours loaded?'

Her answering laugh teased him. 'Aren't you a lucky sod for not having found out?'

In no more than a few minutes Hooke had the Athenas grouped before the open gateway, making last-minute adjustments to their weapons. On Mainwaring's orders, as many as could find them had wrestled into the grubby linen coats of the Spanish prisoners. And with them stood the six blacks of Anne Brixham's crew, a hand or more taller than the English, handling the long Spanish flintlocks with confident ease. The girl had been right. Mainwaring found himself hoping they would fight as well as they looked.

Mainwaring hefted the brace of pistols he had found in the Spanish officer's hut. They were Boutets, French, and lighter and better balanced than the Miquelet. He thrust them into his waistband before picking up the cutlass.

'We're ready, zur,' growled Hooke. Then he beamed, looking past Mainwaring's shoulder. The American turned to see the girl, her hair clubbed severely back into a queue, standing with her weight on one leg and leaning on a musket with all the assurance of a grenadier. The way the cartridge box crossbelt pressed into the cloth of the shirt left little to the imagination.

He gaped at her, and looked at Hooke. The grizzled sailing master, and the Athenas behind him, were grinning like apes at him. 'Damn your eyes, Mr Hooke, what are you staring at?'

'Er – ah – nuffin', zur. Nuffin' at all.'

'Then be good enough to ensure each man is primed and – !'

His words were drowned in a deep, rumbling thunder that filled the air, making the ground under their feet shake and tremble with the heavy, repeating reverberations, blows of sound that punched at their chests. Mainwaring spun on his heel to stare down at the grey bulk of the Iron Castle.

Her topsails and t'gallant masts now centred behind the

fortification, *Hampton Court* was obviously unleashing a furious cannonade at the fort. The smoke was already beginning to rise in thick, billowing columns through the masts as if the ship were afire. Again and again the thunderclaps rang out, the punching, regular rhythm of a British warship's disciplined battery fire. Mainwaring wondered at the chaos of splinters, masonry and flying shot it must be producing within the Castle. But where was the answering fire?

He filled his lungs to bellow over the din, and pointed down the track towards the frightful scene with his cutlass blade. 'Come on!' he cried, and lunged out through the gate.

Fifteen minutes later, the thunder of the cannonading had become numbing, a hammering, endless series of blasts that pained the ears and addled the senses. Mainwaring was pressed with Hooke and the girl at the foot of the rough, scaly stone of the Castle's landward side. Beside them, the Athenas were stripping off the grubby linen coats that had masked their run down the hill. Clustered in the dry ditch below the angle of a shallow bastion, the little group could see nothing of the ferocious gunnery battle going on on the far side. But already, the air around them was dark with reeking, drifting smoke, the ground beneath their feet jarring with the thumping impacts that could have been either the strike of shot or the discharge of the Castle's own guns – or both.

But the din was masking the blows of musket butts that Evans and the *Black Gull* crewman known as Jesse, both men dripping with sweat in the stifling heat, were feverishly bringing down on the rusted, half eaten-away hinges of the low wooden door set in the wall. If eyes in the Castle had seen them, they might still have appeared to be a party from the palisade rushing to aid the Castle's defence. As they pelted down the hill, kit banging and swinging around them,

Mainwaring had winced at an image of *Hampton Court* disintegrating under a hail of shot from the great batteries above them.

'God *damn* that door!' railed Mainwaring. 'Can you not get it?'

'Tryin' – sir – !' gasped Evans. The sweat shone on the Welshman's thick biceps. The huge black swore as his own musket butt missed, gouging chips from the door, but then in the next instant, both men's blows landed at once. The battered hinge parted, and a few vicious blows shattered the lower hinge.

'So much for fortifying places in the bloody tropics!' breathed Mainwaring. 'Stand back, lads!' With a ferocious blow of one boot the door gave way inward, collapsing in an upward puff of dust to reveal a black tunnel.

'Follow me!' Mainwaring cried, and ducked in.

The girl was running behind him, tugging at his sleeve. 'It goes straight,' she was panting, 'then – turns several times – before coming out near the steps to the walls!'

Mainwaring grunted, feeling his way as quickly as he could through the low, murky chamber. Hooke and the girl were close at his heels, the men just behind, cursing as toes jammed on stones and edges on the uneven footing. The tunnel was of arched stone, thick with cloying cobwebs and reeking with rot and mould. A rat scampered shrieking across Mainwaring's boots, and the chamber shook and rang with the repercussions of the guns somewhere overhead. Vision was impossible in the blackness, the air was chill and damp after the heat, and Mainwaring shivered, wishing the sudden fluttering in his stomach would cease. He wondered as he stumbled his way along if the girl, with her damnable calm and confidence, was feeling any fear at all.

Then, without warning, the passage angled up and to the left, pale light flooding down it. Ahead was a gate of rusty

160

iron bars, a glimpse of smoke-wreathed wall visible beyond it. The light flickered with the pink, lightning glare of gun flashes, and Mainwaring could hear the shouts and cries of men, the thump and rattle of gun tools, the bark of orders. As he watched, a party of red-breeched Spanish gunners in shirtsleeves staggered past the opening under the weight of a gunpowder barrel.

Mainwaring spun, pulling Anne close to him. Her eyes, wide and ready, looked up at him in a disarming and disturbing way. He cursed the effect she had on him and forced himself to think. 'The ramparts! Where the gun platforms are! Which way are the stairs to 'em?' he roared, over the din.

'To the right! Only a step or two! Once up you can go round the top, I remember!'

Mainwaring nodded. 'Mark that, Isaiah? We make for the ramparts, and go for the gun crews! Clear?'

Hooke nodded in turn. 'Zur!' He turned and bellowed a blasphemous version of Mainwaring's words to the white-eyed men packed behind him.

'Fix bayonets!' cried Mainwaring. Then, 'Come on!' He burst out into the daylight of the Iron Castle's terreplein, the inner courtyard. His vision seemed blurry, and he had a bright, floating image of a stone quadrilateral with gun platforms atop the walls, several substantial single-storey buildings in whitewashed stone, with red-tiled roofs, and an enormous flagstaff with a Spanish ensign drifting, a smoke-encircled spectre, over the ramparts. Indeed, the smoke was so thick that a clutch of gunners went doubling past, jabbering at one another as they carried a bundle of long gun tools towards the far end of the terreplein, and paid no attention to the small group of armed men crouched, half hidden, in the shadows of the curtain wall.

The air was rent by the ear-splitting concussions of gun

blasts, and overhead the embrasures facing the harbour side were penetrated by a line of guns being served feverishly by at least fifty men all told. Mainwaring was trying to count the guns: two fired simultaneously, followed by a third, with others being swabbed and rammed in haste or heaved forward to the run-out position with their tackles by the straining gunners. What must be happening to *Hampton Court* did not bear thinking on. *Act*! cried his mind. 'This way!'

Mainwaring sprinted out of the shadows through the smoke, lit by the lurid flashes from the gun vents. He made for the rough stone steps that led to the ramparts, and raced up them without a pause, his heart pounding in his throat. Any instant now the reaction would come, the musket ball would smash into him, and he would die in kicking agony; the attack would fail, the Athenas with him would die or rot in prison, and the girl . . .

He was at the first gun, the crews gaping at him with blackened faces, turning too late to reach for muskets leaned against the sides of the embrasures before Mainwaring and the baying pack at his heels were upon them. Out of the corner of his eye Mainwaring saw Hooke rush on past him to the next gun, the huge black named Adam and several others with him. And then a muscular, moustachioed gunner was before him, cursing at him in lightning-fast Spanish, swinging a roundhouse blow at him with a rammer. Mainwaring crouched into a squat, the rammer whistling past his head, and then straightened to swing a backhand blow of the cutlass hilt to the man's temple. The Spaniard's knees buckled and he went down, hard, against the rough *pavé* of the gun barbette.

Mainwaring leaped over him as he fell and was on the next man, a wild, fighting lust controlling him now. He cut down with the cutlass in a blow that missed a thin and fevered-looking man in a tattered tricorne and stained red waistcoat,

162

who fell on his knees away from the blow with a shriek, arms raised in a plea for mercy. With his free fist Mainwaring struck the man on the side of the head, stumbling on over the thin body as it went down.

There was a vivid flash before his eyes and a report that rang in his ears, and he heard a shriek behind him. He turned to see a Spaniard still holding the musket levelled that had just missed him. The American lowered his shoulder and bodied hard into the man. The musket clattered to the barbette, the Spaniard's foul breath gusting into Mainwaring's face as the man grunted and bent away, beginning to retch. Mainwaring smashed him down with a blow of the cutlass hilt.

He kicked the man away, leaping over the rolling body, and plunged on. Somewhere he could hear Hooke bellowing. Now he was at the second gun, seeing a dead gunner slumped across the vent, another rolling in agony by the trucks, clutching at the bloody, horrid wreckage of his face. Mainwaring pulled one of the Boutets from his waistband and pistolled the man in the forehead, feeling a surge of nausea welling up within himself. He shook it off and ran on, thrusting the pistol back into his waistband.

'Hooke! Where are – ?' he roared into the swirling, flash-lit murk. And then a shadowy figure was suddenly before him, and he was doubling over, struck with breathtaking force in the stomach. He fell to his knees, the cutlass clattering out of his hand, seeing in the smoke before him the red breeches and white, dirty gaiters of a Spanish gunner, seeing the rammer that had driven the breath from him, seeing the long tool being swung aloft above a grinning, triumphant face for the skull-crushing final blow. And then a musket blasted, deafening in his ear, the fire flash reflected in the goggling eyes of the gunner even as the heavy ball smashed him away into a twitching sprawl.

Anne Brixham was beside him, musket in one hand, lifting him with surprising strength with the other, her face smudged and streaked. 'Edward! Can you – ?'

'Yes!' gasped Mainwaring. He fought to his feet. 'Christ's guts. He would've done for me.'

'Can't have that. I need my father.'

'Callous bitch, aren't you? Where's my bloody cutlass . . .' He found the weapon, picked it up, and stumbled on, the girl beside him. She was almost chuckling at him.

But in the next instant she stopped, frozen in her tracks. The musket dropped from her hands as she pressed both palms against her cheeks, staring off into the smoke-swirled terreplein below in a pose of horror which might have seemed comic had it not been so palpably real. 'Oh, no!' she wailed. 'Oh, my God! Father! No!'

Mainwaring spun on his heels, following her gaze. Below, a doorway had burst open in one of the whitewashed buildings and two Spaniards had appeared, one with a pistol in hand, the other with musket and bayonet. The man with the pistol was roughly pushing ahead of him a slim, white-haired figure in breeches and shirtsleeves, an older man, his arms pinned back, chains hanging from his wrists. As Main-waring stared, the men rushed the older figure to the flat surface of the curtain wall, spun him round, and pushed him against it. The musketman stepped back a pace or two, hurrying to prime and load his musket, the other man holding the prisoner against the wall.

'No! Don't! Don't shoot him! Please – !' the girl stood wailing, momentarily bereft of her quick action, her very ability to move.

Mainwaring lunged to the barbette of the nearest gun. A musket leaned against the embrasure lip, and he kicked away the hand of the dead Spaniard who lay grasping the stock. He swung it up, checked to see that the pan was closed, prayed that the priming was in place, and pulled it to full cock. He ran to the parapet edge. The musketman was levelling his weapon, the other Spaniard standing back, the white-haired man standing defiantly to meet his death . . .

Mainwaring took a deep breath, let it half out, sighted on the musketman's back, and squeezed the trigger. The weapon bucked against his shoulder, its *ftoom* ringing in his ears. He cursed and ducked under the cloud of smoke, and saw the man with the musket sprawling on his face, the musket beneath him. And now the older man was being held against the wall by the other man, whose pistol had been thrown down, and in whose hands a knife flashed. As he watched, Mainwaring saw the older man's knee come up, the Spaniard going down in brief agony, the older man backing against the wall, waiting for the knifeman to rise and finish the work.

Mainwaring scooped up his cutlass where he had dropped it and sprinted past Anne to the head of the narrow stone stairs. He was down them in three wild bounds and in a dead run across the terreplein as the Spaniard rose again. The man hefted the knife and launched himself again at the prisoner, who stood waiting.

But Mainwaring was there, grunting as he dropped his shoulder into the slighter Spaniard, driving the man away into a tumble across the rough ground. He fell to one knee, and then thrust himself to his feet as he saw the Spaniard recover his own footing with cat-like quickness. The Spaniard's face distorted into a rictus of fury, and he sprang at Mainwaring, the gleaming knife arrowing for the American's throat. It was too far, and too slowly done; and Mainwaring's cut down viciously with the cutlass, seeing the man's hand leap from his wrist, hearing him shriek as he stared at the pulsing stump. And then with the backhand blow his neck spurted scarlet, and he fell away.

Behind Mainwaring, the girl was sobbing, pressed to the

165

chest of the straight, slim man, whose eyes were closed and whose lips moved in tenderness against the dark curls.

The guns of the Castle's battery had ceased firing. Now, in the thick swirl of the reeking smoke, the fighting was ending. The Athenas and the San Andrés men had moved like a wave down the line of guns, overwhelming the astounded Spanish with the ferocity of their attack. And now the surviving Spanish, a dozen or so gunners and a handful of marines, were backed into an angle at the far end of the line of guns.

Mainwaring cupped his hands as he saw Hooke raising his cutlass to order the volley that would cut down the pathetic Spanish where they stood. It was time to end the killing. 'Enough! Enough, Mr Hooke! Cease your fire!'

Even at the distance, Mainwaring could sense the bloodlust leaving the burly master's eyes, the sanity returning. 'Aye, aye, zur!' Hooke growled. 'Hold yer fire, lads. But don't let 'em twitch a muscle!'

Mainwaring looked at Anne, still pressed against her father. The elder Brixham was a handsome man, with clear, open features and the same sea-green eyes that looked at Mainwaring with gratitude.

'Your servant, sir,' said Mainwaring, and bowed slightly.

'It is I who am yours, Captain,' said Brixham. 'I cannot thank you enough.'

'Your pardon, sir. Anne, do you speak Spanish?'

The girl nodded.

Mainwaring pointed to the Spaniards. 'Tell them – tell them to lower their weapons and surrender. They'll be spared.'

She nodded again. The old, strong light began to come back into her eyes, and she cupped her hands to call. As the rapid Spanish phrases tumbled out the fear gradually passed from the hunched forms of the Spaniards, and the weapons came down. They seemed to wilt where they stood, forlorn and defeated.

'Good,' said Mainwaring. He raised his voice again, conscious that he was trembling with fatigue and some other emotion. 'Mr Hooke! Disarm them and find a place to put 'em. And let's get that damned ensign down from the – '

'Cap'n, zur! Cap'n!' a voice shrieked from the ramparts. It was Slade, standing atop a merlon, peering down at the harbour scene below. His voice was cutting through an eerie silence, an almost overpowering quiet. The naval gunnery had ended. 'They've done it, zur! Old Grogham's done it!' Slade was bouncing up and down in excitement, pointing. 'Come look, zur!'

Mainwaring looked at Anne and her father, lost in another embrace, and ran up the stairs to the ramparts. His legs felt weak and rubbery as he climbed, and he noticed for the first time, it seemed, the heaped bodies of the Spanish dead. Had he and his men wreaked that destruction and death?

He put a hand on a gun carriage and vaulted up into the embrasure. But even as he gained his footing he stopped, gazing in surprise at the scene before him.

Below the Iron Castle, at the foot of the rocky slope leading to the water, a semi-circular gun battery stood. How extensive its armament might have been could not be judged, as the wooden structures immediately behind the row of guns were a cloaking matchstick shambles of destruction, evidently wrought by *Hampton Court*'s guns. Ruin was everywhere: guns up-ended in their embrasures; enormous chunks of masonry gouged out of the merlons and barbettes; the sad sprawl of corpses everywhere. Through the drifting smoke Mainwaring could make out perhaps eight or nine guns still on their carriages. But they were silent. Their crews, a ragtag mob of twenty to thirty men, were stumbling and running out of the shattered battery up the hill towards the Iron Castle.

Alone on one barbette, a Spanish officer was waving a sword out towards the English vessels, shrieking something that obviously was a call to return to duty.

But now, in the lower battery's embrasures, an extraordinary thing was happening. Heads were appearing in them. Heads, and cutlass blades, muskets and bayonets. And men were scrambling through, huzzaing wildly. A few musket shots rang out over the cheering, and as Mainwaring watched, an English seaman ran to the battery's small flagstaff, pulled down the Spanish ensign, and swiftly ran up a small Union flag.

'It's the landin' parties, zur!' exulted Slade. 'They've taken the battery from seaward!'

In the water, more boats were pulling in strongly for shore, packed with soldiers and seamen. Barely a pistol-shot off, not one but three ships of the squadron rode at anchor, their decks all activity, the smoke of their broadsides still pouring out of their gunports and open hatches.

'Look, zur!' cried Slade. 'It's *Norwich*, and *Worcester*, and Old Grog's *Burford*, 'isself! Christ, that battery must've shot well. Old *Norwich*'s lost her main t'gallantm'st!'

Mainwaring nodded. *Hampton Court*, seemingly undamaged, had drifted off southward a cable or two, and was coming to a new anchor. Perhaps she had lost a cable in the first furious exchange. Clearly the light winds had made deep penetration of the harbour impossible. But the results of that unexpected focus of power on the Iron Castle and its shoreside battery were bearing fruit, in the form of the capture of the battery itself – and the scrambling mob of Spanish who would, in the next instant, be pounding on the gate expecting sanctuary. And already the English in the lower battery were forming up, giving three more cheers, and scanning the Iron Castle's bulk as if readying for an attack on it.

'Damn your eyes, Mr Hooke, have ye got that Spanish rag down yet?' Mainwaring bellowed over his shoulder. 'The landing parties are in the battery below us, and they'll be assaulting *us* next!'

But even as he spoke the floating flag sank down the tall mast over his head, McComb and Quintal heaving it down with relish. Slade had a Spaniard's red waistcoat on his bayonet tip, and was waving it over his head, hallooing in ecstasy. And there were cheers sounding now, cheers from Mainwaring's men. And now from the English pouring into the battery below.

Slade was pointing with the bayonet, the waistcoat streaming like a flag, jumping up and down in excitement. 'The ships, zur! They're cheerin', too!'

And Mainwaring could hear them, distant but strong, ringing out in short, sharp barks, a wild, triumphant sound. When he spoke, his voice was hoarse with sudden emotion. 'By God! By God, so they are,' he said.

5

'Lieutenant Mainwaring to see you, sir. The cutter's just brought him out from the Iron Castle,' said Edward Vernon's flag lieutenant.

A somewhat dishevelled vice-admiral thrust away the report he had been laboriously penning and beamed at the tall figure which appeared in the doorway of *Burford*'s great cabin. 'Come in, Mainwaring, come in!' he boomed. He rose out of his chair and moved round the desk to grasp Mainwaring's hand in vigorous pleasure. 'The hero of the day, what? You and Commodore Brown. By God, a fine show, sir!'

Mainwaring returned the smile. His face was drawn and tired-looking, and there was a growth of stubble over his chin. He was still in the torn shirt and powder-burned red breeches. 'Thank you, sir. But my Athenas and the men of Mr Brixham's vessel deserve the credit. They – '

'Of course, of course, m' lad. Sit down. I want to know how you achieved this miracle. By God! A rare feat of arms, what?'

Mainwaring sank into the hard chair before the Admiral's desk, as Vernon returned to his own. Out through the stern lights, the heat of a new morning was beginning to shimmer the air over the still waters of Porto Bello harbour. 'We were fortunate, sir,' said Mainwaring. 'And that's the simple truth.'

Vernon nodded, all approbation. 'You saw, I presume, the launch that came out from the town at four bells this morning? Which has since returned?'

'Yes, I did, sir.'

'You may be interested to know that it carried an offer of surrender from the governor. On certain conditions.'

170

Mainwaring sat up. 'That's splendid news, sir!'

'Mind, the conditions set by this fellow Martinez were ludicrous. I have sent him *my* conditions and given him three hours to accept. But I have no doubt the capitulation is assured.'

Mainwaring nodded, pleased for the likeable, warm-mannered Vernon. 'Congratulations, sir.'

'Thank you. But the achievement is that of the men of this squadron. Brown, Rentone – and you, sir. I must say, Mainwaring, that you interpret your orders with the most extraordinary latitude.'

Mainwaring flushed. 'I – er – I'm sorry, sir. Under the circumstances I did what I thought was best – '

'Under the circumstances you did very well indeed. Your capture of the Iron Castle ensured that the lower battery had little choice but to surrender. And that pair of achievements has, it appears, induced the Dons to offer terms. A damned fine job, Mainwaring.'

'May I ask, sir, what actually took place after *Hampton Court* stood in, sir? I – we were too preoccupied to see what actually took place.'

'Were you indeed?' beamed Vernon. 'In point of fact, the light winds made my initial plan impossible. Brown came in as far as the battery and saw clearly that he would not be able to carry on further into the harbour. I gather it was about that time that you were approaching the Castle from the landward side.'

'Yes, sir. We were obliged to take an outlying fortification before moving on to the Castle.'

Vernon's eyebrows rose. 'My word. Did you really? I must commend you again, it seems.' He coughed into a vast handkerchief that appeared from a sleeve cuff. 'At any event, Brown, as the good officer he is, promptly had Captain Dent anchor *Hampton Court* before the battery, and open fire.'

Mainwaring grinned. 'Yes, sir. We heard that. Sounded like an earthquake.'

'Not surprising. She fired over four hundred rounds in twenty-five minutes. A storm of shot, one might say.'

Mainwaring nodded. It was clear why the Spanish gunners had fled their posts. Mere men could not stand before a hail of cast-iron death of that volume.

'Brown reported that the fire from the Iron Castle's batteries on him slackened and died away at that point, leaving only the lower battery answering him. Would that have been when – ?'

'In fact, yes, sir. We were taking possession of the ramparts.'

'Ah. Well, the lower battery – thirty-two guns, if I recollect accurately – only managed to get nine guns responding to Brown. Young Don officer named Garganta commanded 'em, and bravely enough, too. He managed to cut *Hampton Court*'s cable, and she drifted off. *Norwich* and *Worcester* managed to beat up and anchor in her place, however. And we ourselves got a lucky capful of wind. Managed to anchor *Burford* here within pistol-shot of the place. When all three of us went at it, it didn't take long.'

Mainwaring nodded.

'When the lower battery was taken, Mainwaring, had you already secured the Iron Castle?'

'Yes, sir. Took five officers and thirty-five men prisoner. The rest were killed or escaped through the gates or over the walls.'

'Your own casualties?'

'One man, sir. Valero. Musket ball through the chest.'

Vernon eyed him levelly. 'Your men must be bloody hell-hounds, Mainwaring. What?'

'In fact they are, sir.'

Vernon coughed into the handkerchief again. 'Damned

172

good thing, too. Where was I? Ah, yes. We anchored further up the harbour, then. Exchanged some shot with the Gloria Castle. Swines had a lucky shot and cut m' foretopm'st. But we put a ball into the governor's house. I had us anchor down harbour for the night and planned to go in after 'em today, but the Dons sent out the cutter. So we've taken the place. And largely due to you. Where in blazes did you spend the night?'

'In the fort, sir. I sent four men back to recover my boat and bring it round. I've left my sailing master, Mr Hooke, in command.'

'Very well. I'll have Captain Newton see that your lads are relieved directly. When did you sleep?'

'We haven't, sir. There was too much to do.'

Vernon nodded, silent for a moment. Then he said, 'Mainwaring, you've done well indeed. And your men with you. I have word that you freed an English planter being held by the Dons, and his daughter. Is that correct?'

'Yes, sir. And six men, the ones who helped us in the attack.'

'This planter – Brixham, isn't it? – owned a vessel. Would you know the name?'

'Er – yes, sir. The *Black Gull*.'

'I thought as much. Pity. It was sunk during our exchange with the Gloria. At anchor before it.'

Mainwaring had a fleeting image of Richard Brixham's face, lined with fatigue but full of gratitude. And of Anne. It would be a bitter blow to them both.

'You'll send Brixham and his daughter to me, and his people. I'll provide for them as best I can.'

'Aye, aye, sir.' Mainwaring felt an odd pang of loss in his chest.

Vernon's gaze was boring into him. 'Mainwaring,' he was saying, 'you've done enough for ten men in this venture. I'll see that my report reflects that. But I regret that I must make use of your considerable talents – and that speedy Yankee schooner of yours – immediately.'

Mainwaring nodded.

'Captain Dent reported seven cases of Yellow Jack this morning, Mainwaring. And there's sick men in *Worcester*, *Princess Louisa* – damn, the squadron will be rife with it, soon! But I cannot leave without destroying the fortifications, or at least rendering them and their guns inoperable. And there's the town to deal with. So I shall be here at anchor, working each ship's company as hard as I dare. And that means parties ashore, for a week, perhaps a fortnight. Parties that will begin dying. Like flies, poor wretches. And ships at anchor unmanned except for anchor watches. I shall be at the mercy of any Don squadron which might appear off here without warning. But if I can be alerted to their presence, I can get the squadron to sea for Port Royal, or raft 'em into gun platforms.' He paused. 'I need you to be our ears and eyes to the eastward. At least until the *Sheerness* frigate comes in and confirms that Pizarro or Don Blas have taken their squadrons into Cartagena. If they sail for Porto Bello, and we are caught at anchor with our crews ashore . . .' He did not finish.

'I understand, sir,' said Mainwaring. He thought of *Athena*, sleek and beautiful, ghosting back and forth on the seaward horizon of the harbour mouth. He yearned for her in a sudden burst of feeling.

'I'm sure you do,' Vernon was saying. 'Please establish a patrol between here and the Gulf of Urabá. Stand in as close as you dare and then off. If you see Pizarro or Blas, crowd on sail and report to me.'

'Aye, aye, sir. How long, sir?'

'Two weeks, if your stores last. No more.' He smiled

without humour. 'We'll either have finished the job – or be dead of the Jack, by then. Clear?'

Mainwaring nodded. 'Sir. There is one other thing, if you please, sir.'

'Yes?'

'The crew of the *Black Gull*. I'd like to have them in *Athena*, sir. But I don't want to press 'em. Anne – Miss Brixham and her father will need 'em when they resettle. They've got to leave San Andrés.'

'The men are slaves, are they?'

'Yes, sir. But they treat 'em as freed men.'

'No matter. Slaves are property. If you have the Brixhams' permission to transport their property – without reducing your ship's efficiency – then that is your affair, Lieutenant.'

'Yes, sir. Thank you, sir.' Mainwaring paused. 'There's – there's one other thing, sir.'

Vernon glowered, but not unkindly. '*Yes*, Mainwaring?'

'The girl. Miss Brixham, sir. Damned if she isn't a good hand as well, sir. If she – well, if she's willing, sir, I'd like her to sail with us.'

'With that pack of cut-throats – oh, belay that. You've fine men, and I'm aware of that. But a woman in your messdecks *at sea*?'

'Not exactly, sir. She'll use my cabin. And her father as well, if he wishes. I'll bunk for'rard. I feel a certain responsibility for them, sir.'

'Which might be better served by leaving them in *Burford* as my guests, what?'

'Yes, sir,' said Mainwaring. He looked down.

Vernon sighed. 'Oh, confound the proprieties. If she wants to go, that is your affair, Mainwaring. I shall hold you responsible for their welfare, however.' He looked round over his shoulder at the light-sparkled harbour. 'If the Yellow Jack cuts through the way I fear, they may be safer at sea with you in any event.'

'Thank you, sir. Very much.'

'Yes, yes. You may have little to thank me for with a young woman loose about your decks like a gun off its tackles. But never mind.' The admiral's face grew more serious. 'As to your sailing. You'll re-victual as necessary from my purser in *Burford* here. Although from your last report I gather *Athena*, somewhat fortunately, was well stored by the Spanish in her brief service with them. Can you eat all that damned oil and whatnot?'

'Yes, sir. Good bread and well-preserved meat, actually, sir.'

'Very well,' said Vernon. 'Then I suggest you repair to your ship. When dawn rises tomorrow I should like you to be at sea.' And he stood to end the interview.

Fifteen work-filled hours later, a clear moonlight was angling in, ivory, across the settee cushions and the decking in His Britannic Majesty's Armed Schooner *Athena*'s great cabin. The slow movement of the ship to its hawser caused the even squares of light to swing slowly back and forth over the painted canvas. One of the stern lights was chocked open, and from where he sat at the narrow desk, Mainwaring could hear the gentle lap of water under the counter. Just visible to one side, the riding lights of one of the other ships in the squadron were visible, orange glows on a hulking black mass.

Mainwaring took a deep breath, scenting the warm smell of the shore as it came in through the open light. He had let the candle in its stick gutter and flicker out just as he had finished writing the last sentence and signing his report to Vernon. Laying the quill down, he sat listening to the motions and noises of the ship – the creak of timbers, the quiet clump of the duty watch going about its business, readying the last things before *Athena* sailed in the dawn light – and more, to

176

the regular, soft breathing of Anne Brixham, who lay in the small cabin's box bunk.

Richard Brixham had accepted Vernon's hospitality. But he had not stood in the way when Anne Brixham, to the delight of her *Black Gull* men, had said that, by God, she would sail in *Athena*, and was the equal to any man in her. The old man had looked hard at Mainwaring and had smiled, nodding, seeing something in the Massachusetts man's eyes ceding something to him. And Mainwaring had brought her and the blacks along with the landing party in his boat and Vernon's cutter to a joyful reunion with Stephen Pellowe and *Athena*, a reunion that led to endless telling and re-telling of the tale, and the Athenas warming to the small, intense woman whose energy was matched by the sunlit beauty of her face and smile. Then had followed the frantic readying and re-arming of *Athena* for sea.

Mainwaring had insisted that Anne take his cabin, moving his sea chest into the narrow, partitioned cubicle that Pellowe existed in, and sending that chuckling individual off to sling his hammock beside Hooke, forward. And then he had had to write his report of the landing, and she had insisted in her turn that he come in and use the desk. The night had fallen, and the little figure had curled up in his box bunk like a cat, and gone to sleep immediately.

Now, as he looked at the small, still shape, he felt an almost painful tenderness for her flooding out of himself as if to cover and protect her. It was a disturbing and oddly frightening feeling, and he sat up, looking away at the distant lanterns through the stern lights. That one orange point with its rivulet of light below it on the water was likely *Strafford*. He wondered if her ship's company had got over their annoyance at being so largely out of the action –

'You've finished,' she said. Her voice was low and quiet.

'What? Yes. I – didn't know you were awake.'

The girl stirred under the blankets. 'Have been for some time. Watching you write. Watching you think, now.'

'The sea's calm,' he said, after a moment. 'Hardly a ripple.'

She threw back the covers and padded across to the settee, curling up on it and hugging her knees, gravely watching him. The boots were gone, but she still wore the velvet breeches and the baggy, rough man's shirt. Her hair still wisped about her face in dark shadows, and an angle of moonlight found her hands. They were white in the light, and graceful, despite the strength Mainwaring knew they had.

'Do you – often sit and think like this? In the dark?' she said. The moonlight caught faint sparks in her eyes.

'No. Hardly ever, at least. Moments like this – well, rarely happen.' He left the chair, and sat beside her. He could smell her: a faint musk.

She was looking at him over her knees, and they were silent, sharing a long gaze. Then, very slowly, he leaned forward and kissed her. Her lips pursed into a soft cone, and were warm and sweet, moving as she returned his kiss. Her hands came up to hold his face, a low, gentle noise sounding in her throat. As his arms moved about her, her knees came down, and she moved eagerly into his embrace, pressing her firm little body against his. They lingered in the kiss, not wanting to end the touch.

And then his hands were moving, pulling aside the rough shirting, tracing up the satin surface of her body, and her cheek was against his, her breathing quickening. His hands found her breasts, and she caught her breath in a little gasp as he held their silky, hot fullness, his lips seeking hers again.

Abruptly she was away from him, standing as he gazed at her in surprise. She shrugged out of her shirt and thrust off the breeches, standing in the next minute in a shaft of the moonlight that angled through the stern lights. Her breasts were full and round, their dark nipples moving as she turned

178

towards him, holding out her arms to him. The moonlight played over the smooth muscles of her stomach and down, over the swelling curve of her hip.

'Oh, Edward. Edward, my dear love. For God's sake, don't just stare at me!'

Mainwaring burst out laughing, laughing in sheer pleasure and delight. And then as he rose, she was in his arms, all naked and wanton, her lips hungry on his, and with a flying joy ringing in his heart he sank with her into the pool of moonlight on the decking.

Athena lifted in a long, swinging motion over a white-capped swell and sank back with a roar into the boiling foam under her bows. The sun was climbing towards the zenith, and under its scintillating rays, burning down from the cloudless sky, the sea was a deep, dark blue, alive with the flickers of the white-caps under a steady easterly Trade Wind.

The schooner was ten leagues due north of the western headland of the Gulf of Urabá, steering on the inshore leg of a pattern that, since dawn – which had brought the savage wind with it – she had been tracking over. Close-hauled on the larboard tack, *Athena* carried a single-reefed main and foresail, with her headsails shortened down as well. Aloft, the square foretopsail was tightly furled against its yard. Even with its power thus reduced, the schooner was driving its way off to the south-east with a speed that left a cauldron-like wake boiling and hissing behind her, and she lifted and powered over the swells, taking them on her shoulder with a *c-crunch* and a burst of spray that haloed the bows and drenched the lower sails, leaving the decks gleaming and wet.

It was grand, glorious sailing, and in the hot wind the men braced on *Athena*'s deck joked and laughed with one another over their work, excited and exuberant at such rushing freedom after the fetid stillness of the Porto Bello anchorage.

Edward Mainwaring appeared up the forward companion-way, hatless. He squinted at the mainmast pennant, feeling a shiver of delight at the roaring wind and the taut, curved arches of the sails towering above him. He had been below with Abner, listening patiently as the loquacious gunner had taken him on a tour of *Athena*'s cramped little magazine and recited the precautions Mainwaring had had him undertake. He had finally left him and his mates rigging the felt curtains round the magazine, that in action would be drenched with water, as a precaution against fire.

'Fair day, zur!' boomed Hooke beside the wheel. Evans was the helmsman, and he was grinning in good-humoured effort as he wrestled with the schooner's corkscrewing motion. The muscles on his brown, bare arms flexed and worked under their deep tan.

'That it is, Isaiah. What's the state o' things?' He was looking around. Looking for the small figure. *Athena* heaved under him, catching him off balance, and with a self-mocking snort Mainwaring braced himself against the weather rail. The schooner buried itself with a thunderous roar into a swell whose breaking crown was almost too bright to look at. A hiss of spray, glittering like diamonds, shot over the bows and pattered like rain on the deck. Mainwaring wiped his dripping face on his sleeve and grinned at Hooke.

'Nigh on a gale, zur. Due easterly. Course sou' east by south. Jib an' stays'l wiv a single reef, an' a point taken in the fore an' main. Starb'd watch on deck. An' I figure we'll raise th' headland off th' bows in 'bout a glass or two, zur, accordin' to Mr Pellowe.'

'Very good.' He still could not see her. 'Where's Miss Brixham?'

Hooke beamed and pointed aloft with a thumb. 'Foretop, zur! Gettin' the hang uv it. Jewett's wiv 'er, zur. 'Ee'll not let 'er fall.'

Mainwaring squinted up, feeling his heart thumping in his chest. A petite figure in the fore crosstrees, hanging on with monkey tenacity as the schooner heeled, was waving at him, the wide, happy grin visible. Jewett, the burly, capable topman who had spoken up before the land assault on the Iron Castle, was hovering behind her.

'Dear God,' breathed Mainwaring.

Hooke laughed. 'A prime little sailor, that 'un. There's no ill luck to havin' '*er* in this ship!'

Mainwaring thought of how she had cuddled against him in the shadows of the box bunk.

'No, Isaiah, there isn't.' He made himself tear his eyes away from her, to look forward over the bows at a sea made into rolling billows of gold by the sun. 'No sightings this watch? You've still doubled up on the lookouts?' If he allowed it, the thought and need for her would overwhelm his duty. And that he must never allow. Neither for the ship's sake, nor for its people.

'Aye, zur. Two aloft, besides Jewett an' Miss Anne. An' two in th' bows. Not a scrap o' sail.'

Mainwaring nodded. 'All right. As soon as we raise the Darién coast we'll put about, as before. Any squadron'd stay well offshore, to my mind.'

'Zur. Abner tell ye he's finished th' tackles an' breechin' lines on th' new guns, zur? Gives us a right proper armament, t' my mind.'

Mainwaring looked along the glistening, pitching deck to where the gunner and his two mates had come on deck and were kneeling beside one of the new three-pounders Mainwaring had managed to secure at Porto Bello. *Athena* now mounted four three-pounder truck guns a side: four in the waist, two just forward of the break in the forecastle, and two in the confines of Mainwaring's cabin. Added to these were the four one-pounder swivels now set by their yoke pins into

181

strongbacks on the quarterdeck rail, two to a side. It was not enough to confront a frigate, let alone a French or Spanish fifth-rate, but the increased armament had given *Athena*'s men a sense of being better armed, if not well-armed –

'Deck! Deck, there!' The cry rang down from aloft. It was Jewett's voice.

Mainwaring snapped his head up, cupping his hands. 'Deck, aye?'

'Sail, sir! Larboard bow! Tops'ls an' t'gallants!'

Hooke was at Mainwaring's side. 'That Jewett's a hawk-eyed one, sartin. Seen 'er afore the lookouts.'

Mainwaring filled his lungs to call over the sea noise and the rush of the wind. 'Can you see colours, Jewett?'

A pause. 'No, sir!' Another pause. 'But she's a Don or a Frenchman, sir!'

The hair tingled on Mainwaring's neck. 'How so?'

'Sails, sir! White as snow! An' the cut of her t'gallants! I know the look of 'em, sir!'

'Jewett's an experienced man, sir,' said Stephen Pellowe. The youth had appeared up the forward companionway at Jewett's first cry. 'I'd take his word for it.'

'Then I shall as well, Mr Pellowe,' said Mainwaring, briskly. 'Bring the ship to Quarters, if you please!'

Within a half-minute Slade and Winton were dodging about the ship, loosing ear-splitting calls on their silver pipes down the hatchways and bellowing into the gloom below. 'D'ye hear, there? Hands to Quarters! Lively, there!'

The men who had been drafted into *Athena* from *Hampton Court* had been given precious little time to learn their stations, let alone become familiar with their messmates. But they were man o' war's men, and went to their posts alongside the more experienced Athenas as quickly as they could, guided by the brisk instructions of Pellowe and Hooke in the purposeful silence characteristic of an English warship. The small truck guns quickly had their tackles loosed and set up, the tompions pulled and vent covers taken off, the tools laid out in their cradles on the deck nearby, a deck quickly made more sure underfoot by sand scattered over the wet, slick planking. One man of each gun crew had scuttled below to Abner's newly readied magazine for the charges in their leathern buckets, while aft, the men manning the swivels had their small shot and charge boxes open on the deck before them, quickly loading the ugly little guns.

Athena punched through a gleaming, green-shouldered swell and heeled sharply as a gust caught her, the men coming up from below slipping and slithering as they made their way to their guns.

'Abner!' Mainwaring barked at the gunner. 'Keep your vent covers on! They'll not fire if wet!'

The gunner nodded, his 'Aye, aye!' lost in a new roar under *Athena*'s bows, but already the gun captains were slapping the lead plates back over the vents after the loading and priming of the little guns were completed by the quickly working crews. Mainwaring was pleased to see how equally Abner had divided the gun crews, putting knowledgeable men alongside inexperienced ones. One after another, the three-pounders' breech rings were slapped as a sign the priming was home and the vent cover on, and on the cry 'Run out!' the guns snorted out through their gunports, the crews hauling with rhythmic grunts at the squealing side tackles.

Mainwaring looked up. Jewett had crossed, upside down, on the triatic stay to his fighting post in the foretop. And lower down, the small, quick figure of Anne Brixham, her dark hair riffling in the wind, was coming down a maintopmast stay hand over hand. As Mainwaring stared, aghast, she reached the rail, leaped lightly down to the deck, and flashed a radiant smile at him, hands on hips.

'Plannin' a fight, are ye, Cap'n?' she said in a superb mimic of a Yankee twang, and Mainwaring would have grabbed her on the spot, fighting back the impulse only in the nick of time.

'Yes. I don't have a good feeling about that Don, if that's what he is. I think you should – '

'He's a Spaniard, all right. Jewett's got good eyes, but I've got better. He's a Don. A *guardacostas*, in fact.'

Mainwaring looked at her sharply and then glanced away to the eastern horizon. Only a speck of white showed there, the vessel's hull being behind the earth's curvature. 'Now, how in hell would you know – ?' he began.

'Oh, Edward. I've sailed the *Black Gull* from San Andrés to Cartagena and east o' there a dozen times. There's two or three of the *guardacostas* you come to recognize. That one's the best of the lot. Or the worst, I suppose.'

'You can identify her? At this distance?'

The girl nodded. 'Has a funny look to its foretopm'st. That's the *Aguerra*, I'm sure.'

Mainwaring straightened as if he had been struck. 'You're certain of that?' His eyes were hard points.

Her face sobered. 'Yes, I'm sure. Why are you looking at me like that? Do you know the *Aguerra*?'

Mainwaring's mouth was a tight line. He was gripped by a sudden tension. Tension, and the beginnings of awakening anger. 'She was the one who took us. The picket for the Spanish *flota* we escaped from. Damnation, if that means Pizarro or Blas is astern of him and tracking for Porto Bello . . .' He did not finish.

Heedless of the activity around them, she moved closer, looking up disarmingly into his eyes. 'What are you going to do?' Her hand touched his arm.

Mainwaring's eyes were fixed on the distant white rectangle, larger now. 'If that's *Aguerra*, then I shall fight her. And take or sink her.'

184

She was by his side, her hand stealing now into his. 'Why, Edward? Won't you just give things away by doing that, if he escapes? You still look like a privateer. Why not turn tail and run, like one would – ?'

Mainwaring shook his head. 'No, Anne. That game'll not do, now. The Dons know the squadron's here, and no ruse will persuade 'em otherwise. And I think they will have recognized *Athena* as you did them.' He looked at the distant topsails. 'I'll have to fight.'

'It wouldn't be best to put back to Porto Bello?'

'What would that solve? I might outrun that fellow, or I might not. I'd have no word of where the Don *flota* really is – we've had no word from *Sheerness* cruising off Cartagena – and I'd as likely lead that bastard right to Vernon.'

The girl nodded. Her hand squeezed his, a warm, strong grip. 'All right. And I'll fight too. Where's Adam and Jesse?'

Mainwaring gripped her shoulders. 'No, damn it! I want you below, this time. Out of harm's way.'

The girl shrugged off his hands and looked hard at him, lifting her chin. 'No. Edward, I said that I'm not one of your tars, and I'm not! Where are they?'

Mainwaring pointed forward. 'There. They've taken over number two gun, larboard side. Likely below getting shot and cartridge. But they – '

'Then I'm manning that gun with 'em,' said the girl briskly. 'Not the first time I've served a gun. Edward, you need every capable pair of hands you can find!'

Mainwaring, about to say something more, bit it back. Had the girl not proven she was as capable as a man already? And had she not saved his life in the bargain?

'You owe me a favour, my love,' Anne said, in the glory of a sudden smile. 'I *did* save your luckless hide, back there in the Iron Castle.'

185

'I was just thinking that. You don't make things easy, do you?'

'Certainly I do. Just don't try to stop me doing what I can to help you. To help *us*.'

Mainwaring could see when he was beaten. 'All right. Man your gun. But keep your head down and your wits about you. Please.'

But she was already striding quickly forward, calling to the *Black Gull* men as they staggered up the companionway, laden with cartridge buckets and gun tools.

Mainwaring looked aloft once more, cupping his hands.

'Foretop, there! Jewett? Can you make out colours?'

There was a pause.

'Aye, sir! Spanish!' came the cry. 'Red hull, sir! Looks like a *guardacostas*.'

It was *Aguerra*, thought Mainwaring. He could feel in the pit of his stomach that the girl had been right. It was the sleek, crafty stalker that had taken *Athena* before. Tricked him, killed his men, taken his ship. 'Mr Hooke! Mr Pellowe!' he barked, bringing both men to his side in an instant. 'D'ye know who that is out there?'

Hooke's face had an odd look of satisfaction. 'Aye, zur. The greaser what done fer us. Th' one as was a picket t' their squadron afore.'

Pellowe stared at Mainwaring, his youthful features pale despite his tan. '*That* ship? Dear Christ!'

'Listen, both of you,' said Mainwaring. All three men spread their feet, reaching for handholds as *Athena* thumped into a swell and heeled, Evans cursing behind them at the wheel. 'We know what she is, this time. There'll be no trickery. But I want that ship. I want her badly.'

'We – ah – understand, sir,' said Pellowe after a glance at Hooke.

'I'm sure you do. Now listen. She's got a vicious broadside,

186

we know. And good gunnery. But we've speed and weather-liness on our side.' He glanced forward at the gun crews. 'And we're a little better armed.'

''Ee can still outrange us, Cap'n,' said Hooke.

'No matter. We'll soon close the range. Stephen, you'll command both batteries. Keep 'em manned, both sides, and don't pull a crew from side to side unless we lose a crew. We'll engage both sides quickly enough. Clear?'

The midshipman's mouth was set in a line of resolve. 'Aye, aye, sir.'

'Good. Isaiah, that pack of sailhandlers will be your charge. I'll want quick work, because I intend to manoeuvre to avoid his broadside until I can close him and try to board. You'll have to be damned fast at it.'

'No fear, zur.' The burly master was actually rubbing his ham-like hands in expectation.

'I shan't. Stephen, ensure Jewett and the other two in the foretop are sent up muskets and cartridge boxes. They can sharpshoot from there. Tell 'em to aim for the quarterdeck, officers and helmsmen first targets. And get those weapons tubs on deck, fore and aft: cutlasses and pikes, and as many pistols as Abner managed to fit with flints.'

He paused. 'There'll be one other thing,' he said. 'There'll be no quarter when we board. Not until I give the word. I want no man hanging back. Questions?'

Both men shook their heads, faces grim.

'Carry on, then. And quickly!'

Mainwaring glanced at Evans' binnacle, and then up at the foresail leech, looking for the tell-tale shiver that would say Evans was pinching the wind too closely. But the towering arc of canvas was rock-still. The Welshman was a consum-mate steersman, and *Athena* was racing along under his grip in perfect balance.

He looked forward at the horizon. The Spaniard was well

up over the line now, even squares of brilliant white sails, so different from the tan, workworn English canvas, taut over a dark, red-hued hull. The ship was pitching slowly, overhauling the swells, a flash of white showing rhythmically under her bows.

Dear Christ, thought Mainwaring. *Here he comes, like a damned shark smelling blood. No clewing up, no preliminaries.* He turned to Evans. 'Ease her a point. Steer sou' east by south. Keep her clean full.'

'Sou' east by south, aye, sir,' said Evans. And *Athena* bent anew to the power of the wind.

His Most Catholic Majesty's *Gaurdacostas Aguerra* lifted under the fresh power of her newly set topgallants, the sea roaring in almost continuous thunder under her forefoot. Antonio Lopez stood once more at the foot of the quarterdeck ladder, squinting up at the figure of the Chevalier Rigaud de la Roche-Bourbon.

'The lookouts have confirmed it, señor. It is the same vessel. The English schooner we took, and which afterwards escaped.'

Roche-Bourbon's eyes seemed to glitter under the shade of his elegantly feathered tricorne. 'Sweet Mother of God!' he whispered. 'How you do favour me!'

'She is undoubtedly the picket for the squadron of the Englishman, Vernon, señor. Should we not – ?'

'What we *shall* do, Lopez,' said Roche-Bourbon icily, 'is allow you to show me how well you fight this ship. And how you took him last time. I am most interested to see.'

Lopez wiped his mouth with the back of his hand and looked forward at the small, plunging shape of the schooner.

'*Madre*. She is fast, señor. And the Englishmen fight well –'

'Are you afraid, Lopez?'

'The Spaniard spun. '*Afraid*? By the Virgin, señor, no! But – '

'Then you will bring your ship to Quarters. And I shall enjoy watching you close that whoreson *bostonnais* craft and take her. There is a man in her I am most interested in seeing face to face one more time.'

Roche-Bourbon's eyes sought out *Athena*, and his hand moved to the hilt of his hanger, the knuckles whitening as his grip tightened. *Holy Mother, how kind you are*, he thought. *To bring him to me, rather than making it necessary to seek him out. To bring him to me, and make his killing easier.*

'Thank you,' he breathed.

'Here, sir,' said Quintal. He handed Mainwaring the remaining Boutet pistol and the cutlass he had picked up in the taking of the Iron Castle. The pistol had been carefully cleaned, loaded and primed, and the polished cutlass was hanging in a scabbard and shoulderbelt.

'Thank you, Quintal. Did you make this leatherwork?'

'Aye, sir,' beamed the man. One eye was still half closed below the cutlass cut Quintal had received during the fight ashore. 'Yew need a proper carriage, sir.'

'I'm honoured, then. Thank you again.'

Quintal knuckled his brow and padded off forward. Mainwaring settled his hat lower over his eyes, clutching at the weather rail again as *Athena* heeled to a gust.

'Christ, it's blowin', sir!' offered Evans. His broad feet were planted wide on the decking as he controlled the helm with smooth motions of his powerful arms.

'Aye. Just see you keep her way on. Now is not the time to haul her wind and lose it.'

'Aye, sir.'

Pellowe was coming up the quarterdeck ladder. The

189

youth's waistbelt bulged with a theatrical-looking brace of huge Spanish dragoon pistols. As he arrived, the small arms tubs were being wrestled into place at the foot of the fore and main masts, beside their fife rails. Several carefully coiled grapnel lines were laid out with them.

'Ship's at Quarters, sir,' he reported. 'Guns loaded and primed, run out, but vent covers on.'

'Very good.' Mainwaring took a deep breath to try and still the sudden shaking in his legs, and the equally unpleasant flutterings that had developed in his stomach. 'Where will you stand to direct your batteries?' There was something almost pathetic about using that term for a handful of tiny guns throwing a fly-swat broadside.

'Er – just there, sir. For'rard of the gratings. Why?'

Mainwaring harrumphed. 'Miss Brixham. Please keep an eye on her. I know she's capable, but – '

At the second gun on the larboard side Anne was leaning her weight into the hauling of the side tackles as the little gun was run out. Beside her, the huge figure of the black named Jesse loomed, dwarfing her.

Pellowe nodded, understanding in his eyes that oddly irritated Mainwaring. 'I shall, sir,' said the youth.

Mainwaring harrumphed again and looked forward, scanning to set the rapidly developing situation in his mind. The weakness in his knees and stomach made him curse himself for a coward, and he wondered if Pellowe or any of the men could see or sense his fear. And, God prevent it, if *she* did . . .

The sea was now a rolling, shimmering gun-metal prairie under the clear sky, brilliant sun and fierce, hot wind. *Athena* was close-hauled on the larboard tack, beat in spray-haloed plunges off to the south-east, her people ready at their posts, watching in attentive readiness the approach of *Aguerra*. Although Mainwaring had not spoken of the vessel's identity except to Hooke and Pellowe, the word had spread rapidly that the vessel in sight was the same *guardacostas* that had humiliated the schooner; in the expressions of the original Athenas, and even in those of the new men who knew the tale, there was a hard-eyed determination that Mainwaring was glad to see.

Far to windward, *Aguerra* had moved directly into the path of the sun, and was now a black shape, lofty and menacing, moving steadily down the roiling golden pathway towards the schooner. The Spanish vessel was no more than a half-league away now, and even in the brilliant light-and-shadow glare Mainwaring could see the foam driven to either side under her bluff bows as she overhauled the swells in slow, curtseying majesty.

'Damn me, that's a fine ship!' breathed Mainwaring to himself. The Spaniard would have the added advantage that, being a bluff-bowed square-rigger, she made a better gun platform than the heeling, fore-and-aft-rigged schooner. To bring Pellowe's guns to bear so that they could be quoined up or down to any reasonable degree would mean bringing *Athena* either dead into the wind – or dead off it. Either reaching or tacking, *Athena* would have the advantage of speed over the Spaniard, but would virtually be unarmed. Mainwaring swore and spat over the lee rail. It was not going to be easy. But then it had not been the last time.

'Mr Hooke?' he called. Hooke was standing with his knot of sailhandlers at the mainmast foot.

'Zur?'

'Be ready to move quickly. We may tack or wear suddenly, without much warning. And when we do, sheet home quickly! Whatever we do, we must not lose way!'

'Aye, aye, zur!'

Aguerra was perhaps a thousand yards off now. The sleek red and gilt hull was clearly visible, the tall, translucent pyramids of canvas floating like a cloud above it. From the

191

foremast truck a thin white pennant was streaming in floating delicacy forward over the lance-like bowsprit and jib-boom.

Pellowe was pacing behind his guns, simply dressed in plain breeches, shirt and boots, a cutlass resting almost casually against his shoulder. The great pistols had been put aside at the mainmast foot.

'Ready your linstocks!' he intoned. The captains had taken the smouldering slow matches from their notches in the match tubs, set amidships behind each gun, and wound them round the short staffs with their forked heads, blowing on the match to ensure fire in the gusty, spray-rinsed conditions. 'Starkey, look to your priming. That vent cover's loose. Adams, overhaul that side tackle. The gun'll slew round if it fires like that!'

Six hundred yards. *Aguerra* came bowling down the wind towards them, her course one that would put her square athwart the bows of the close-hauled schooner. Mainwaring could see knots of men moving about her decks or scrambling aloft into the tops, slung muskets gleaming on their backs. Now, suddenly, the ship slowed visibly as the courses crumpled up towards their yards, gathered in by the rhythmic hauling of buntlines and clewlines. 'Clewin' up fer action, zur!' came Hooke's unnecessary cry.

Mainwaring glanced up. *Athena*'s maintruck pennant streamed like a scarlet flame off to leeward. Below it, in the crosstrees of the foremast, Jewett was visible in his perch on the swaying, pitching mast, his musket barrel trained out towards the approaching *guardacostas*. As if he had sensed Mainwaring's eyes on him, he cupped his hands and bellowed down. 'Closin' fast, sir! An' prime targets on th' quarterdeck!'

Mainwaring waved a reply. *Aguerra* was no more than three hundred yards away now, suddenly very close, a few minutes away from sweeping past *Athena*'s bows, those beautifully faired gunports already gaping open to reveal the red-

192

muzzled snouts of the long guns within, the squeals of their trucks sounding down the wind as they were run out. Mainwaring bit his lip. If he took *Athena* off the wind several points, the schooner would add several knots to her speed. That might mean a chance to cross the Spaniard's bow, and give Pellowe the opportunity to throw shot high at *Aguerra's* rigging, if the angle of heel made a shot at deck or hull level impossible. But would the Spaniard sit there and hold his course while –

No!

'Wearin', zur!' came Hooke's bark. 'Turnin' his starb'd battery towards us!'

The same damned quick-footed reactions, thought Mainwaring, seeing the square-rigger heel, the bowsprit turning off, the row of guns swinging to bear. In the next instant the killing broadside would roar out . . .

Mainwaring sprang beside Evans. 'Ready about, there!' he cried. 'Down helm, Evans! Take her round!' He cupped his hands as Evans slapped the great wheel over. '*Helm's a-lee!*'

Forward, Hooke and his men were diving for the sheets as *Athena* heeled alarmingly and swooped into a lifting, plunging turn into the wind. The bows thundered into the swells, spray hissing in sheets back over the decks, and aloft the canvas suddenly went mad, booming and thumping in long, shadowed ripples that set the deck under Mainwaring's feet shaking. *Athena* swung on, and he had a vision of *Aguerra*, huge over the starboard bow now, rushing by at breathtaking speed. And then the schooner was around, Hooke's men hauling as if possessed at the sheets, and the schooner leaped ahead like a greyhound on the starboard tack.

At that instant, *Aguerra's* side exploded in consecutive flashes of flame and punching, chest-thumping reverberations. The ragged broadside sent towering geysers jetting up just off *Athena*'s counter, toppling back in drifting curtains of mist that glimmered with short-lived rainbows.

Athena steadied as Evans 'met her', checking her swing as Hooke's men hauled home the sheets. *Aguerra* swept on, wreathed in a huge cloud of her own gunsmoke . . .

The smoke!

'Ready about!' Mainwaring barked. Then, with scarcely a breath, 'Down helm! Helm's a-lee, there!'

Again the wild, thumping, chaotic turn into the sun and wind, the spray shivering high, the canvas a living thing. *Athena* swung, and the watching, sodden gun captains saw the smoke-swirled shape of *Aguerra* draw into their line of fire on the starboard side.

'Now, Stephen, before we sheet home! As your guns bear, *fire!*' Mainwaring cried.

Pellowe's own cry in the next instant was lost in the sharp, banging reports of *Athena*'s starboard battery. The two guns in the waist leaped back against their breechings, the 'huff' at the vents jetting up like pink tongues as the linstocks arced down. The wind curled the sudden billows of reeking smoke back over the rail, streaming like wind-driven fog over *Athena* and off to leeward.

Mainwaring started in spite of himself as the two swivels near him barked in vicious, ear-ringing blasts. And then he was at the rail, coughing in the smoke, straining to see if the Spaniard had taken any damage.

Beside him, McComb, feverishly swabbing out his smoking swivel gun, was cackling, pointing with his chin. 'Look'ee, zur! Did in 'is stern lights for 'im!'

There were gaps in the stern lights of the ship, and as *Athena* heeled away, Mainwaring could see more evidence of Pellowe's guns: a section of transom rail gone, a vang of the lateen mizzen yard adrift and trailing in the wind.

Pellowe was vaulting up the quarterdeck ladder, his face

wet with spray. 'Sir! It's just no damned good, sir. Won't do. Those hits were pure luck. Can't quoin the guns down far enough!'

'I know, Stephen. Do what you can. Get back to your guns, sir!'

The youth looked at him oddly, then responded to the order, discipline triumphing over distraction.

Mainwaring squinted forward at *Athena*'s track, then back at *Aguerra*. The Spanish vessel had held its course, and the schooner was now well past the *guardacostas*' stern, working more to windward each moment. But how to avoid her next turn to deliver those damned broadsides –

'She's turning, sir!' Pellowe was calling. 'Going for his other broadside!'

Mainwaring swore inventively. Damn the Spaniard! Her captain was a cunning bastard, bearing up a point or two, putting *Aguerra* on to a broad reach instead of a run. Somehow he had sensed *Athena* would fight, and not run, and had given up the weather gauge, turning now to present his larboard broadside to the heeling, defenceless schooner.

'Fall off!' Mainwaring barked. 'Hooke! Ease the sheets, fore and main! Gybe the fore across if you must, and set 'em wing and wing! Helm up, Evans! Run down on her!' He pointed at Pellowe. 'This will give you your stable platform, Mr Pellowe! If your guns bear, for God's sake make it count!'

Now *Aguerra* was on a broad reach, showing more of her quarter to the schooner. Her guns would bear in the next instant. But her target was suddenly narrowed, for *Athena* was swooping off the wind now, her counter roaring and the great sheets rattling out through their blocks as the schooner turned wide off the wind, her bowsprit arrowing for *Aguerra*'s side. With three men dragged like monkeys on a vine on the foresail gaff vang, the foresail went over in a thumping gybe that shook the deck. *Athena*'s headsails fell slack, but under

195

the press of the wing-and-wing fore and main, the schooner overtook and boiled through the swells, rushing down on the square-rigger.

Fire now, you bastard! said a cry in Mainwaring's mind. And in the next instant *Aguerra* did. A rippling thunderclap flashed down the elegant gilt and red hull, twenty-foot flames lancing out from the grinning red muzzles in the larboard battery, the smoke a curling, billowing wall whipped by the wind up and around the tall shape of the sails. There was a sound like ripping linen in the air, and then in the next half-moment a forest of towering shot splashes jetted up, masthead high, around *Athena*, enormous, glittering columns that disintegrated into a cloud of drifting mist through which the schooner plunged.

Mainwaring looked quickly round, cuffing at his dripping face. 'Damage anywhere?' he cried.

Hooke was calling at him from the mainmast timber bitts, where he was snugging down the firesheet. 'None, zur! Christ on a crutch, she missed us clean!'

Mainwaring sprang to the rail, ducking to see out below the main boom. Several men were tugging the boom tackle, a purchase that was set forward to keep the huge spar from gybing. The schooner surged downwind, the flashing red of the ensign rippling out from the gaff peak as the sleek little vessel closed on the bulkier shape of *Aguerra*. The Spanish vessel was trim and beautifully handled, but her bluff, apple-cheeked hull had nowhere near the speed of *Athena*. With the sea roaring under her, her sails drawing like great wings, the schooner swooped on her larger antagonist like a swallow after an owl.

Behind Mainwaring, Evans cursed in frustration. 'Look there, sir!' he called. 'She's wearing round! Going to give us the starboard battery again, he is!'

Mainwaring's voice was like a knife. 'Shut your mouth and

hold your course. But be ready to move when I tell you!' He cupped his hands. 'Mr Hooke! Stand by to board her! Larboard side to!'

'Aye, aye, zur!' came a bellowed reply.

Mainwaring ran forward to the rail overlooking the waist, his eyes locked on the red wall of *Aguerra*'s side. A singing certainty had taken hold of him, an uncaring and ruthless hunger to smash in alongside the *guardacostas* and attack it with his bare hands, if necessary. He felt all the anger and humiliation of the loss of the last encounter, the deaths of his men, the cable tier in *San Josefe*, the interrogation and the beatings in Roche-Bourbon's cabin rising like a bubble of fury inside him. Caution and care seemed gone. *Aguerra* was his prey, and he would kill her or take her. Now.

'Mr Pellowe!' he barked. 'Secure your guns and stand to the small arms! Muster your gun crews on the fo'c'sle! You'll board from there! Mr Hooke?'

'Zur!'

'You and your party fill your hands and muster aft, here! Both of you, see you get grapnels over the minute we strike!'

The deck exploded in a general dive for the weapons tubs, and Mainwaring drew the great cutlass, swinging round on Evans.

'Put her in hard alongside, larboard side to! When you see the grapnels hook on, leave the helm and follow Mr Hooke! You swivel men as well! Get to her quarterdeck, and try to take her helm. And if you can strike her colours, do it! Clear?'

Before the men could reply, there was a shriek from aloft. 'Broadside, Cap'n!'

Mainwaring sprang back to the rail. *Aguerra* had turned more quickly than he had expected. Barely a hundred yards away, the square-rigger had not waited for *Athena* to come up in her suicidal rush, but had hardened up into a reach across the wind, keeping *Athena* abeam. And in the gunports

Mainwaring could see the Spanish gunners working with frantic speed to load their guns, to fulfil the will of whatever cunning mind was driving the Spaniard . . .

And then Mainwaring saw him. A slim, elegant figure in blue and scarlet, near the wheel on *Aguerra*'s quarterdeck. Was it his mind, or did he hear the mocking laughter ringing across the water?

'*You*! God damn and blast your cleverness, you – !' spat Mainwaring. He cupped his hands, a new resolution gripping him. 'D'ye hear, there! We'll ram the bastard! D'ye hear? *We're going to ram*!'

'Jesus, sir, the jib-boom'll snap clear off – !' began Evans.

'Evans, I won't tell you again to be silent!' said Mainwaring, savagely. 'Put the jib-boom dead amidships in her!'

Evans paled. 'Aye, aye, sir!'

Athena hurtled in. And ahead, in the sudden close, plunging and rolling mass of *Aguerra*, heads were appearing all along the rail, pointing at the schooner as it rushed in, mouths opening in sudden awareness and fear. Now, even over the roar of wind and sea, Mainwaring could hear voices raised in a jabber of alarm.

And then, in the next instant, *Aguerra*'s side exploded in a wall of flame. With the schooner barely fifty yards off, at point-blank range, the Spanish had fired their entire starboard battery broadside as one thunderclap of sound.

For Mainwaring, it was a sheet of lightning flashing before his eyes, and a physical blow that struck him like a fist. He could feel himself reeling back, stumbling over Evans' feet, the air all around him suddenly thick with a strange yellow mist, full of fragments and black shapes that hung within it. His hair was streaming, his hat gone, and there were pulls and tugs at his clothing, something hard tinging into the brass of the pistol at his belt. Beside him, one of the men at the swivels kicked over backwards to the deck, hands half raised to the bloody welter that had been his face. A six-foot section of the waistdeck rail lifted as if on hidden strings and cartwheeled towards Mainwaring, catching Evans in the midsection like a scythe, sweeping him away in a tumbling sprawl against the transom rail, mouth agape, the breath dashed from his lungs.

Spray was raining down on the schooner from shot splashes and suddenly sound rushed back into Mainwaring's ears, as if he had been momentarily deaf. A splintering crash sounded overhead, and as he stared the great winging face of the foresail collapsed in flapping, ballooning waves as the gaff, its throat and peak halliards parted, hurtled down. It struck with a banging crash, a crazy, snaking mass of lines and rigging whiplashing round it into a chaotic tangle, falling over the hunched forms of Pellowe's gunners at the break of the forecastle. Mainwaring heard a brief shriek, and saw Abner throw up his arms in a hopeless gesture an instant before the jaws of the gaff smashed him into a broken, twitching huddle on the deck.

Mainwaring fought to his feet, the nausea foul in his throat. Anne! his mind cried. Dear God, have I killed you – ?

Smoke was everywhere, billowing round the schooner, flowing over her decks in a momentary backwash of the wind. With a curse at himself Mainwaring spat to clear the sick, dry feeling in his mouth and lunged for the spinning wheel. *Athena* was beginning to slew around, turning her flank to the Spaniard under the press of the mainsail. And from the red and gilt hull, dimly visible through the thick smoke, cheers and cries were ringing. Cries of triumph. And now muskets were flashing, pink flickers in the murk, the reports thin and sharp, the balls thwacking and thumping into the deck beside Mainwaring. He reached the wheel and seized it, checking its spin, seeing out of the corner of his eye Evans struggling to get up, face contorted in a grimace. *Athena* checked her turn as Mainwaring threw his full weight against the wheel, feeling the thrum of the rudder. For a moment the wounded schooner paused, lifting over a swell, the smoke wreathing away from her now. And then the bowsprit swung back, the jib-boom arrowing again for *Aguerra*'s side, the headsails filling with a *crump*.

Mainwaring was baying at the top of his lungs. 'Stand ready to strike! Board her over the 'sprit!' Ahead, figures were scrambling out from under the foresail wreckage, weapons ready. It would be only an instant more . . .

And then, with a horrid rending impact, *Athena*'s jib-boom crashed through *Aguerra*'s rail and slid onward, and upward, the headsails ballooning and collapsing, the masts and sails of the Spanish vessel shaking and trembling with the impact. Under Mainwaring's feet the deck shook, and from ahead more splintering, tearing sounds blasted as the enormous fabric of wood, rope and canvas of the two vessels locked together in a death grip. And over the din came the sound of voices in *Aguerra*, voices raised in rage, or in oaths and orders. And cries of agony.

With the unheeding fury boiling within him, Mainwaring pulled the cutlass from its sheath and leaped down into the wreckage-strewn chaos of the waist, fighting his way forward. As he passed men groping to their feet he caught them by an arm or shoulder, lifting them upright, thrusting them forward. And then he was at the bowsprit foot, and Hooke was there, and Pellowe, and a wild-eyed knot of men with weapons, staring at him as if he were an apparition.

With a bound he was atop the slanting, slippery bowsprit, pointing with his free hand at the Spanish ship, teeth bared, his face transfigured by the fighting fever that had taken hold of him. 'Board her!' he roared. '*Come on*!'

With a savage cry they were at his heels, and scrambling and slipping up the narrow spar, dodging past the spider-web of lines and rigging, plunging over the humped, tent-like mounds of the collapsed headsails, on over the rail of *Aguerra*, into the murk there where the smoke pouring up from the Spaniard's hatches on the gundeck shrouded the weatherdeck in a grey, swirling miasma of reeking fog.

Then Mainwaring was there, the decking of the Spaniard seemingly hundreds of feet below him, and he was leaping recklessly down, seeing only at the last second the shocked Spanish seaman who had appeared below, gap teeth bared in a snarl, thrusting a pistol up at him with both hands. Mainwaring's boots struck him square in the chest, and the Spaniard thumped to the deck, the pistol's report deafening in Mainwaring's ears, the ball whizzing by his head. He hit the deck awkwardly and off balance, and fell to one side in a sprawl, suddenly tangled round with trailing lines from *Athena*'s bowsprit that clutched at him like a net on a wild animal. With a terror of being held there he fought to get free. All about him was deafening tumult, the clash of steel on steel, pistol and musket blasts, the thump and scrape of cursing, struggling men, the shrieks and moans of the wounded, the deep baying of *Athena*'s men, the jabber of the Spaniards. Christ, would he never get free!

Abruptly, he was stumbling free of the ensnaring tangle, and staring into the eyes of a Spanish officer, a pot-bellied, bewigged caricature in laced scarlet and egret feathers. But in the next half-second a gleaming sword blade in the caricature's fat paw was arrowing for Mainwaring's chest in a lightning-quick fencing lunge, the Spaniard grunting with the effort. With a growl Mainwaring parried the thrust hard, the steel ringing, and without a pause cut a vicious backhand blow of the heavy cutlass at the man's neck. The blade thudded into the flesh, and the Spaniard gobbled horridly, sinking to his knees, his sword clattering out of his grip.

Mainwaring wrenched his blade free, a froth of scarlet

bursting from the man's neck as he fell forward. But he was stepping over him, heedless of the bile rising in his throat, the rage still gripping him. A blow tore at his shoulder, and he spun to see a small bare-chested Spaniard with frightened eyes thrusting weakly at him with a boarding pike. With his free hand Mainwaring gripped the weapon's haft and with a twist of his wrist, tore it out of the smaller man's hands. The Spaniard stared at him, wailed something, and ran off, vanishing into the smoky tumult of struggling bodies.

'*Athena! Athena!*' Bellowing at the top of his lungs, Mainwaring pushed towards the foot of the quarterdeck ladder, shouldering his way through the struggling men, his voice cracking with strain. He cut left and right with the cutlass, grunting in savage satisfaction with the blows, feeling them strike home in bone and gristle, the shrieks of the wretches deafening in his ears as he thrust the struggling, half-seen forms and the contorted faces from him. Now he was at the ladder foot, a Spaniard halfway up it kicking at his head until with a lunge Mainwaring buried his cutlass to the hilt in the man's belly. As he yanked out the scarlet blade the man fell on him, mouth wide in a soundless shriek, and he thrust the body over his shoulders in a grotesque tumble behind him to the deck. In the next instant he was on the quarterdeck, running to the foot of the staff where the great, pale Spanish ensign streamed out amidst the smoke. With the cutlass he hacked at the thin halliard, and the ensign crumpled, collapsing down over the transom rail.

And then he was spinning away, gasping in pain at the vicious cut that had opened on his left shoulder, the shirt torn away, the dark blood welling up. He fell back against the transom rail, tangling in the folds of the ensign, feeling the faint and the nausea rising within him. And he stared in disbelief at the elegant blue and scarlet figure that hovered before him, circling blade centred on Mainwaring's throat. 'Dear Christ!' Mainwaring gasped. '*You*!'

The Chevalier Rigaud de la Roche-Bourbon eyed him with a glittering, cold smile, a picture of controlled power seemingly untouched by the carnage and struggle that raged all about them. His teeth gleamed, and he licked his lips, his eyes like points of steel. 'Yes, Mainwaring. You owe me a little debt, it would seem, *hein*? A pity I must collect in so thorough a manner!' And on the last word Roche-Bourbon lunged, the slim blade whistling for Mainwaring's jugular.

But with a desperate effort Mainwaring was twisting away, and the blade slid through a fold in his shirt. And then he was hacking viciously at the elegant figure, forcing Roche-Bourbon back, forcing him to parry and parry again as the heavy cutlass blade drove at him.

The Frenchman recoiled a few paces and grinned mirthlessly at the gasping American. Mainwaring felt his head spin, the pain of his bloody, dripping arm taking over, making him will it back.

'Such animal energy!' snarled Roche-Bourbon. 'Very commendable. But skill is also necessary, Mainwaring. Or were you never taught that as you played with your colonial fishpots?' The blade flashed in the sunlight, the Frenchman advanced in the foot-slapping classic style, and with a speed that Mainwaring could barely see the slim weapon was licking at him like a serpent's tongue, cutting at his wrist, cutting at his sword arm, and then, with a lancet of pain, whistling past his eyes to lay open a thin, bloody cut on his cheek. 'How nice to leave a mark where it is evident!' crowed Roche-Bourbon. 'And now for the other cheek – !' The lightning blade whispered in.

But with the pain of the cut the red rage had risen again in Mainwaring, and he parried the blow in a ringing clash that stopped Roche-Bourbon in his tracks. With a snarl he bodied into the slighter Frenchman, sending him reeling back against *Aguerra*'s binnacle box, following him. He smashed at Roche-Bourbon in crude, crushing blows of such power that the Frenchman could not duck away or do anything but parry them, with one and then two hands, the gleam of confidence that had been in his hard eyes fading slowly to a more desperate look as Mainwaring pressed in.

'I'll thank you ... to be ... respectful ... to a ... king's officer!' raged Mainwaring, the blows raining down again and again, forcing the Frenchman to his knees, until Roche-Bourbon's face was a contorted mask of fury, humiliation, and now, fear. And then, in a last, struggling effort, Roche-Bourbon lunged in the interval between Mainwaring's hammer blows, his blade centred on the latter's midsection. But Mainwaring saw it coming, turned his body, and trapped the blade under his arm. With a twist of his shoulders, he wrenched the weapon from Roche-Bourbon's grasp.

'Your time is not yet, it seems, M'sieur! Not yet!'

And with a backhand blow of his fisted free hand, Mainwaring smashed the ashen-faced, staring Frenchman into a senseless sprawl against *Aguerra*'s transom rail.

He stood, gasping for breath, staring down at the unconscious figure, feeling the waves of nausea returning, feeling the fiery pain in his bloody arm. A light-headedness came over him, and he clutched at the rail for support. Then he became aware that the din of fighting had stopped: there was no clash of steel, no voices raised in shouts or screams. He turned, and saw the chaotic image of *Athena*'s bowsprit and jib-boom projecting incongruously over *Aguerra*'s waist, the rigging of the two vessels locked together in a twisted tangle, the decks of both vessels strewn with wreckage and bits of equipment. *Athena* was grinding against the Spanish vessel's side under the wind and swells, and through the mist that seemed to cloud his mind Mainwaring knew he had to get

Athena pulled free, before even more serious damage took place. Why were his ears humming so?

Mainwaring shook his head, trying to clear it. Remnants of smoke drifted away from *Aguerra*'s deck, over the bodies strewn here and there, a few writhing as they lay or struggling to get up. The Spanish still standing were being herded together, and were tossing down their weapons, their faces abject in defeat or burning in humiliation.

And Hooke was there, grinning at him, his face blackened, his cutlass blade scarlet from guard to tip. 'Yew've done it, zur! Took 'er, by Christ!'

Mainwaring felt his legs trembling. He was looking, searching the faces. He saw Pellowe helping Jewett to his feet, saw Slade and Sawyer pushing a thick-set Spaniard twice their combined size into a clutch of his disarmed fellows. Where was she? Oh, God, had he killed her too . . .

Hooke was at his ear. 'She's there, zur. Behind th' mainm'st. I kept 'er wiv me th' whole time, zur. Fought like a cat, she did!' Hooke was beaming in pride.

But Mainwaring was oblivious to him. He was conscious of her eyes as they found his, and of her small shape running up the quarterdeck ladder. And then of her rush into his arms, the smell of her hair, the murmurs of her lips against his neck.

Hooke was grinning at them both. And in the next instant he was calling for the cheer, the three exuberant huzzas ringing out over both ships, and around the man who clutched the girl to him amidst the shambles of the struggle, and could think of nothing at the moment but that she was alive and in his arms.

Epilogue

Vice-Admiral Edward Vernon, in sweat-stained shirtsleeves, looked up in irritation from the welter of papers that were strewn over his desk in His Britannic Majesty's Ship *Burford*. His flag lieutenant, the sallow look of fever in his face, coughed into a handkerchief as he leaned in the cabin door.

'What the devil do you want, Flags? If it's another report of dead, I simply cannot – '

'No, no, sir. Nothing like that. The *Sheerness* frigate has just come in, sir. She's reported that the *flota* of Don Blas has anchored at Cartagena. Either they've not heard we're here, or don't wish to know, sir.'

'What?' Vernon glanced out at the heat-shimmered water of Porto Bello harbour. 'That's splendid! I know Blas. If he suspected we were here he'd have tried to attack us, you may lay to that. Word must not have got to him. It'll take days for it to arrive by land. Thank God!'

'Er – the captain of *Sheerness* thinks he knows why Blas didn't hear, sir. There was a fast picket vessel sent out, amongst others, that had a mad Frenchman in command. Fellow apparently was sure we were here, and was coming to make sure before reporting.' He paused. 'Apparently it was the same chap who gave our young Yankee Mainwaring such a difficult time when they captured him. Was coming back to even the score after Mainwaring's escape. Mainwaring had apparently knocked him about a bit, it would seem.'

'A fast picket?' said Vernon. 'What kind?'

'*Guardacostas*, sir.' The flag lieutenant coughed into the

206

handkerchief again. 'Small frigate, virtually the same as a French corvette. Mainwaring took it, sir.'

'I beg your pardon?' Vernon's look was incredulous.

'He took it, sir. Met up with this French fellow – Roche-Bourbon, his name is, I think – off Urabá and boarded him.'

'What, took it by *boarding*? With that corporal's guard of a crew?'

The flag lieutenant smiled. 'You can see for yourself, sir. The schooner's in the offing. A bit torn up by the fight, by the look of her. But he's leading in the Spaniard, and they're both under English colours, sir. Listen, sir. You can hear the hands cheering 'em.'

Vernon listened. Muffled, but distinct, he could hear the cheers. From *Burford* and the other ships in the pestilential, fever-ridden anchorage, ringing out like a fresh note of optimism and hope, again and again. 'Damned rare sound, that,' muttered Vernon. 'By God, Flags, if that young colonial's bought us time – '

'I think it's clear he has, sir,' said the flag lieutenant, quietly.

Vernon beamed at him. 'Then I think I shall grant myself a turn on deck,' he said. 'And perhaps voice a cheer of my own!'